...always fun, fresh, and fabulous!

—Arial Burnz, *USA Today* bestselling author of *Midnight Eclipse*

"Amy Lillard's novels are funny, sweet, charming, and utterly delicious. Reading her stories is like indulging in gourmet chocolates: You'll savor every delightful page, and when you reach the end, you'll always wish there was more!"

—Michele Bardsley, *New York Times* bestselling author of *Your Lycan or Mine?*

"Amy Lillard's characters will tug at your heartstrings and leave you wanting to meet more!"

—Laura Marie Altom, author of *Stepping Over the Line*

"At the top of my autobuy list, Amy Lillard's romances always leave a smile on my face and a sigh in my heart."

—A. J. Nuest, RONE finalist

"Amy Lillard is one of my go-to authors for a sexy, witty romance." —Kelly Moran, Readers' Choice finalist

"Amy Lillard weaves well-developed characters that create for lovers of romance a rich fabric of love."

—Vonnie Davis, author of the Wild Heat series

"Funny, warm, and thoroughly charming. Make room on your keeper shelf for Amy Lillard!"

—Karen Toller Whittenburg, author of *Just What the Doctor Ordered*

Titles by Amy Lillard

LOVING A LAWMAN
HEALING A HEART

Healing a Heart

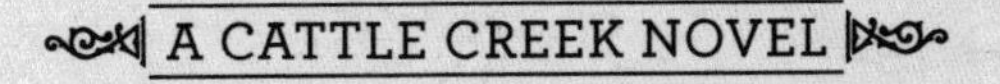

Amy Lillard

BERKLEY SENSATION
New York

BERKLEY SENSATION
Published by Berkley
An imprint of Penguin Random House LLC
375 Hudson Street, New York, New York 10014

ISBN: 9781101990957

First Edition: February 2017

Printed in the United States of America
1 3 5 7 9 10 8 6 4 2

Cover art by Annette DeFex
Cover design by Daniela Medina
Book design by Laura Corless

To everyone who has ever loved and lost—
whether friend, family, or lover.
May you always find the courage to love again.

Chapter One

It was official. Jake ripped off his leather work gloves and shoved them into the back pocket of his jeans. He was going to kill Jessie.

This was all her fault. And she was going to pay for it one way or another.

He raised his binoculars to get a better look at the little white car that had so recently pulled into the drive at the Diamond Duvall Ranch, better known around these parts as the Diamond. A convertible Volkswagen Beetle. Not a ranch car by any stretch.

How many did this one make? Seven? Eight? He didn't know. He'd lost count early on of how many "cowbride" wannabes had shown up on his doorstep—literally—to get a shot at Texas's fifteenth most eligible bachelor. Heaven help them all if he had scored any higher on the scale. They'd be wading through women. He had a ranch to run. He didn't have time to fend off ladies with wedding gleams in their eyes while his sister-in-law sat back and laughed.

Though this one seemed a little different. Field glasses

still magnifying the scene, Jake peered at her. She wasn't wrapped in some slinky, stretchy second-skin dress that showed off every curve. Instead she wore faded jeans and a hippie-looking shirt with elaborate stitching on the front. Her leather sandals weren't appropriate ranch footwear, but it was a sight better than a pair of those god-awful heels women seemed to prefer these days. The word *hippie* sprang to mind once again.

He lowered his binoculars and cranked the four-wheeler, then whistled for Kota. His blue heeler perked up at the summons and ran ahead toward the ranch house.

Best he took care of this one on his own. The last time he left it up to whoever answered the door, Grandma Esther had invited the woman in and had all but interviewed her to be the next Mrs. Jake Langston. And down the aisle was one place Jake never intended to walk again.

She started for the door, but stopped, apparently deciding to wait for him to greet her. She turned and shielded her eyes, and his heart gave a painful thump. Something about the motion was so familiar. . . .

He was only a few yards away when he recognized her. Austin. And that one fantastic night . . . but her name . . .

He killed the engine and slung his leg over the side of the four-wheeler, his hands suddenly sweaty, his mouth dry.

But she wasn't here to find him because she missed him. Or wanted a repeat of that one incredible night.

Damn that article. She was only here because she had realized that he wasn't a poor workaday cowboy, but one of the wealthiest men in West Texas—oil excluded.

She smiled.

He scowled.

Damn, he wished he could remember her name. Had they even exchanged names? It would be so much easier to kick her gold-digging rear off the property if he could call her by name.

"Jake." She said his name as if she were trying it on for size.

He stopped and propped his hands on his hips. He really didn't have time for this.

Kota had no such reservations and continued on toward the interloper. He sniffed his way toward her.

She held her ground but gave the dog a cautious glance. "Will he bite?"

"Only if you break from the herd."

She nodded, then a nervous laugh escaped her. "I—"

He broke in. "Let me save us both the trouble and the embarrassment. I know why you're here."

"You do?" Her brown eyes widened. He might not remember her name, but those melted-chocolate eyes were burned into his soul. Along with the feel of her underneath him, on top of him . . .

"The article in *Out West* magazine."

A frown wrinkled her brow, and she tilted her head to one side as if needing a better angle on the situation.

You're going to need more than that, sweetheart.

The hot Texas sun glinted off the chunk of purple in one side of her seal brown hair. That he didn't remember. Purple?

"And you should know, you'd better just clear on out right now," he continued. "I'm not interested in it."

The frown deepened. "It?"

"It." He waved a hand in her general direction. The word had sounded so much more forceful in his head.

"I don't think you understand."

"I don't think *you* understand."

"Can we go inside and talk?"

"Nope."

"It's hot out here and I just—"

"If you don't like the heat, stay out of Texas."

She thought about it a second, then gave him a small smile. "That was a joke."

"I'm trying to be as nice as I possibly can, but I've had more women crawling around here in the last few weeks than I ever imagined. It's best you just go on home." He turned to walk away, hoping she took the hint. Maybe if he went back into the house without inviting her, she would lose interest and leave.

Yet the feeling that something about her was different panged at his midsection.

"Jake?" Grandma Esther stood on the large stone porch. "Aren't you going to invite her in? It's mighty hot out."

"That's true, Grandma, so get on back in the air-conditioning."

"Jacob Dwight! How are you ever going to find yourself a bride if you don't invite these women in?"

He closed his eyes and sucked in a deep breath, his feet stuck in the dirt somewhere between the driveway and the big house.

"Are the women coming here to marry you?" she asked from behind him.

"He is the seventeenth most eligible bachelor in Texas."

"Fifteenth," he corrected, then winced at his own words. He wasn't making this easier on himself.

Her laughter rang, sweet and clear like a babbling brook.

Wait . . . what?

The sun had to be getting to him. He whirled around, wondering why she hadn't left.

Then he realized what was so strange about the situation. Why would a hippie chick want to marry a cowboy? True he'd shown her a few tricks in the saddle, as they say, but one completely incredible, fantastic, amazing night did not a lifestyle change make. Or something like that.

"I don't want to marry you," she said. The light in her eyes told him she wasn't lying. "But I do need to talk to you about something."

Just as bad.

"Come on in this house, girl." Grandma Esther waved her in with the business end of her cane.

The brunette—why couldn't he remember her name?—edged past him.

Kota nipped at her heels.

She yelped. The cow dog had never actually bitten anyone, but Jake knew that his nips and nibbles could be a bit unnerving if you weren't used to them. He hid his smile as she skipped to the house.

Reluctantly, he followed behind.

Grandma Esther stepped to one side as she entered the house. He watched her rear disappear into the shadows of the cool foyer.

The porch offered a reprieve from the blistering sun, but another heat filled Jake. Memories of that one night when he had let his guard down. When he'd lost his resolve and tried once again to find the answers at the bottom of a bottle. He hadn't had a drink since then, but he didn't count days sober. It wasn't like that for him. But he knew with so many ghosts of could-have-beens and should-have-beens haunting him that the alcohol could take over in an instant and it was best to just stay away.

But that one night . . .

"Esther, what is going on out here?" His mother skidded to a halt when she caught sight of their visitor. But Evelyn Duvall Langston was nothing if not composed. She brushed down the sleeves of her rose-colored, pearl-snap shirt. "Hello."

"Hi." The brunette flashed his mother a nervous smile. Bre? Was that her name? No, but it was close. Briana? Nope. That wasn't it either.

"I wasn't aware that Jake had a guest."

"She's not a guest." He frowned to silently instruct his mother to drop the matter.

Mama opened her mouth to speak—she never was much at following his wishes—but Grandma Esther stepped in, her cane rattling against the stone floor. "Come on, Evie, let's give these two some privacy."

For once Jake was grateful for his grandmother's interference. He certainly couldn't toss her out on her pretty little behind with his grandmother and mother watching. Well, he *could*, but he would never hear the end of it.

He watched Grandma Esther lead his mother into her office, then turned back to his unwanted guest.

Once again she shot him that nervous smile. She hadn't been so nervous three and a half months ago when they had—

"I don't know how to say this except to just say it." She sucked in a deep breath. "I'm pregnant."

He went numb as his gaze flickered to her midsection hidden under her blousy, gauzy shirt. A bus could be parked under there. Or maybe that was the point.

"Pregnant?"

Was this true? Would she even be here if it weren't? Maybe. He had become such a target lately. Slowly he raised his gaze to hers. She was telling the truth. Somehow, someway, he knew it.

His heart constricted and the air left his lungs even as he tried to speak.

His worst nightmare.

His stomach clenched and his fingers tingled with a combination of adrenaline and terror.

Nothing would ever be the same again.

"Get rid of it." His lips barely moved. Fear gripped him. Fear like he had known only once before. He was the dutiful brother. Reliable. Dependable. The caretaker. The responsible one. Always responsible. He'd never been careless. Never.

That night in May flashed through his mind and mixed with one fall afternoon down by the river with Cecelia. A picnic meant to bring the spark back into their marriage. And yet all it had brought about was her death.

The night with this stranger blurred and frayed until the two merged into one and all he could think about was the fear.

"I—I beg your pardon." Her voice was no more than a whisper. But it held the weight of the ages. Betrayal, disbelief. He'd never meant to hurt her.

"Get rid of it."

She trembled, her own nervousness eclipsed by an emotion he couldn't discern. She opened her mouth and when she spoke, her voice was no more substantial than an incredulous wisp of smoke. "You mean like an . . . an abortion?"

"That's exactly what I mean." An invisible hand clutched and clawed at his throat until he could barely breathe. This couldn't be happening.

"Jacob Dwight Langston!"

His mother stormed toward them, but Jake couldn't think, couldn't move.

"I'm sorry, Miss . . . Miss . . ."

Evelyn looked to him.

"Bryn," he croaked. Oh, *now* he could remember her name.

"What my son means to say, Miss Bryn—"

"Talbot," she corrected, then shifted from one foot to the other and adjusted the strap of her enormous orange handbag.

"Miss Talbot," his mother started again, but Bryn shook her head.

"I . . . ," she faltered. "I just thought you'd want to know."

She spun on one heel and headed for the door.

Out of all the possible scenarios she had expected, this was not one of them. Weren't cowboys supposed to be noble?

Bryn shook her head at herself and palmed her keys. What the heck did she know about cowboys anyway? Just that one sizzling night where she had done the unthinkable and hooked up with a man she didn't even know. A perfect stranger.

Not perfect at all.

She tripped down the steps and hurried toward her car. This stop had put her behind schedule. But she had thought he should know. Didn't every man deserve that much?

She just hadn't expected his reaction. Disbelief maybe. Denial, probably. Even anger.

Coldhearted bastard. Except he hadn't been so cold that night. He'd been more than warm that night. Hot, burning up, dazzling.

As if.

"I should have never come here," she muttered. But she hadn't expected his reaction.

Still, there was something in his eyes when he said the words, that unthinkable act. Sadness, remorse and . . . guilt?

She pushed the thought away and slid behind the wheel of her car. What did he have to feel guilty about? They had entered that hotel room together.

"Looks like it's just the three of us again." She pressed a hand to her rounded belly and glanced over at the urn sitting in the passenger's seat. "Just the three of us." She cranked the car and put it into reverse. The best laid plans.

"Miss Talbot?" Jake's mother came rushing out the door and over to where Bryn had parked. At least she thought she was Jake's mother and the older lady his grandmother, though neither one looked particularly like the man. Neither had those fabulous green eyes. Or that dark hair that just begged a woman's fingers to—

Bryn rolled down her window. "Yes?"

"Won't you come back into the house?" Mrs. Langston stooped down where she could look into Bryn's car. Her gaze flickered to the passenger's seat, then back to Bryn. She'd be damned before she would explain herself.

"I don't think so." She shot the woman her most polite, Southern smile and turned to get a good look out the rear window as she backed up.

Jake's mother clutched her arm. "Please, Miss Talbot. Come in. Let me apologize for my son's behavior."

She whipped around, but shook her head even as she made no move to leave. "There's no need." He didn't want the baby they had created. So be it. She did. The child she carried was a new beginning. A fresh start. One she so desperately needed.

"I believe there is."

Something in the woman's voice had Bryn putting the car into park, had her cutting off the engine.

"Just for a bit." His mother smiled encouragingly, then moved back so Bryn could get out.

Her limbs were stiff and jerky as she opened the car door and stepped into the Texas heat once again. It was different than Georgia. Not as humid by far, but hot all the same.

Together the two of them walked back to the sprawling ranch house. It was a beautiful structure, though Bryn had been too nervous before to truly appreciate its majestic beauty.

"Let's go into my office where we can talk." She led the way, then turned back to face Bryn. "I'm Evelyn, by the way. Jake's mother."

"It's nice to meet you," Bryn murmured. Southern manners kicked in where all else failed. At least she had called it right. "This really isn't necessary," she said.

Evelyn ignored her and opened one of the large doors to a leather and bronze office complete with a gently worn sofa with a brown-and-white cowhide tossed over the back. Bryn was fairly certain it was the real deal and not a designer version from Pottery Barn.

"Go ahead and have a seat. Grandma Esther went to get us some refreshments."

"Really," Bryn gently protested once again. "This isn't necessary. I don't want anything from Jake. I—"

"Sit." The one word was spoken like a woman who was accustomed to getting her way. Always.

Bryn perched on the edge of the sofa, while Evelyn eased into the overlarge chair behind the desk.

"How did you and Jake meet?"

Bryn shook her head. This was not going at all as she had planned, but then again, what did she really expect?

That she could come in, announce that she was having Jake's baby, and they would just let her waltz out the door without so much as a by-your-leave?

A girl could hope.

But when she got back to Georgia, she was having a long talk with Rick about personal boundaries and bad advice. A girl had to depend on her best friend to help her through tough situations. So far he had encouraged her to latch on to a cowboy—the very same cowboy who'd gotten her pregnant—and pointed out his picture in *Out West* magazine, thereby negating her arguments that she didn't even know his last name. That night, trivial matters like surnames just never came up.

"I was in Austin in May. I believe Jake was there for a weekend conference. He really didn't tell me." She shook her head. She was making a mess of this.

She stood. "Listen, you don't owe me an apology. I'd rather just be on my way."

"Carrying my grandchild."

Bryn made a face. "She sort of has to go with me." She placed one hand protectively over her growing mound of a baby. No matter how much she watched what she ate, she seemed to be packing on the pounds.

"It's a girl?" Evelyn asked. Her voice was barely audible.

Bryn shrugged. "I just want it to be."

Jake's mother smiled. "So did I, but I ended up with five boys."

"Five?"

"I'm afraid so." But her smile took all the venom from her words. "Jake didn't mean what he said. He . . ." she started, then shook her head, "he had a tough time when his first wife died."

"He's a widower?" Of course he had been married. The women in Texas knew a good thing when they saw it.

"Cecelia, that was his wife, she died giving birth to their daughter, Wesley."

He has a daughter? Bryn sank back to the couch cushion. "I see."

"He just needs some time to adjust to the idea of being married again. And having another baby."

"I'm not marrying Jake." The idea was ludicrous. They didn't know each other. A baby did not a marriage make. "It was a mistake coming here." Bryn pushed to her feet and slung her purse over one shoulder.

Evelyn was on her feet in a heartbeat. "I told you, Jake didn't mean what he said."

Bryn pinched the bridge of her nose and pushed her sunglasses back into place. "This has nothing to do with what he said. Well, maybe a little, but we don't know each other. We can't get married."

"You know each other well enough to have made a baby." Evelyn's words stung with the truth.

"That's not really the point, now is it?"

"Why are you in such a hurry?"

She spun around. Grandma Esther stood in the doorway with the promised refreshments.

"Oh, you know. I'm a busy girl with things to do."

"If you're going back to Austin, then I hope you'll leave your number and address so we can keep in touch."

"I'm not going back to Austin."

"Your car has Georgia plates," Esther said.

"That's right. That's where I live."

"You're from Georgia?"

"That's right."

"You never did answer me," Esther pressed.

"I have a . . . meeting on the West Coast." That was a great way of putting it. Surely beat the heck out of *I'm dumping my baby sister's ashes in the Pacific*. "I'm supposed to be there day after tomorrow."

"Then you have plenty of time." Esther waved away Bryn's protests with a flick of one gnarled hand.

"That's right," Evelyn said. "You can have dinner and spend the night here."

"I—"

"We won't take no for an answer," Evelyn said.

"Besides," Grandma Esther interjected, "it'll save you the hotel charge."

Money wasn't an issue. But staying with these people . . . that was. She should get out now while the getting was good.

"Please." Evelyn's voice was filled with heartfelt emotions. "Please give us a chance. We need to get to know you. After all, you're having my next grandchild."

She didn't want anything from these people. In fact, if it hadn't been for that blessed magazine, she wouldn't be standing here now. But she had wanted to give them the chance, let them know that in six months' time another Langston was entering the world.

"How do you even know I'm telling the truth?"

Evelyn smiled. "If you were just trying to trap Jake into marriage, why would you walk away?"

Chapter Two

Jake laid his head against the rough cedar paneling of the hallway and tried to get himself back together. He could hear his mother, his grandmother, and Bryn Talbot in his mother's office talking about nothing and the most important things in his life. He felt trapped, hopeless, like a calf who had gotten tangled up and no one was around to free him. Oh, how he wished he could hop in his truck, crank up Van Halen, and just drive.

But if he was wishing, he might as well wish he could go back and relive that night. Change something—*anything*—that would keep them from being where they were right now. Or maybe he just wanted to go back a half an hour or so and figure out a better response to Bryn's shocking news. There had to be at least a hundred.

He shook his head. Going back wasn't an option. Going forward was all he had left.

Lightly, he rapped on the door and entered without waiting for a response.

Grandma Esther hung about the fringes, holding a plate

of nachos as if presenting them to the queen. His mother leaned against her large mahogany desk while Bryn perched on the edge of the big leather couch as if she might bolt at any second. She seemed confident, yet wary. In control, yet ready to call the whole thing off. And beautiful.

She looked beautiful. And he was slammed with memories from that night. Heated sighs, soft touches. Vivid yet surreal, like a dream he couldn't quite shake. But this was no dream.

All heads turned in his direction as he entered, but he only had concerns for the woman on the couch.

"Can I . . . uh, talk to you for a moment?"

There was a split second when he thought she might say no, then she gave a small nod.

"Come on, Esther. Let's give them some privacy."

"Not on your life." His grandmother shook her head and dug in her heels. "I wouldn't miss this for the world." She grabbed one of the nachos from the plate and shoved it into her mouth before offering some to the both of them.

Bryn politely shook her head, but somehow the small gesture seemed to break some of the tension.

"I'm sorry," he said. The words too simple and not enough, but all he had just the same.

Her gaze was steady as she studied him. "Sorry that we're having a baby or—"

"Sorry for what I said."

"Okay." She dipped her chin as if to say she understood, but her eyes remained distrustful. Wary.

"Esther." His mother hovered at the door, but Grandma Esther simply ate another nacho and looked from one of them to the other as if she were at a tennis match.

"And you're right. I did need to know."

She remained silent. He had no choice but to continue, though the words seemed to be getting harder and harder to say.

"Can you stay for dinner? Give us some time to work out the details?"

"We can call Seth and Jessie," Grandma Esther said. She abandoned the plate of nachos on the desk and headed for the door. Her cane rattled with each step she took. He supposed she was going into a different room to use the phone, but Jake was grateful to have one less person be witness to his humiliation.

"I'll just . . . ," his mother started, then pressed her lips together and let herself out of the office.

The door hadn't even shut behind her when Wesley raced in, her blond hair flying out behind her. "Daddy! Daddy! Daddy!" These days she had two speeds: full blast and asleep. She flung herself into his arms as if she hadn't seen him in days instead of just minutes. "I finished my snack, can I go out to the barn? Joe Dan said he'd keep an eye on me."

"Joe Dan has work to do." Jake brushed her hair back from her face and resisted the urge to kiss her jelly-smeared cheek. She was getting to the age where random kisses were not allowed. Still, he could eat her up he loved her so much. The feeling alone made his heart ache in his chest. "I tell you what. If you will go play in your room for a few more minutes, I'll take you to the barn myself. Deal?"

"Deal." Her grin was sly as she slid down his side. Her boots clunked on the floor as they touched down. She started to turn for the door, then stopped. "Who's that?"

"Bryn," he choked out. There were so many answers but none that he could give his daughter.

"Hi." Wesley walked over to Bryn as pretty as you please and extended her hand for the woman to shake. "It's nice to meet you, Miss Bryn."

"Likewise."

Then his daughter turned back to him. "Is she here about the cook's job?"

Jake shook his head.

"Oh, okay, then." She nodded sagely.

"Go on and play now."

"'Kay, Daddy." She skipped from the room as if she hadn't a care in the world. That was his job, to make sure she didn't.

"I'm just going to go now." Bryn waved a hand toward the door in a gesture that looked like a fish flopping on the banks of a creek.

"I thought you were going to work out some details with me."

She shook her head and turned away, but not before he saw the tears in her eyes. "I'll send you an e-mail." Without waiting, she made her way to the door and out.

It happened so quickly Jake blinked twice before realizing that she was gone. "Wait," he called, finally setting his feet into motion behind her. "You don't have my e-mail address."

Her footsteps never slowed as she darted across the foyer and out the front door. "I'm sure the ranch has a website."

She was almost to her car when he caught her arm and spun her around. She might have had a good head start, but his longer stride was to his advantage.

"Why are you running away from me?"

She shook her head and gently pulled her arm from his grasp. "I just need to go." Thankfully her tears had disappeared, if they had ever really been there to begin with.

"And we're going to decide the fate of my child over e-mail?"

"Our child," she corrected. "And yes. I see no problem in handling this through e-mail. In fact, maybe we should just consult attorneys and let them sort through it all."

Jake shook his head. "They might get to draw up the papers, but you and I have to decide."

"I need to go," she repeated.

"What's so urgent that you can't stay for an hour or two? I mean, you came here. Surely you didn't think you could tell me that you're having my baby then waltz back out again like nothing ever happened."

"You're right. I should have never come here."

"But you did."

She stopped trying to get away from him. "I have an appointment." She had said that before.

"I understand, but this is important. More important than to take care of it with a string of e-mails."

She shook her head. "We're going in circles."

He crossed his arms. "The solution?"

"I don't know," she whispered.

"Why don't you stay and let's work this out?"

"I can't. I can come back."

"Come back?"

"I promise. I'll come back after my . . . appointment."

They were at an impasse. What could he do but tell her okay? "So be it."

Bryn was all too aware of those green eyes following her as she backed out of the driveway. She imagined that she could feel his stare but she knew she was just being overly dramatic.

And yet . . .

She waited until she got to the farm road before punching the address of her hotel into the GPS. Four and a half more hours until she got to El Paso. Four and a half hours of wondering why she agreed to come back.

"You are on the quickest route to your destination."

"Great," she muttered, adjusting the air. Then she dialed the familiar number and turned on her hands-free.

"Hair Flair Unlimited."

"Rick?"

"Girl, I have been worried about you. I thought you'd call before now."

His familiar voice brought tears to her eyes. She blinked them away. One thing she had learned in the last couple of years: tears didn't help a thing. Not. One. Thing. "Yeah . . . ? Well, I'm sorry. I didn't mean to worry you."

"So," he said. She could almost hear him rubbing his hands together in anticipation. "Did you see him?"

Six foot plus of handsome cowboy flashed through her mind. Dark hair, green eyes, strong jaw, unyielding lips. "Yeah. I saw him."

"And . . . ?"

She shook her head. "And nothing."

"Don't give me that. I need details, and I need them two hours ago."

"There isn't much to tell." It was both the truth and a lie.

"Was he surprised to see you?"

Bryn turned on her blinker indicating that she was turning out onto the highway even though it didn't appear there was anyone around for miles. "That word works."

"Oh, you! Spit it out. What happened?"

"He seemed angry." Though for the life of her she couldn't figure out why. It'd really been more than anger, and he looked a bit scared. And that was where she got confused. What did he have to be afraid of?

"Angry?"

"I know, right? It's weird. But I just got the feeling . . ."

"And . . . ?" Rick asked.

"And nothing. I need to get to El Paso before dark, and I told him I had to go."

"There's something you're not telling me, and it's big."

And that was what she got for being best friends with Rick McFadden since seventh grade. "I don't know," she said truthfully. "It was just strange."

"How else did you expect it to be? Not every day you go tell a man you're having his baby, never mind the fact that you barely know him."

Those hard green eyes flashed through her thoughts. "I don't know him at all."

"Only in the biblical sense," Rick quipped.

"Will you be serious?"

He coughed. "Sorry. Why are we being serious again?"

"I don't think I can go through with this."

"Well, it's a little late to be changing your mind."

"Not about having the baby. About including him. I mean, we don't know each other and—"

"Hush your mouth," Rick said. "You can't keep this child from him."

Bryn sighed. "I know, but—"

"No buts."

"He's not what I expected."

"How so?"

She resisted the urge to close her eyes and think about it. He wasn't what she had expected in so many ways. "Well, he's wealthier than I thought, and he's got a little girl."

"He's married?"

"Widower."

"That's tough. How old is his daughter?"

"Four. Maybe five."

"Honey, are you going to be okay?"

"I will."

"What are you doing now?"

"Driving."

"What?" he screeched. "Why aren't you back at the ranch house with your cowboy?"

"First of all, he's not my cowboy. Second of all, I made a promise that I intend to keep."

Rick sniffed. "I'm sure Emery would understand. You need to work things out with this man. And the sooner the better. You can't do that driving to California."

"You don't understand. I was standing there, his grandmother's trying to serve nachos, his mother wants to talk to me about the future, his daughter comes running in. I just couldn't take it. I had to leave."

"So you tucked tail and ran, using your sister's ashes as an excuse."

"Hey," she said. "I told him I would come back."

"Now, I know you better than that. You have no intention of going back to that man's house."

What could she say? It was the truth. She didn't have any intention of going back. Why couldn't they handle everything by e-mail? In this new day and age, she didn't have to be right there with him, staring into those green eyes as she tried to make life-altering decisions about the child she carried. She just couldn't do it.

Maybe it was time to talk to somebody. But she managed her grief this far. Still, she knew that she had a lot of changes in the last few years starting with the death of her stepmom and her dad.

A freak accident, everyone had said. Freak or not it still resulted in her and Emery losing the two most important people in their lives. Emery had been seven at the time. Since then Bryn raised her sister the best she could.

"Bryn, he has rights, you know." Rick's voice had lost all of its teasing.

"I know."

"Promise me you'll go back on the way home."

"Rick, I—"

"Promise me," he said again. "I have a feeling that he wouldn't skip out on you. You can't do the same to him."

"Wasn't it you who also told me to go buy that cowboy a drink?"

Rick chuckled. "I seem to remember something of the sort."

"So why should I do what you say now? Look what that got me into."

Rick chuckled again. "You'll do it because you know I'm right."

Jake stood in the driveway and watched until she was good and truly gone. His heart felt like it was being squeezed in a vise. She wasn't coming back. She could promise all she wanted, but he could see the panic in her eyes. It was primal and instinctive. She could no more hide it than the color of her hair.

With a sigh he turned and made his way back into the house.

"Jake?" his mother called as he opened the door.

"Ma'am?" Good man. Delay the inevitable.

"My office. Now."

His footfalls sounded heavy upon the hardwood floor as he made his way to her office. His knees were stiff. It was like being fifteen again and called in front of her because the foreman caught him and one of the ranch hand's daughters in the hayloft.

He resisted the urge to salute as he entered.

She pointed to the couch, the very same place where Bryn had been sitting just minutes ago.

Jake crossed his arms and refused to sit.

"Well?" she asked.

"Well what?"

"Where is she?"

"She's gone."

"You let her leave?"

"Yes, Mama. In case you haven't forgotten, this is a free country and holding someone against their will is a federal offense."

"Don't get sassy with me."

He pulled his hat from his head and tossed it onto the couch. Then he ran his fingers through his hair, needing some sort of action to relieve the stress building inside him. "I'm sorry, it's just—"

"—been a long afternoon. I know." She leaned back in her chair and eyed him. "So what are you going to do?"

"I don't see that there's a lot I can do." He shrugged. "Let the lawyers handle it I guess."

"Would you like to tell me what happened?" Was she talking about that night in Austin?

"Not particularly." He pulled his phone from his pocket and texted Seth.

Can you come to the house tonight? Need to talk.

"I think you should decide what you're going to do." His phone chimed.

I can come now. See you in twenty.

OK, Jake texted in return, then pocketed his phone. "I don't want to talk about it." He left off the *with you.* He wouldn't hurt his mother's feelings for anything in the world. But she was too wrapped up in the family and appearances for her to see everything else. If he had his way and in a perfect world, he would marry Bryn. They would magically fall in love, have the baby and live happily ever after. But this wasn't a perfect world. And the chances of him getting his way were slim to none. At this point all he could do was pray that she would be okay. That she would be strong enough to have the baby. That nothing would go wrong.

Let me get this straight." Seth set his beer on the patio table and squinted his eyes, as if that would help bring everything into focus. "You met this woman in Austin, in May, and I'm just now hearing about her?"

"I can't say it was one of my finer moments." That wasn't exactly true. Deciding to let his guard down and have a drink wasn't something he was proud of. But those hours he'd spent with Bryn, upstairs and away from all the noise and company, had been something else entirely.

He'd felt alive in her arms. Alive for the first time in a long time. It was both liberating and terrifying. And when he'd left early that morning, he looked at her there in the bed and thought about leaving a note, something, anything so she could get in touch with him if she wanted. Then he'd changed his mind and quietly let himself out.

"You must have done something right." Seth picked up his bottle and raised it in toast.

Jake shook his head. "I'm beginning to think God is punishing me."

Seth rolled his eyes. "It's a baby, Jake. Not the end of the world."

And suddenly he felt like the biggest heel in Texas. "I didn't mean that." He shook his head. How could he be so insensitive? It had only been a couple of months since Seth and his wife Jessie had lost their baby to miscarriage. They'd almost split up over the loss, with Jessie on her way out of town before Seth convinced her that he loved her and he wanted her to stay and be his wife. The declaration of his love was still painted in bright red letters across the city's water tower. And since Seth was the sheriff of Page County, Jake didn't think it would ever be removed.

"It's okay," he said. "We've both lost something very important. Just don't let it cause you to lose more than you have."

Chapter Three

"You can do this," Bryn muttered to herself as she got out of the car. Once again she was on Langston property. She had buried her mother, her father, and her baby sister. She had driven across the country and sprinkled her sister's ashes in the ocean, but facing Jake Langston again? Now that was really something she didn't want to do.

But Rick was right. She would have to share her child with the Langstons. It was better by far to spend some time with them and find out who they really were before she carted her baby off for the rest of the summer.

The thought made her stomach hurt. But what choice did she have? And all because one night she took a chance on a cowboy. And what a chance it was.

"Well, I'll be."

Door still open, Bryn looked up to see Jake's grandma Esther standing on the porch. She was dressed in typical granny attire, pull-on, denim-look pants and a cotton T-shirt, though Bryn noticed it had been silk-screened to look like a Western shirt. On her feet she wore black orthopedic shoes, but Bryn had the feeling she wore her boots when she thought no one was looking. "Hi."

The elderly woman shook her cane at Bryn. "I knew you would come back. It's a good thing they didn't bet me." She shook her head. "Bah, those boys welch on their bets with me all the time anyway."

What could she say to that? "That's terrible. They shouldn't welch."

Esther shook her head. "That's what grannies do. Let their grandkids get away with murder. You know, once Jake had this fund-raiser at school. He used to come over to my house all the time and pilfer around and ask for things to sell. Then he would come the next day and try to sell me my things back."

"Did it work?"

The old woman smiled with the memory. "Every time." She motioned toward the house. "Come on in. I'll help you find a room."

Bryn shook her head. "I'm not staying here."

Esther stopped. "But you're not leaving town."

"I thought I would drive on in to Cattle Creek and get a hotel room."

"Trust me, you do not want to do that. There's a bed-and-breakfast, then the motel where the kids go to watch dirty movies." She lowered her voice as if repeating state secrets. "Like we don't know that's what they're doing in there. You just need to get that idea out of your head and get on in this house."

The offer was generous, but she couldn't accept. Yet she had the feeling that the more she argued with Esther Langston, the harder it would be to win.

"Well, now don't just stand there. Get on in here so we can commence with the getting to know each other."

Bryn laughed and followed the woman inside.

"Evie," Esther called just inside the door. "Bryn is here."

A door opened down the hallway and Jake's mother

appeared. She wore a relieved smile that perfectly complemented her pristine white Western shirt and immaculately starched jeans. "You came back."

"Yeah." She nodded, feeling more than a little awkward. "I figured we could benefit from getting to know each other better."

Evelyn nodded. "Jake's in town right now."

"He's not here?"

She shook her head. "He and Wesley went into town to get everything she needs for school. And, of course, to make sure that we'll have a bus to pick up the kids each morning."

Emery would have been starting the seventh grade this year. Bryn pushed that thought away and tried to concentrate on the fact that Jake wasn't there and she was. "I should have called to let him know when I would be here." But she hadn't, because she really hadn't known if she would actually come back until she found herself in his driveway once again.

"That's okay, dear," Grandma Esther put in. "He knows the way home."

As if to back up her words, the sound of tires crunching gravel sounded from outside.

The old woman's eyes twinkled. "And that's him now."

A few seconds later the front door opened, followed by "Nana! Nana! Nana!" Wesley came running into the office and flung herself into Evelyn's arms.

She noisily kissed Wesley's cheek, then let her slide back to the floor.

"I did it! I'm going to school in the fall." Wesley did a little dance, the heels of her pink cowboy boots clunking against the floor during her jig.

Evelyn caught Bryn's eye. "Kindergarten," she mouthed over the top of Wesley's head.

Bryn gave a nod but stopped as Jake came into the room. Damn, but the man was more handsome today than he was the last time she had seen him. Of course he had been scowling then and shooting green daggers with his eyes.

"You came back," he said in lieu of a proper greeting.

Bryn stood. "I said I would."

He gave a quick nod. And she knew then that he'd had as many doubts about her return as she did.

"Jakey-boy, go get her things out of her car and I'll check the linen closet for clean sheets. I think we'll put her in the room next to yours."

"No." Bryn shook her head.

"It's the nicest guest room we have," Esther explained.

"I mean, no, I can't stay *here*."

Esther patted her hand. "I thought we had already covered this. You don't want to stay in town. Not enough options. Plus, if you are going to try us on for size, don't you think it's better to spend as much time with us as possible?"

Was that what she was doing? Trying them on for size? Did it matter if they fit? She was having this baby, whether Jake liked it or not. Yet how would she get to know them if she spent more time driving back and forth from town than she did actually at the ranch?

"I'm just staying a week," she said.

Esther shook her head. "Nonsense. You stay as long as you like."

"Come on," Jake said. "I'll help you get your things."

They passed a couple of doors on the way down the hall, but Jake didn't bother to point out which one belonged to him. Bryn didn't bother to ask. Knowing he was so close was bad enough. She surely didn't need to know *exactly* where he was. That might be too much temptation to bear.

Half an hour later, Bryn was all moved into the "spare room next to Jake's." And if his room was anything like hers . . .

A tall ceiling complete with raw cedar beams soared over her head. The floor was composed of wide wood planks making her think of the pallet floors she had seen on the Internet. Two walls were covered with the same cedar paneling while the third was rugged sandstone. The fourth was a bank of glass that overlooked the swimming pool. A sliding glass door bisected the windows and led to a large verandah that seemed to stretch the length of the house. All in all, the effect was masculine and rugged, but it welcomed her all the same. There were two doors besides the one that led into the hall. One opened to a large walk-in closet while the other led to a long narrow bathroom. There was another door on the opposite side of the bathroom. It was locked, but she figured it led to the bedroom next door, like the Jack and Jill bathroom in *The Brady Bunch* sitcom.

Bryn crossed to the bed and sat on the microfiber coverlet. It had the feel of suede and was the pale tan of a newborn fawn. Cinnamon- and teal-colored pillows added a little color to the décor along with a Navaho-print blanket.

Well, she was here. Maybe she should call Rick and let him know she arrived safely. She checked her watch. It was almost supper time here, which meant it was past that in Georgia. Maybe she should just text him instead. She reached for her phone and typed in a short message. Just as she hit send a knock sounded on the door.

"Come in."

Her breath stuck in her throat as Jake stepped into the room. "You get all settled in?" He pulled the door closed behind him and leaned back against it.

She nodded. "As much as I can be." It wasn't like she had a lot of clothes with her. She hadn't planned on being on this trip as long as it was turning out to be.

"Listen, I think I should warn you that Grandma Esther is determined that I get married again." He shook his head. "Ever since Seth and Jessie got married."

She had heard those names before.

"Seth's my brother. Jessie is his wife. They're coming for supper tonight. You'll get to meet them then."

"That's nice. Your mother told me you had four brothers."

"Seth is the only one close. He and Jess live in the old ranch house." He jerked his thumb over one shoulder in a gesture she knew to mean *kinda close but over there*. "Chase still lives here, I suppose, but he's off on the rodeo circuit. And . . . anyway, Tyler is in the service and Mav . . ." He shook his head. "Mav walked out fifteen years ago, just after Dad died, and he's not been back since."

"How sad," she murmured.

"Just don't bring it up."

"Got it."

"Or Chase." He shook his head. "I didn't mean to come in here and air all the family's dirty laundry, but I think you should be aware of a few things. Seth and Jessie got pregnant this summer. Then they got married and lost the baby."

"And they're still married?"

"Yeah." He grinned. "Jessie's like the sister we never had. You'll like her, but I wanted to tell you about the baby. Just in case."

Bryn laid a protective hand over her stomach. She was past what most considered the danger zone of miscarriage, but she'd had too many friends lose babies even after their twelve-week mark to take anything for granted.

"I really didn't mean it, you know."

She didn't have to ask what he was talking about. "It's all right. You don't have to keep saying that. I want the baby and that's all—" She stopped. She had been about to say *that's all I care about*, but she couldn't afford to be that selfish now. "This baby means the world to me," she finally said.

"I'm glad." He pushed off from the door and turned to leave. "Supper's in about an hour. Seth and Jessie should be here soon."

Her heart gave a hard pound in her chest. Showtime, as they said. "I'll just freshen up and meet you . . . where?"

"On the verandah. Grandma Esther likes to have a beer before supper." He gave her a sheepish grin. "You can't drink."

She shrugged. "That doesn't mean I can hide out in here." Though after the day she'd had, the week, the year, she would like nothing better. She just needed some rest. And tonight, in this big old bed, she was hoping to sleep like a baby. Surely she couldn't hear Jake through all the sandstone and cedar.

"See you in fifteen?"

She stood and stretched, her back popping like firecrackers. "Better make that twenty."

Jake let himself out of Bryn's room, stopping there in the hallway and sucking in a deep breath. He slumped against the wall needing a couple of minutes to get himself together. Damn, what a time this was turning out to be. The last thing . . . the very last thing he wanted to do was get married again. But she was carrying his baby. He wasn't sure if his mother or Grandma Esther would excuse him for this one.

The one time—*one time*—he had let his guard down and this had to happen. They had been careful. They had used protection, but it seemed that fate had another plan.

He pushed himself from the wall and continued back toward his mother's office. It'd be another fifteen or so minutes until Seth and Jessie arrived. Might as well get this over with.

He rapped lightly on her door and let himself in at her summons. Then he shut the door behind him and sprawled on the couch.

"Sit up straight," his mother commanded.

He didn't move.

"What are you going to do about this, Jake?"

He hoisted himself upright, but his legs were still

sprawled out in front of him. "I don't think there's a lot I can do. Maybe convert her room into a nursery. That way the baby will have someplace to stay."

His mother pushed her reading glasses down on her nose and glared at him. "Does that mean what I think it means?"

"It means that I'm not the only one making decisions here."

"So because she doesn't think you should get married, you aren't?"

"I'll be the first to admit that this is not the optimum situation. But I can't make her marry me."

"Nor do you want to."

"Maybe I don't."

"You can't make a different outcome by not marrying her."

And for that he had no response. He was willing to make anything—*anything*—different this time in order to keep her safe. "But I can't make it different by marrying her either."

"Jake, it's best—"

He cut her off with a quick shake of his head. "Mother, as much as I appreciate your concern and input, we are both grown and can handle it."

"But—" she protested.

"No buts. If Bryn doesn't want to get married, then we won't. And there's nothing that will change that."

But if she did . . . damn. This day was definitely not turning out as planned.

Hesitantly, Bryn stepped out onto the verandah. It was only seven o'clock and the sun wasn't ready to go down, but the sky held the orange promise of a beautiful West Texas sunset.

Was she ready to face Jake and his family? She took a steadying breath and ran a hand down the front of her lilac smock top. She had paired it with white skinny-legged capris and tan-colored cork wedge heels. By far it was the dressiest thing she had brought with her on this trip, but that wasn't saying much. Yet it seemed the occasion was more casual than she had anticipated.

Jake was standing next to a man who could have been his twin. His doppelganger was dressed in jeans and a polo shirt, a gun belt and badge strapped around his narrow hips. That must be Seth.

The two of them were talking to a slim woman with curly red hair. Undoubtedly Jessie, though Bryn didn't see Evelyn, Esther, or Wesley anywhere.

Jake saw her first, looking up and catching her eye as she came near. "Hi," he said. He seemed in some sort of trance as if he too was having trouble believing that this was all real. But he looked handsome. Oh, did he look handsome. He had changed since she had seen him last. Now he wore a shirt much like his brother's except where Seth's had some sort of crest, Jake's held what looked to be a brand. Jeans were expertly pressed and dark brown boots shined to perfection.

"Hi," she greeted. Somehow keeping her voice steady when all she really wanted to do was drool.

"Bryn, I'd like you to meet my brother Seth and his wonderful wife, Jessie."

Seth shook her hand and Jessie gave her a hug, both working overtime to put her at ease. And for that she was grateful. She was a stranger in a strange land and she had no idea how to proceed.

"Does everyone in these parts carry a gun or are you studying to be an outlaw?"

Jessie chuckled.

"Seth here is the sheriff of Page County," Jake explained.

"A lawman in the family. That's always a plus." Bryn smiled.

"Don't count on it," Jessie said. "He arrested me twice!"

"That sounds like quite a story."

Jake nodded. "It is at that."

Jessie looped her arm through Bryn's and turned her toward the house. "Sit by me at dinner, and I'll tell you all about it."

Bryn looked out over the pool to the ranch beyond. The buildings and other fenced areas created an L around the property, and she wondered what they were all used for. She had no idea the ranch would be this . . . sprawling. But it seemed as if that was the measure of Texas. Sprawling.

Even the table they had eaten at was a huge entity that seemed to go on for miles.

But it had been fun. She had worried about sitting at a table with a bunch of strangers. That was what they were to her, strangers. Even Jake.

And that was the weirdest part of all. They were having a baby and they didn't know the first thing about each other. But come tomorrow, that was one thing they were going to have to work on. Just how did one go about getting to know the father of her child?

She moved a little further out onto the patio, staring up at the billion stars in the sky. Maybe it was because the land was so flat or maybe things really were bigger in Texas, but it seemed that there were twice the number of stars here than in Georgia.

She heard a clicking noise and looked to see Kota padding across the patio. She didn't know a lot about dogs, but he seemed friendly enough. What was it Jake had said? As long as she didn't break from the herd. She wasn't exactly sure what that meant but she could guess.

"Come here, doggy." She lowered her voice and stooped over a bit, holding her hand out toward the pooch. He really was the craziest-colored dog she had ever seen. Mostly black, white, and gray with rusty patches thrown in for good measure. Kind of like a German shepherd that had been liberally flecked with bleach. She supposed he was some sort of herding dog, though she had no idea of the exact breed. Wait, weren't they just called cow dogs?

Kota came closer, slowing and finally coming to a stop right in front of her. He sat on his haunches and stared up at her expectantly.

"You're a good dog, right?" She hesitantly scratched him behind one ear.

He tilted his head to the side and she took that as a good sign.

"Yes, you are," she said, gaining more confidence where he was concerned.

"Nice night."

She nearly jumped out of her skin. Dog forgotten, she whirled around, hand pressed to her pounding heart. "Jake! You scared me!"

"I didn't mean to."

She lurched to the side and apparently Kota considered her breaking from the herd. He nipped at her heel, effectively keeping her in place.

"Ow," she exclaimed more from surprise than pain.

Concern immediately took over Jake's expression. "He didn't hurt you, did he?"

She shook her head. "He just scared me a bit."

Jake nodded, though he let out a high-pitched whistle. Kota immediately left Bryn to stand at his side, though she could tell Kota really wanted to make sure she behaved. Well, according to a cow dog's standards anyway.

"What are you doing out here?" she asked.

"Same thing as you, I guess. Enjoying the evening."

"Wesley in bed?"

"Finally." He chuckled. "She was pretty wound up at supper."

"She's a wonderful little girl."

A silence fell between them, broken only by the sound

of the night. There were no cars or horns. No sirens out here, just the low of the cows and the occasional bark as one of the other dogs heard something it didn't like.

Kota's ears stood up and he let out a small whine, but he never left Jake's side.

"Go on," Jake commanded.

The dog took off into the night.

She could hear the dogs barking, then things grew quiet once more.

"What are we going to do?" she quietly asked.

"Get married."

She shook her head. "I can't marry you." Though her heart leapt at the prospect. *Down, girl.* He might be one of the most handsome men she had ever met and the fifteenth most eligible bachelor in the entire state, but she didn't belong here. And he surely wouldn't pick up and move to Georgia. So where did that leave them? "I guess we should talk about visitation and that sort of thing." It sounded cold, like they were talking about something other than a living, breathing child. Something less.

"Why not? I have a good job, enough money to take care of you and the baby, and all my own teeth."

"This is not why I told you about the baby."

He took a step toward her. A menacing step, or was that a trick of the shadows where he stood? "Then why did you tell me, Bryn? You obviously don't want money or a ring. So why come here and tell me when you have no intention of letting me be a major part of the child's life?"

"Maybe this was a mistake."

"You think?" He took another step, this one bringing him close enough that she had to crane her head back to meet his cold green gaze.

"Not the baby." She waved a hand around as if to dismiss that idea. "Coming here."

"That's what I'm talking about as well."

She swallowed hard as he continued to tower over her.

"So why did you?"

"I don't know," she whispered in return.

Something changed between them, shifted, until the night seemed to hold something each one had been searching for but had never managed to find.

"Could it be you want to know if what we shared that night was real?"

"Of—of course it was real," she sputtered. Deliberately obtuse was not her best look.

"You know what I mean." He reached up a hand and brushed her hair back from her face. "I don't remember the purple," he murmured.

"Rick—my friend I was with that night—he thought it would be fun."

"Does he always advise you?"

"Sometimes." When had he gotten this close to her, and why had she only noticed now? It would take only a breath and he could swoop in and capture her lips with his own. Or maybe she should raise up on her toes and see if his kisses were as hot and sweet as she remembered.

And if they were? What then?

She wrenched herself from his embrace, only then realizing that somehow his arms had gotten wrapped around her.

"No." The one word was breathless with anticipation and disappointment. "You can't manipulate me this way. It's not fair." She backed away from him and fled to her room.

She could not fall under his spell again.

Chapter Four

Bryn opened her eyes, blinking a couple of times until she remembered where she was, Jake's house.

She rolled over and glanced around the room, unable to see a clock. She had no idea what time it was. She had stopped wearing a watch long ago. Once they knew that Emery's time was limited, they stopped measuring it in minutes, simply living each day in events. Trips to the zoo, the movies, out to sidewalk cafes for lunch, or simply a hot chocolate. There had been no need to tell time then, while it was ticking away faster than she cared to acknowledge.

With a sigh, she stretched and stood, then stretched again. Lord, she felt like her belly had grown twice as big overnight. It seemed no matter how closely she watched what she ate, she gained weight. It wasn't that she minded the extra girth, but she knew the doctor would fuss at her for health reasons. At her next appointment they would do the glucose tolerance test, and she was a little apprehensive that they would tell her that she had gestational diabetes.

But until then . . .

She made her way to the bathroom and took a quick shower, brushed her teeth and dressed, then headed out of her room to find the rest of the household.

It couldn't be too late. She never slept past eight in her life, but she suspected that for the Langstons, eight a.m. was more like mid-morning.

"You're still here!" At least Wesley's unusual greeting sounded happy.

"I'm still here," Bryn said, taking quick note that only Grandma Esther was around to take care of the young girl. They were making pancakes dubiously shaped like Mickey Mouse. Or maybe they were supposed to be caterpillars. Hard to say.

The pair looked much the same as they had the day before. Esther wore pull-on jeans, a novelty T-shirt, and her black walking shoes. Wesley looked as if she had been through a windstorm with her hair in a haphazard ponytail that looked like she had slept in it. Her clothes appeared clean, even though the denim shorts had red gingham trim that clashed a bit with her purple *Cowgirl Princess* T-shirt. Once again she wore cowboy boots, but that was to be expected.

"Are you hungry?" Esther asked. "I can make you some pancakes too."

"Starving," Bryn admitted with a quirk of a smile.

"Would you like three or four?" she asked.

"One."

"What's wrong?" Wesley asked. "You like pancakes, don't ya? Everybody likes pancakes, right, Grandma Esther?"

"Well, I'd say most folks do, but there are some I suppose . . ."

Maybe she was hypersensitive, but that sounded suspiciously like a challenge to fit in.

Bryn waited until Wesley's attention was centered on the pancake shaped like half the Olympic symbol before patting her growing belly. "I seem to be getting bigger by the minute."

That was one more thing she and Jake hadn't gotten around to talking about. What they were going to tell Wesley. And when. Far be it for Bryn to come in spouting off secrets and trying to explain why she wasn't there to cook but she was giving Wesley a baby brother or sister.

"You're growing a baby in there. You need more than a single little puny pancake." It seemed Grandma Esther wasn't opposed to spilling a family secret to the little ears in the house.

"I was hoping for maybe some fruit or yogurt. Maybe some nuts."

Esther nodded her head toward the large stainless steel refrigerator. "Should be some oranges in the icebox. Maybe an apple. Not sure about yogurt." She winked. "Not much call around here for it."

Bryn smiled her thanks and headed to the fridge. She was going to have to take a trip into town to buy a couple of things to eat. Not that the Langstons hadn't provided good food up until this point, but at the rate she was putting on the pounds, she wouldn't be able to fit through the door come the end of the week.

"Anyone else want an orange?" She grabbed a couple out of the fridge just in case.

"I only like my oranges cut in pieces," Wesley informed her.

"You only eat them that way so you can make an orange peel smiley face."

"That's exactly the way I like them too," Bryn said. "Would you like me to cut one for you?"

"Yes, please." Wesley smiled and looked so much like her father it took Bryn's breath away. She may not favor him in hair color or eye color, but she certainly had his mannerisms.

"Chopping board is over the oven," Esther told her. "Knives are next to the microwave."

Bryn retrieved the items and set out to slice the oranges.

"You said you weren't here to cook," Wesley said after a minute.

"You think this is cooking?"

Wesley shrugged, that one-shoulder motion just like her father. "It's kitchen work."

"As opposed to?" She shook her head and rephrased her question. "What other kind of work is there?"

"Barn work, of course. Riding fences. Daddy says there's horse work and cow work." She wrinkled up her nose. "But he won't teach me much of it yet. He says I'm too little." Her expression told exactly what she thought of that.

Bryn hid her smile. "I'm sure what he meant was he loves you and doesn't want to see you get hurt."

"I guess so."

"Wesley." Esther's voice was soft yet full of reprimand.

"I mean, yes, ma'am."

Esther gave a small nod of approval. "Come on and sit down with us." She motioned Bryn over to the kitchen table.

Unlike the dinner table where they had eaten last night, this one sat off to one side in the kitchen. And though it would have easily seated eight, the backless benches made it seem a little less formal.

She slid onto the bench across from the two of them and bowed her head so Wesley could say grace. Just like Emery had at that age, she recited the children's blessing. "God is great. God is good. Let us thank Him for our food. By His hand we must be fed, give us, Lord, our daily bread. Ah-men."

"Amen," Esther repeated, but Bryn couldn't get anything past the lump in her throat. Stupid pregnancy hormones had her tearing up at the worst times.

"Are you all right, sweetie?" Esther quietly asked.

Bryn nodded and managed to blink them back. "Fine,"

she lied. But *fine* was a relative term. She could be fine. She would be fine. And she had it better than most.

"Jake didn't mean what he said, you know . . . about the . . . you know." Esther shot a pointed look at Bryn's belly.

There was one thing about this family that was undeniable: they were sure protective of each other. And it made her miss her own family so much more.

"I know," she said. She had forgiven him long ago, but it was touching how everyone rallied behind him in support.

"Look." Wesley stuck her orange slice in her mouth and grinned, showing nothing but the peel as she giggled and did her best to hold it in place.

Bryn ate her slice, then did the same. Together the two of them looked to Grandma Esther, but she had already stuck her orange across her teeth and was grinning back at them like a Cheshire cat. Well, one with an orange plastered across his teeth.

They all started laughing like it was the funniest thing, sitting at the table eating orange slices and lopsided pancakes.

Let's go out to the barn and look at the kittens." Wesley made a face. "Well, they're not little kittens now, but they're not cats either. You want to go see them?"

It was after breakfast, after their quick cleanup. Grandma Esther had hobbled off to check the weather. From where Bryn stood it looked to be just like yesterday: sunny and hot.

"Where do you suppose your daddy is?" she asked Wesley. Not that the girl would truly answer, but she could hope.

Wesley tilted her head to one side and seemed to think hard about the question. "He's probably out checking fences."

Not quite the response she had anticipated, and that made her wonder if Wesley did indeed know what her father was doing at that moment. "Okay. That sounds like it takes a long time."

Wesley nodded. "A real long time. You want to go see the kittens now?"

And if it took a long time, chances were she wouldn't have an opportunity to see him or talk to him until supper.

She sighed. Her visit was unexpected. She couldn't demand that he drop everything and entertain her for the next six days, but it would have been nice to spend a little time with him today. She just needed to get to know him better was all. For the baby's sake. No other reason.

Wesley tugged on her hand, bringing her back to the here and now. "Miss Bryn, dontcha want to see the kitties? If we wait too much longer, they'll end up as just plain ol' cats."

Bryn laughed. The child was precious. "Well now, we can't have that. I tell you what. You let me brush your hair and then we go straight out and look at the kittens before they turn to cats. Deal?"

Once again Wesley adopted that thoughtful pose, mulling over the proposition. "Deal," she finally said, skipping off down the hallway toward their bedrooms, leaving Bryn to follow behind.

Wesley's room was an eclectic combination of rodeo and baby girl. Pink seemed to be the theme, with a touch or two of purple to keep things interesting. But everything in the room centered on horses, cowboy hats, and boots.

She scampered onto her bed, one leg swinging off the side as she issued her instructions. "My brush is over there." She pointed toward the large oak vanity. An array of ponytail holders, bows, and other hair ties were scattered about, creating a kaleidoscope of color. "But I brushed my hair already this morning."

"You did?" Bryn crossed the room noting that the rug was a large pink sheriff's star. Where did a person find such a thing? Only in Texas. "All by yourself?" she asked.

"Uh-huh." Wesley nodded. "I mean, yes, ma'am. I brush it every morning."

Bryn found the brush and joined Wesley on the big four-poster bed. "And do you put it in a ponytail as well?"

"Of course. I am a big girl, you know."

"I know." Bryn hid her smile as she tried to get the green ponytail holder out of Wesley's blond curls. "I hear you're starting school soon."

"Ouch," Wesley complained as Bryn hit a particularly tough snarl.

"Sorry."

Wesley caught her eye in the vanity mirror in front of them. "Why is your hair short?"

"Because I cut it."

"Why is it purple?"

"My best friend did that. He thought it would look nice."

"Your best friend is a boy?"

"Uh-huh."

"Doesn't that make him your boyfriend?"

"No." Bryn stifled a laugh. The child was precocious. "Rick is not my boyfriend."

"I like purple," Wesley said.

"Me too." Bryn continued to brush her hair.

"What about Daddy?"

"What about him?

"He's your friend too, right?"

"Of course." She didn't know what to call her and Jake's relationship. But friend didn't cut it.

"Does that make him your boyfriend?"

"Not really."

"Oh." Wesley seemed disappointed.

Bryn wanted to press, to see if Jake went on dates or maybe had a favorite girl to scratch an itch, but she couldn't find the words to delicately ask a five-year-old about her father's dating habits.

She finished Wesley's hair and wrapped it in a fresh ponytail.

Wesley critically eyed herself in the mirror. "I like it," she said. "You can do my hair again sometime."

"I'm so very honored that you are pleased." Bryn stood and gave her a small bow.

"Can we go see the kitties now?"

"Are you sure they aren't cats by now?" Bryn asked as she walked to the door and waited for Wesley to follow.

"I hope not." Wesley took off down the hallway at a dead run, and Bryn had to wonder if the child walked anywhere. Maybe if she hung around Wesley for the next week, she wouldn't have to worry so much about gaining weight. The girl would run the pounds off her.

Wesley skipped across the yard toward one of the outbuildings. It was closest to the house and on the short side of the L that made up the ranch buildings. A white-fenced corral stretched from the red-painted building toward the road, giving it the picturesque postcard appearance.

"They're in here." Wesley pranced into the barn like it was her second home, leaving Bryn to follow behind. "Here, kitty-kitty-kitty," she called.

Bryn heard their meows before she saw them, four gawky kittens with legs too long for their growing bodies. Still, they were beautiful. One had full orange stripes, while another was orange striped in patches over the white. The third kitten was black and tan striped, while the last one was a beautiful solid black.

Wesley beelined for the black cat, scooping him into her arms before he could scamper away. "This one's my favorite." She hugged the cat close even as it struggled to get down. "Joe Dan said we should name him Ebony, but I don't like that name." She made a face, without words clearly expressing what she thought of Joe Dan's name choice. "I want to name him Susan."

"Susan?" Bryn nearly choked.

"It's a good name for a cat."

"Sure. A girl cat. Didn't you just say it was a boy?"

The cat had finally settled into Wesley's arms sensing that escape was not forthcoming, but his struggles started anew when she lifted him into the air, straight above her head. "I don't know that I believe them. I think they just don't want to call her Susan. They keep turning her over and saying that it's a boy. But I can't tell any difference in the bottom of her feet."

Bryn stifled another laugh and rescued the kitten from Wesley's hands. She was no expert in telling boy cats from girl cats, but from what she could tell, Susan was a boy. "I think Joe Dan may be right."

Wesley stomped her foot. "Gosh darn it!" Then she seemed to recover. "That's okay," she said, reaching for the cat. She plucked him from Bryn's embrace, kissing him on the top of the head. "He's still my favorite. Even if I can't name him Susan. But I don't think Ebony is a good name either. I don't even know what that means."

"It's another word for black."

Wesley scrunched up her nose and shook her head, her ponytail bouncing from side to side. "Is there another another word for black?"

"Several, but I've got an idea. Why don't you name him something that is black?"

"Like Crayon? I have a black crayon."

Honestly, the child was precious. "How about Midnight? The sky at midnight is dark like a black kitty."

"Yeah." She dragged out the word until it was a mile long. "Sometimes the sky is black. Come on, Sky. Let's find the cat treats."

"Not exactly what I had in mind," Bryn muttered as Wesley carried the cat into a small room off to the right. This must have been a common ritual as the kittens followed behind her like the mice after the pied piper.

"Daddy said we can't have any more cats," Wesley said

as Bryn came into the doorway. "Uncle Chase brought these home a while ago."

Chase . . . that was the rodeo brother, if Bryn remembered correctly.

"He's always bringing home animals of one kind or another. Dogs, cats, rabbits. But I don't think he's going to bring any more home whether Daddy says he can or not."

"Why is that?"

"Because the last time he left he was real mad. He and Uncle Seth got into a fight and—"

"Wesley!"

She stopped abruptly at the sound of her father's voice.

Bryn turned to find him standing in the doorway. He was backlit so she couldn't see his features. His entire body was thrown into silhouette. And what a silhouette it was.

"There's no need to talk about that with our guest." He stepped into the barn looking even more handsome than he had last night. Last night when he had almost kissed her.

Another man stepped in behind him, followed by the ever-faithful Kota. The dog dropped to his haunches at his master's feet.

"Yes, sir. But he was mad. Don't you think?"

"Joe Dan was going to show you a rope trick," Jake continued.

"I was?" the other man asked.

"Yes, you were." Jake cut his gaze toward the door in a not-so-subtle hint for the foreman to take his daughter out of the barn.

"Oh, that's right, I was." But instead of taking Wesley's hand, he extended his own for her to shake. "Joe Dan Stacey," he said with a charming smile. "I'm the ranch foreman."

She returned his smile. "Bryn Talbot, nice to meet you."

Joe Dan was a husky bear of a man with a short beard and twinkling blue eyes. Bryn could immediately see that he was a trusted member of the Langston ranch.

Jake cleared his throat. "That rope trick."

"Right," Joe Dan said. "C'mon, little sister. Let's get ourselves some sunshine." He led her from the barn, and once again Bryn found herself alone with Jake.

"I should have known this would come up sooner or later."

"What?"

"Family drama. See, Chase used to date Jessie. Sort of. They were always a couple, but not." He stopped. "I'm not making much sense, am I?"

"A little. But Jessie is married to Seth—oh."

"Yeah. Something happened between Seth and Jessie, they got married, and Chase is a little upset about it."

"Is that why Chase doesn't come around much?"

"Yeah, but Chase isn't the kind to stay mad long." He shrugged, that same one-armed motion as Wesley's. "It's only a matter of time."

She nodded, unsure of what to say. Her family had always been small. Though now with Emery gone, it was just her and the baby.

Jake gave an uncomfortable chuckle. "I didn't mean to come out here and air the family secrets."

"And I didn't really come out here to hear them." She gave him a smile she hoped looked encouraging. But somehow it felt stiff and plastic.

"Why did you come out here?"

"Wesley wanted to show me the kittens."

"I could show you around the ranch later."

Bryn had never been on a working ranch before. She nodded. "I'd like that."

An awkward silence descended between them.

"Thank you for coming out here with Wesley. She always wants to show the kittens to anyone who steps foot on the property."

"She's adorable."

"Thank you," he murmured.

"I take it she looks like her mother."

And just like that a shutter descended over his expression, effectively shutting her out.

"I'm sorry," she stammered. It had been at least five years since his wife's death, but it seemed that was something they didn't talk about.

"It's okay," Jake said.

But despite his words, she understood that there was only one thing that could make him so guarded when it came to Wesley's mother. Jake was still in love with his late wife.

Chapter Five

The last person he had expected to see when he'd come into the barn was standing just a breath away, looking like something out of one of those women's magazines at the grocery store checkout. Frayed jeans that ended well above her ankles, gauzy shirt that billowed when she walked, and those same leather sandals she had worn the first day he'd met her.

"About last night," she started, then shook her head. "I don't want anything from you. I mean, you don't have to woo me or whatever." She gave an awkward shrug, then another.

"Is that what you think I was doing?"

"I just think it's better if we don't do anything like that again."

What was she talking about? They hadn't done anything at all, but he had a feeling that if she hadn't skedaddled to her room, the morning would have found them together. But she was right. That would only complicate matters further.

"We still have to figure out what to do about . . ." He nodded toward her midsection. She was already starting to show. A lot. Which meant she was either carrying a big baby or she was further along than she said. But that would mean . . .

He looked into those brown eyes and knew that she was telling the truth. It was insane to trust her so quickly, but he did.

And that night . . . it came back to him at the oddest times. Like now. When he could remember every touch and every sigh.

Her eyes widened. She remembered it too. "I don't know," she whispered.

He swallowed hard, then gave a quick nod. "Tomorrow," he croaked. "Let's talk about it tomorrow."

She shook her head. "Tonight. We need to get this straightened out as soon as possible."

She was leaving in a few days. But the thought was no consolation to him. Until she left, she was underfoot, a constant reminder of his shortcomings.

Last night he had only wanted to talk to her, but some baser part of his nature seemed to take over and the next thing he knew, she was in his arms. She fit there like a lost puzzle piece, and that was really and truly what unnerved him. She was a stranger to him.

A stranger who was having his baby.

But still a stranger.

She was not some mythical other half of himself. He didn't even believe in such hogwash. She was simply a woman.

So why couldn't he seem to get her off his mind?

He ducked out of the barn, but she was nowhere in sight. That was good. He didn't know what to say to her anyway.

And every time he did try to talk to her, he seemed to foul it up.

Joe Dan laughed at something Wesley said, then stopped when he saw Jake.

"I think it's time to go in now."

Wesley looked up and nodded, but her disappointment showed. She wanted to be right in the thick of everything, and it worried Jake to death. He was having a hard enough time knowing she was heading to school in just a couple of weeks. That was something he didn't have much control over, but whether or not she was around a bunch of bucking horses and heavy hoofbeats, was something he could manage.

"You know she's going to be a horsewoman like her grandmother, right?"

"That's a long time from now."

Joe Dan shook his head. "Not really. She could be barrel racing in just a couple of years."

"Don't remind me."

"I'm just sayin'. You take her out riding fences and let her have free rein in the barn."

"That's different."

"It may be to you, but I don't think it is to her."

"I'm going to the house. I have some invoices to pay."

"That wouldn't have anything to do with your house-guest, would it?"

Jake shook his head. "Not willing to discuss it."

"The boys in the bunkhouse are betting she's pregnant. Any truth to that story?"

"Not willing to discuss it." Jake headed for the house with Joe Dan close behind.

"So it is true."

"Joe Dan, there are some things a rancher shares with his foreman and there are things that a rancher keeps to himself."

"Right. And I take it this is one of those second choice things."

Jake stopped on the porch so suddenly that Joe Dan nearly ran into him. "You got it right. Now get back to work."

Joe Dan tipped his hat, but continued to grin. "Whatever you say, boss. Whatever you say."

Small and insignificant. The two best words to describe how she felt.

Bryn shifted in the padded armchair in front of the desk and tried to make herself feel a little less small and a little less insignificant. But that was the job of the large polished desk and the even larger leather chair sitting behind it.

She shifted again.

The last place Bryn had wanted to find herself after supper was in Jake's office once again. The place was huge and hugely intimidating. Framed diplomas and certifications just added to the foreign atmosphere. He sat behind the desk to separate the two of them. With the width of the desk between them, surely there wouldn't be a repeat of last night.

Right?

"I guess we have to think about visitation times." She hadn't wanted to bring it up, but wasn't that the best way? Face your fears and all that? Well, this summed it up. Her worst fear, having to ship her baby to Texas. But she had known when she pulled into his drive that it would come to this.

"Getting married is still on the table." And he looked so serious when he said it.

"Will you stop that? I cannot marry you."

"Why not?"

She rolled her eyes, refusing to answer.

But moving to Texas would make it a sight easier. She pushed that thought away. "I'm sure we can come up with a solution that suits everyone."

He leaned forward in his chair and all at once she was grateful for the desk between them. "How do you suppose we do that?"

She didn't have the first clue.

"You know this would be a lot easier if you would agree to get married. Then we wouldn't have to worry about who gets the baby for Christmas each year."

She tilted her head to one side. "You really think that's going to help? I only plan to get married once."

"So did I."

The words fell like a boulder between them.

"Maybe we should get a lawyer to help us."

"We haven't even started," Jake pointed out.

Bryn shook her head. "I don't even know where to begin. You can't have her for her first Christmas."

"Why should you get to spend the first Christmas with the baby alone? You both could come here."

Christmas with the Langstons. The thought made her heart soar and sink all at the same time. She missed her family so very much, but adopting the Langstons would not bring her parents or Emery back. And she would always be on the fringes here. Not quite part of the family, but allowed in all the same. She wasn't one of them and no certificate could change that.

She jerked her thoughts to a stop. She was coming dangerously close to regretting her impulsive decision that landed her where she was now, but regretting that was a little too close to wishing she wasn't pregnant at all. And that was something she wasn't. She was so very grateful to have this second chance at a family.

"Surely we can work this out," she murmured. But the words were more for her benefit than for his. "We have a lot of time before we have to worry about where she spends her first or any Christmas."

Jake stood and came around the desk. He leaned against it, still a good foot away from her but so much closer than he had been. "This ranch is the only life I've ever known. I've not seen much of Texas. Even less of the world. But this is the best place I can think of. Fresh air. Great family and open spaces. I'm glad I'm raising my daughter here. I want this baby to be able to experience that as well. Is that too much to ask?"

He didn't give her time to answer, instead reaching out and pulling her to her feet.

"Don't." Having him so near was confusing. Wonderful. She shook her head to clear her thoughts. "We have time to think about it. Work it out." She pulled her hands from his grasp. "We've got months before we have to make any decisions." Not exactly what she was saying last night, but this was proving to be more difficult than she ever imagined. Maybe once she knew them better . . .

For a moment she thought he might protest. "Fine," he said. "We'll take a little time to think about it."

She moved away from him, needing Jake-free air to keep her thoughts clear.

"But it's not going to change anything. You live there, and I live here. Getting married is our only solution."

She started for the office door. Maybe, just maybe, a little bit of time would bring about a different solution. But as much as she wanted to be hopeful, from where she stood the situation was bleak.

Chapter Six

"Stay." He said the word even as she started out the door.

She stopped half in and half out, not turning around, as if she had imagined his request.

"Stay for a while. Let's talk."

She turned to face him then, but he could see in her eyes that she would refuse him. "What do we have to talk about?"

"See?" he said. "That's the problem. We have to find out what to talk about. Discover our similarities." He must have hit on something. She nodded and came back, though she stood behind the large armchair that squatted in front of his desk.

"What should we do? Play some party game to get to know each other better?"

"If we have to."

She shook her head. "Two truths and a lie is not going to solve our problems."

"It can't if we don't give it a try."

She seemed to think about it for a moment. "Okay, then.

But we can't stay in here with you behind the desk." She shook her head. "It's a little off-putting, that big desk."

"I know the house may look large, but there's not much privacy around here. This is one of the few places where I can go and be undisturbed. Then again Grandma Esther probably has a glass pressed to the door right now."

She laughed, the sound like music. Or maybe he just didn't hear laughter enough these days. Not even from Wesley. The thought was sobering.

"So the living room is out," she said, settling back into the armchair. "Who goes first?"

"Ladies, always." He slid onto the edge of his desk, his booted feet almost brushing her knees.

"Okay." He could almost see the wheels turning in her mind. "I went on my first date when I was nineteen. I've never owned a dog. I wasn't born in Georgia."

"And I have to pick out the lie, right?"

"Yes."

"The date one."

She shook her head. "I was sort of a geek in high school. Well, not geek-geek. Artist-outcast is more like it."

He gave her a sad look. "What is wrong with the boys in Georgia?" he said, then watched the pink creep into her cheeks. Was that all it took to make her blush?

"Your turn," she said.

He searched his brain trying to think of something to say. Then her answers hit him again. "You've never owned a dog?"

"Both my parents were biomedical engineers at the CDC. They just didn't have time for pets."

But he heard something else in her voice. "What about you?"

"They didn't have a lot of time for me either." She sighed. "I loved them but . . . my mother died when I was fifteen."

"Ouch," he said. He didn't know a lot about mother-daughter relationships, but he knew enough to know that fifteen was a critical age in a girl's life.

"We weren't very close. Sometimes I think she got pregnant to experience the biological aspects."

"Seriously?"

"Some women just aren't maternal."

"I suppose not," he murmured.

"After she died, my father married his lab assistant."

"And he found his true love?"

"I don't know. I think it was based off of mutual love for the field. I'm just happy that his assistant was a woman."

He laughed. "That bad?"

"Worse," she said. "But then they had Emery and gave me a family I never knew I was missing. So no, there wasn't much time for a dog. I was going to get one, then she got sick. We were spending so much time in Memphis at St. Jude that I was sort of glad that we didn't have a dog. But it makes me sad that she never got to have a dog of her own."

He watched in horror as tears filled her marvelous brown eyes. He moved without thinking, pulling her up from the chair and wrapping his arms around her.

She was warm in his embrace, soft and pliant, solid and sound. Everything he needed her to be and more.

"Everyone should have a dog," he murmured into her hair. "At least one time in their life." He rocked her from side to side, thankful at least that she wasn't sobbing. Her tears wet the collar of his shirt where she had buried her nose in the crook of his neck, but each breath was steady.

"She used to have this collection of stuffed animals—just dogs. All sorts. I bought her a new one every time we went to treatment. It was silly, I know, but I wanted her to have something. Even if she couldn't have the real thing." She pulled away and reluctantly, he turned her loose. He would have much rather gone on holding her until . . . until . . . well, until. That was all.

"It's not silly. Where are they all now?"

"I took them to the hospital for the other children. I figured that would be the best way to honor her."

"And you took her ashes to the Pacific?"

Bryn nodded, her tears seemingly under control, but somehow he knew they hovered just below the surface. "I dropped some into the Atlantic too."

"You loved her very much."

"I was seventeen when she was born. With parents who could carry on about corpse reanimation but couldn't sit through a school play, she became more like my own daughter than just my sister."

She wiped the last of her tears from her eyes. "This was supposed to be about us getting to know each other, not just Bryn tells all."

"What do you want to know?" He slid back onto the desk, but she remained standing, so close all he had to do was reach out and he could easily tug her into his arms again.

"Have you always wanted to run the ranch?"

"There was a time when I thought Mav would run it. He's the oldest. But . . ." He shook his head.

"What happened?"

"No one really knows. Or they're not saying." He knew his mother had her secrets. "I was away at college when he left. Then right after that, Dad had a heart attack and I came home and took over everything."

"Did you ever finish school?"

"I did. I managed to take correspondence courses and the like. I majored in business, which was easy to do online, and here we are."

"Business?" She seemed surprised.

"That's what we have here, a living, breathing business."

"I know but . . ." She shrugged. "It seems different somehow. Like . . ."

"Like being a cowboy isn't an occupation?"

"More like ranching is a way of life."

Now she had surprised him. "It is, but it's a business too."

"And would you be happy running a McDonald's on the interstate? That's a business."

"No," he said simply. He couldn't imagine doing anything other than what he was doing now. And that had been the problem between him and Cecelia. She had thought he could be different. "I'm a cowboy. And that's all I'll ever be." And it was one of the very reasons why he needed Bryn close. Leaving Texas wasn't an option for him.

"You say that like it's a simple thing."

"It's simple enough for me."

But then simple turned complicated, more than complicated as something shifted between them. She took a step closer to him. She bumped into one of his knees and he moved his legs a little farther apart. He was still sitting on the desk, but now she could move in. It was an invitation and a challenge. A dare and a hope to have her come near enough to kiss.

But after last night, she would have to be the one.

"What are we doing?" she asked.

"Getting to know each other better."

"Is that all we're doing?" she asked. "Getting to know each other better?"

"It's supposed to be." Why were those words so hard to say?

She inched closer still. He wanted to pull her the rest of the way to him, but he managed to keep his hands on his thighs. He wouldn't be accused again. This one was all on her.

"Why does it feel like more than that?"

"Maybe because it is." It was the only answer he had. He'd known from the first time he saw her that Bryn was different. Special. Even through the dull senses and haze of alcohol, he'd known.

"I'm getting mixed signals from you," she whispered, still so close and yet so far away.

"How's that?" he asked in return. His fingers twitched to entwine themselves in her hair but somehow he refrained.

"Your eyes say you want to kiss me, but you seem distant."

"This one's on you, sweetness."

"What's that supposed to mean?"

"It means if you want a kiss, you have to come get it."

Did she want a kiss? Could she explain this force that seemed to pull them together no matter how hard they resisted? Or would she talk it away?

A mischievous light sparked in her eyes. Or maybe it was desire. "Are you saying I can come kiss you and you aren't going to hold me?"

"That's right."

"Take over the kiss?"

"No, ma'am."

"Try to make more of it than just a kiss?"

He swallowed hard. He'd like nothing better than to make it more than a kiss. "Nuh-uh."

"Are you serious?"

"Just trying to be fair."

All of a sudden he felt like he'd thrown down a gauntlet.

She took that one last step to bring her as far as she could come into the V of his thighs. The sides of her growing belly brushed against him as she came closer. He shouldn't have thought it sexy but it was. They were having a baby together and heaven help him, he found it extremely—

She cupped his face in her hands, and then her lips were on his. Her sweet, sweet lips.

Her kiss was tentative and explosive all at the same time. Suddenly he realized that maybe she hadn't had many dates in high school or even many more after. She hadn't been a virgin when they were together, but there was an innocence in her kiss that he had never tasted before.

His hands jerked, but he managed to keep them in place.

He fisted his fingers, fighting the urge to pull her even closer, lift her onto his lap and . . .

She seemed to enjoy being in control, taking the kiss one step further. Her tongue slipped between his lips exploring, rediscovering.

They had more than kissed that night in Austin and he remembered it in sweet fuzzy sections. Yes, he'd had too much to drink. Hell, she had too. And he'd always believed that what the two of them had shared was a trick of the lighting, misplaced emotions tacked onto a time that didn't deserve them. But this . . . this kiss told another tale.

It took every ounce of willpower he had to not snatch her to him. He'd made a promise, and a cowboy always kept his word. No matter how much it killed him.

Sadly . . . No, it was thankfully. Thankfully, she got her fill and stepped back.

She licked her lips as if tasting him again. Then shook her head like she was having trouble collating her memories with the present.

"I'm not sure what just happened here." She took another step away from him and he let her. He was pretty sure he was as confused by the kiss as she was.

"You kissed me."

"Thanks, Jake." She rolled her eyes and shook her head. "I don't think we should do that again."

"What, let you be in control? I thought you did all right."

"Kissing. We shouldn't be kissing." She turned away but not before he heard her say under her breath, "It's too confusing." She started for the door, then whirled back around. "I mean, the last thing I need to be doing is going around kissing cowboys."

Jake shifted, trying to get into a more comfortable position to watch her leave, but that kiss had just been so . . . "Just for the record, sweetness, since you're carrying my baby. I'd better be the only cowboy you're kissing these days."

* * *

Bryn shut the office door behind her and rested against the wall. What was she doing kissing Jake Langston? Had she lost all her good sense?

She was going home in just a few days. The last thing she needed as a souvenir was a crush on Jake. And that seemed to be right where she was headed. Two days and he had her eating out of the palm of his hand. Somehow he knew exactly what to say and the right time to say it. Except for his marriage proposals. She couldn't marry him. She was a Georgia girl through and through. She had no business in Texas. If it hadn't been for Rick and his love of the drummer from Synthetic Cowboy, then she would have never been in Texas on that fateful May night.

But she was.

And now she and her real cowboy were having a baby.

Except Jake wasn't her anything. Baby daddy, maybe.

She pushed up from the wall and made a face. Baby daddy. How . . . quaint.

She started and jumped nearly out of her skin as the office door opened and Jake stepped out.

"What are you doing out here?" he asked.

"Leaving," she said, somehow managing to get her legs in motion. She might have been in control of the kiss but she wasn't in charge of much else.

"Chicken," he muttered as she headed down the hallway.

She turned back to face him, pinning him with a hard look. "You never took your turn at the game."

"Game?"

"Two truths and a lie."

"You want me to do this now?"

"Yes, please." She crossed her arms and shifted her weight as she waited for him to say his three.

He thought about it a moment. "The first girl I ever

crushed on is Wesley's preschool teacher, I get regular pedicures, and my first car was a '79 Firebird."

"The car." She shook her head. That couldn't be right. He'd most likely been driving trucks since he could see over the steering wheel. "The pedicures. No, wait."

"Don't hurt yourself." He laughed. "Why don't you sleep on it and we can talk about it over breakfast?"

He pushed past her and was gone in a second.

Over breakfast? Sleep on it? Like she would be able to sleep at all picturing him crushing on Wesley's teacher.

And that kiss . . .

It was going to be one long night.

Bryn dragged herself out of bed the following morning, once again wondering why everyone in the house let her sleep. Maybe that was their policy with guests. Let them fend for themselves.

It was late enough when she got to the kitchen that both Esther and Wesley were nowhere to be seen. And they seemed to be treating her like just another Langston. There was a note pinned to the coffee maker.

Sweetness—

I heard you wanted fruit and yogurt, so I sent Ol' Buck into town to get you some. It's in the fridge just waiting on you.

Come on out to the barn when you have a chance. We're saddle breaking a few new horses. Could be something a Georgia girl might like to see.

Jake

The food was in the refrigerator as promised. He'd even thought to get the low-fat kind. She laughed when she saw the peaches. She sighed. She was glad she was only staying for a few more days. She wasn't sure she could protect her heart for any longer than that. There was just something about that man.

She took her yogurt to the window overlooking the corral. Several men milled around, but she had no trouble spotting Jake. Something in the way he walked, the way he carried himself. How could she barely know anything about him yet pick him out of a crowd of cowboys in a heartbeat?

He looked particularly wonderful today in a deep red shirt and worn chaps. She caught only a glimpse of his jeans as he turned back to the man beside him, but what a glimpse it was.

She gave the spoon one last lick and somehow peeled her gaze off him. The spoon went into the dishwasher and she was out the door, heading for the cluster of men just to the other side of the barn.

He looked up and caught her gaze. But how did he know she was coming? Could he sense things about her like she felt she could about him? She pushed the fanciful thought away.

It was just lust. Lust brought on by hormones. She'd read it was possible. But that kiss last night . . .

She had stayed awake half the night reliving every second of that wonderful kiss, then chastising herself for taking him up on his challenge. That was what it was. She knew it now. But at the time, she had been too close to the action to see things clearly.

Well, it wasn't happening again. Something told her that he still loved his wife. The haunting look in his eyes whenever someone brought her up. The occasional look he gave Wesley at the dinner table. They were small looks, quick as a wink, but they were there all the same. Just another reason why she couldn't marry him. It would be hard enough to compete with all the live women who wanted to be the next

Mrs. Langston. She could never win with the late mother of his child.

She waved, and he returned it, though most of his face was shaded by the brim of his cowboy hat.

The men standing around Jake all turned to watch her come near. Even the fellow in the middle of the corral holding on to the horse's bridle stopped to watch her.

"Good morning." Jake said, tipping his hat in that charming cowboy fashion. That was another thing she could get used to real quick.

"Morning."

"I trust you slept well."

"Like a baby." *Liar.* But he had started this insane competition between them. And she would be damned before she backed down to him.

"Hey, boss, you gonna introduce us?"

"I hadn't planned on it." He threw the words over one shoulder, then turned back to Bryn. "You ready for this?"

"What exactly is this?"

"Ranch hands." He turned back around and started rattling off names. Bryn nodded politely at each of the men. There were five in all not counting the man in the center of the corral. Now that she was closer she recognized him as Joe Dan Stacey, the ranch foreman. "And this is Ol' Buck."

The man had to be pushing ninety. He had skin like leather, bowed legs, and a back that was bent nearly in half. He reached out a gnarled hand to shake. "Nice to meet ya, girlie."

"Thanks for going to town for me."

"'Tweren't nothing."

"Well, I still appreciate it."

"Uh-oh."

Bryn followed the ranch hand's gaze. A car was pulling up into the drive, a cute little red convertible. And behind the wheel, a beautiful blonde.

"A friend of yours?" she asked Jake.

His lips were pressed thin and he shook his head. "Nope." Then he pulled off his work gloves and started for the car.

"Bobby, you timing this?" one of the hands asked.

"Yep."

Then the bets started to fly.

Bryn held up one hand. "Are you betting on how long it'll take him to get her on the road again?"

"Of course." This from Bobby.

"And did you make bets when I drove up?" After all, Jake had believed she was here for the same reason as Miss Little Red Mazda.

Bryn had never seen a cowhand blush, so the flush that stained his cheeks was a new experience for her. Come to think of it, she wasn't sure she had ever seen a grown man blush.

"Yeah, but it's all in fun."

"That's it," one of the guys said. "She's backing up."

"What's the time?" another asked.

"Three minutes ten seconds," Bobby answered.

"Hot dog!" A wiry cowboy slapped his hat against his thigh. "Okay, everybody. Pay up."

"Yeah, yeah," one man grumbled.

The cowboys all pulled five-dollar bills from their pockets and handed them to the man. Bryn had the feeling that they had been passing around the same five-dollar bills since the magazine article went to print.

"You're a lucky skunk, Delbert," Bobby said and handed over his own money.

"What'd she want, boss?" one hand asked.

"Directions. Everybody back to work."

The hands scattered, most of them scrambling onto the fence to watch the show.

"You give directions often?" Bryn asked with a grin.

"Shut it," he said with mock seriousness. "You're going to jinx me."

Joe Dan came over to the fence leading the horse, who

plodded docilely behind him. "You wanna see if you can do anything with him?"

"I guess." Jake climbed up the fence and slung his legs over, dropping to the ground in one fluid motion.

Bryn braced her arms across the top board and watched as he prepared to get on the sleek black horse. "This is the horse you're riding?"

"Yeah."

"He doesn't look wild. I mean you have a bridle on him."

Jake nodded. "He's bridle-broke. And we can put a saddle on him, but any more weight than that and he bucks like crazy."

"And you're going to get on him?"

"How else is he going to get broke?"

"How else?" she muttered as he settled his hat a little further down on his head and reached for the reins.

For a moment after he swung his leg across the horse's back, Bryn thought he might be okay. Or maybe he had exaggerated the condition of the beast.

Then the horse tossed his mane, his eyes rolled back in his head, and all hell broke loose. The beast arched his back, then kicked both back feet in the air, doing everything in his power to unseat Jake.

The horse kicked again and again, shaking Jake all around on the saddle, but still he hung on. The cowhands on the fence whooped and hollered. A couple even whipped off their hats and cheered. The horse's black coat glinted in the sun as he rose up one last time, pitching Jake off his back.

Bryn gasped as he hit the ground with a thud, face-first. Dust flew up around him, momentarily hiding him from view. Joe Dan rushed over and grabbed the horse's reins, but once Jake was off, the beast had immediately calmed.

Bryn hurried down the fence closer to the spot where Jake had been thrown. "Are you okay?"

Nothing.

"Jake?"

"Damn it!"

Well, at least it was something.

He rose up on his hands and knees, sputtering as he tried to stand.

"Are you sure you're okay?"

"I'm fine," he said. "Just . . . dirty." He pushed to his feet, dusting off his chaps as he stood. But the mess on his chest . . .

Bryn wrinkled her nose. "Is that what I think it is?"

"Yes, ma'am. That would be horse shit."

She covered her mouth to keep from laughing. The cowboys around them had no such qualms.

"Is that a new perfume, boss?" one of them asked.

"Yeah, yeah." He slapped his hat against one thigh, then settled it back on his head. "Joe Dan, I'm headed to the shower."

"We'll be here," the foreman answered.

Unlike the first time when Jake scaled the fence like a teenager, this time he walked around to the gate. His gait looked a little stiff.

She held her nose as he came nearer. "Are you sure you're okay?"

"Of course. It's not like this is the first time I've ever been thrown from a horse." But he winced as soon as he was on the verandah and out of view of the corral.

"You are hurt!"

He shook his head. "I just got the wind knocked out of me. I'll be fine."

"Should I get the doctor?"

He stopped just a few steps short of the French doors that led back into the house. "If you're going to hang out with cowboys, you need to learn not to insult their masculinity." Then he continued on into the house without waiting for her response.

Is that what she had done?

With a shake of her head, she followed him inside. "Do you need something for the pain?" she asked, just trying to see how far she could push him. "I only have Tylenol."

His steps faltered as he started down the hallway toward his room. He didn't bother to answer.

"No worries. I'll just check the freezer for an ice pack."

"Don't you dare," he growled, but never looked back.

She laughed and continued on to the kitchen. She might have been teasing about the ice pack, but a cool drink of water sounded amazing.

She remembered where the glasses were from breakfast the morning before and found one easily. Using the dispenser in the door of the fridge, she filled the glass and stood drinking it, gazing out the window that overlooked the corral.

There was something undeniably beautiful about the bucking horse. The fluid motion, the arch of his back. The perfect kick that looked so practiced it was almost as if the whole dance had been choreographed.

Her fingers itched for her sketch pad. It had been so long since she'd experienced the urge to design that she had almost forgotten what it felt like. She gulped her water down in a single swallow, then hurried to her room.

She took a sketch pad everywhere she went and had since she was twelve. But she hadn't drawn anything since just before Emery died. It was as if her brain was so focused on her sister that it couldn't take the time for anything as frivolous as a jewelry design. And since then . . . well, she had been worried for months that her muse was gone. Poof. Disappeared like smoke in the wind.

She grabbed her pad and pencils and sat on the edge of the bed, her fingers flying through the many sketches before her brain even realized them. The symmetry of the horse's kicks, the curve in his back, the toss of his mane. On and on she drew little pieces here and there. Jake on the ground. The crown of his hat, even the way his chaps moved when he walked.

She shifted uncomfortably. That was the worst part of being pregnant; she was just sixteen weeks and she felt like she had to pee all the time. Heaven help her when the baby got bigger. She wouldn't be able to get two feet from a restroom.

Thoughts and images still racing through her mind, she hustled over to the bathroom door, wrenched it open, and stepped inside.

And there was Jake.

A couple of things registered in her mind all at once: the bathroom was steamy and warm, and Jake was naked. Well, naked except for the teal-colored towel wrapped around his waist. Lucky, lucky towel.

Er . . . "What are you doing in here?" Those were the only words her numbed brain could produce.

He winced as he raised one arm above his head and peered in the mirror. "Showering."

She shook her head. "I know that." She resisted the urge to stomp her foot. She wasn't as angry with him as she was with herself for losing all sense of self when faced with a naked chest.

Well, not just any naked chest. Jake Langston's naked chest was a sight to behold. Smattering of dark hair over strong muscles. Muscles she knew hadn't come from a gym. And a huge bruise just starting to form under his heart.

She started to go to him, touch the skin, ask if it hurt, but there were more important matters on the table. More important questions that needed answering.

"Why are you showering in here?" There. It may have taken three times longer than it should have, but she asked the question and that was the important part, right?

"Because this is my bathroom."

When she had placed her things in the room, she hadn't thought she would be sharing it. She'd simply deposited her toiletries on the counter, knowing she would have to pack them again real soon. She hadn't thought to look *inside*.

She opened the cabinet door to one side of the mirror. Towels, washrags, and generic toiletries. They could have belonged to anyone. She marched around him, careful not to touch him as she passed. The other cabinet told a different tale. Aftershave, razor, toothpaste. Again they could have belonged to anyone. Any *man*. But since he was the only man in the house, she knew they belonged to him.

She looked up to the door directly across from the one that led to her room. "So that's your room?"

"You are quick."

She eased the toilet lid down and sat on it, the urge to pee long gone, lost somewhere in her desire for him and her shock that they were sharing a bathroom all this time and she had never figured it out. It was a miracle she hadn't run into him in here before now.

"When they told me my room was next to yours I didn't expect—" She waved a hand around.

"You didn't expect to share a bathroom with me."

"Well . . . no."

"And you have a problem with this?"

Like they hadn't shared so much more.

"It's not a good idea."

"No?" He turned and braced his behind against the bathroom counter and crossed his arms. His bicep muscles bulged and once again she was keenly aware of him. The way he smelled, fresh from the shower. How tall, how strong. What a fantastic kisser he was.

And how easy it would be to lean in and taste him.

Wait . . . what?

"No," she said. "It is most definitely not a good idea." She shook her head. "And why do these rooms connect anyway?"

"When I married . . . we built onto the house. Instead of building us a new wing, we built Mama and Grandma Esther one."

"And you took the old rooms."

"You're sleeping in Seth and Ty's room."

"Fantastic."

"Oh, come on. We're adults here. Surely we can share a bathroom for a couple of days. I mean, do you really want to move all your things now?"

He was right. She hadn't been thinking clearly. Wonder why. She wasn't staying past Friday. After that she was heading back to Georgia. Back where she belonged.

"Okay, fine." She wanted to issue a bunch of ground rules and such to outline who got the bathroom and when, but once again words failed her. "Fine," she said again. "Now get out of here. I have to pee."

She all but shoved him out of the bath and back into his own room. He'd hang his towels up later, he thought as he pulled a new pair of jeans and another shirt from the closet. He slipped on his underwear and went over to the full-length mirror behind the door. The large bruise just below his heart had already turned an ugly shade of purple, the blood raising the skin. It was just about the size of a hoofprint.

He wasn't sure how the horse managed to pitch him, but he did. Jake was a much better rider than to let a horse throw him that way. He was distracted; that was all he could say. Once he'd seen Bryn standing by the fence, he knew he was sunk. Why had he even invited her out this morning anyway? Because he couldn't get that kiss off his mind. And if he couldn't kiss her—smooching in front of half the ranch employees was definitely off-limits—the least he wanted was to see her.

Of course it didn't hurt that he was a wily one, that Last Dance. Jake had thought the name fanciful when he'd bought the beast. Now he knew a different meaning. Climb on his back and it may very well be your last dance.

Gingerly, he slipped his arms into the clean shirt and fastened the snaps.

That kiss last night. It had been building between them ever since she pulled into his drive. They could deny it all they wanted, but there was something brewing between them, something strong and sexy. But he knew she was leaving in a few days. Exploring what this *thing* was wouldn't serve any purpose if he couldn't make her stay.

At first he had wanted to get married. It was only the right thing to do. But the more time he spent with Bryn Talbot, the more he just wanted her gone.

Chapter Seven

Bryn somehow managed to avoid Jake for the rest of the week. At least as far as the bathroom was concerned. During the day he was working, and she either played with Wesley or sketched on the verandah. The landscape here was so different from Georgia and she found a strange beauty in the harsh ground.

"Something's up," Rick said. "I can hear it in your voice."

Bryn stood on the verandah, cell phone pressed to her ear when she should have been inside packing. She needed to leave tomorrow bright and early, and she wanted to get to Shreveport before dark. From there it was straight on to Atlanta. Two days from home and yet she felt so removed somehow.

"I don't know." She sighed. That wasn't exactly true. She did and she didn't. It was Jake and his family and all the crazy reasons why she didn't want to leave tomorrow. She could tell herself that she needed to get to know them better, but the truth of the matter was she wasn't ready to go home. Not by a long shot. Even sharing a bathroom with Jake couldn't dampen her time here. Not that he was a slob or anything. If not for his damp toothbrush in the holder, she wouldn't know that he had been there at all. "I'm enjoying myself here."

She could almost hear him shrug. "Then stay."

"You make it sound so simple."

"Honey, it is simple. You're the one making this complicated."

She shook her head. "It's not like I've been invited or anything."

"Then move to the hotel in town."

"I've started sketching again."

"Oh, honey, that's great." Excitement filled his voice. "Then you definitely gotta stay."

"I'm mean it's not jewelry or anything, but I'm drawing."

"I think it's fantastic. Maybe your cowboy is a good muse."

Scenes of Jake on the back of the bucking horse, Jake stepping from the shower, even Jake at dinner the night before flashed through her mind's eye.

"I suppose." Or maybe she just wasn't ready to face the big ol' empty house where Emery had grown up. There was no need for one person to have a house that large. Even with a baby coming. But putting it on the market would be like losing another part of her sister. One day, there wouldn't be anything left. When that happened she wasn't sure what she would do.

She ran a hand over her growing stomach. "I have a doctor's appointment anyway." In fact, this whole trip had put her a week overdue for her next checkup.

"Then quit dragging your feet and get to packing."

Bryn smiled. That was just like Rick. Get right to the point and move on. "Yes, sir."

He chuckled on the other end of the line. "Seriously though, be careful and call me when you get to Louisiana."

"I will," she promised.

She hung up the phone and turned to go back into the house.

"Bryn? Is that you?" Grandma Esther came out of the kitchen, a mug in one hand and her cane strangely absent.

"It's me," she said.

"Good. I want to talk to you."

For a moment she wasn't sure what to say, but in the end she simply nodded.

The older woman led the way into the living room, easing down onto the sofa and motioning Bryn into one of the armchairs.

"Where's your cane?"

"Posh," she said. "I only carry it because Evie's afraid I'll fall. Hell, I've tripped on that thing more than I've tripped on my own."

Bryn didn't try to stop her smile. The woman was a jewel. "So when she's not around you leave it behind?"

"Ex-actly." She took a sip of what looked to be tea, then brought herself up. "Did you want a drink?"

Bryn shook her head. "I'm fine."

Esther nodded. "Okay, then. I've been thinking, and I think you should stay here a bit longer. Evie's gone and Jake's always working. How can you really get to know us if we're always off running around?"

She'd just been given the perfect excuse to stay and now she couldn't accept. "I have to go to the doctor."

"We have doctors in Texas, you know."

"Of course, but—" She stopped.

"But what?"

"I don't think I should go to a different doctor. I mean, that is what you're suggesting."

Esther shook her head. "Baby's gonna come when a

baby's gonna come. All these trips to the doctor ain't gonna change that."

Bryn wasn't about to debate the merits of good child care with the woman. Still, there was a little bit of truth in her words. Babies were a mystery the rest of the world was still trying to figure out. And going to a new doctor for one visit wouldn't hurt anything. It might even be helpful to get another opinion. Though she knew, new doctor or not, she was going to be fussed at for her weight gain. She was as big as a house. Yet she wasn't uncomfortable, not yet anyway. And since she had taken care of the last of Emery's wishes, she felt better than she had in the year since her sister's death.

"You don't have to decide right now," Esther said.

"I'm supposed to leave in the morning."

The older woman gave a quick nod then stood. "That should be plenty of time to decide to stay."

Jake," Esther called the following morning. "Tell her she needs to stay."

Bryn, Esther, and Wesley were sitting at the kitchen table as he came through the glass doors. He looked good. Better than good in his standard cowboy/rancher attire. Even the scowl he wore couldn't detract from his handsome features.

Why was he scowling? Wasn't that what he wanted? For her to stay. If they got married, did he expect her to head on back to Georgia? She would never understand men.

"She's a grown woman, Grandma. Perfectly capable of making her own decisions."

Was she? Bryn had spent most of the night thinking about staying and the rest of it talking herself out of the idea. She couldn't hide out in Texas forever. Did she really like it here or was she just avoiding the inevitable, walking back into the house knowing it was time to let it go?

Jake got a drink of water and turned back to her. Their gazes caught and held as he sipped from the bottle.

"I have a doctor's appointment."

She thought for a moment that he paled a bit under his tan, but she decided it was a trick of the lighting. The brim of his hat still shaded his face a bit.

"She can go to the doctor here. Tell her, Jake."

"You're leaving?" Wesley pinned her with those wise yet cheerful brown eyes.

Suddenly guilt flooded her. She hadn't told Wesley she was staying, but she hadn't told her she was leaving either.

"Midland," Jake rasped. "You could go to the doctor in Midland or San Angelo."

Esther shook her head. "Dr. Gary is a good boy, and he's a damn sight closer."

Bryn shrugged. "It's just one appointment." But she could tell that Jake was uncomfortable with the idea. Or maybe he was ready for her to leave and too polite to say as much.

"You're staying?" Wesley asked. Her brow furrowed in confusion. She looked from her father to Bryn and then back again.

Jake nodded, his gaze locked on Bryn. "If that's what you want."

But he couldn't hide that panicky look in his eyes. Or was that fear? She knew that Wesley's mother had died in childbirth, and she could understand his concerns. But Bryn's faith was strong. Life was about love and loss, and there was no getting around it.

He turned and headed back out of the house.

"It's best this way," Esther said. "Evie won't be back for a couple more days."

She would like to get to know Jake's mother better. Bryn had no sooner got to the ranch than Evie had to leave. Bryn thought it a bit odd that she had left like that, but she chalked it up to ranch work. It wasn't like her trip had been planned months in advance. She couldn't expect everyone to drop their entire lives just because she was around.

"Excuse me." She stood and started after Jake.

She caught him before he stepped off the large stone porch. "I won't stay if you don't want me to."

His eyes were unreadable. "You do what you have to do."

"What exactly does that mean?" She was done playing doublespeak with him. Kiss and not kiss. Stay and leave.

He propped his hands on his hips and exhaled heavily. "Of course I want you to stay. I asked you to marry me. If I didn't want you to stay, would I have done that?"

She shook her head. "I guess not. No."

"But you need to go to the doctor in Midland. Mama will be back tomorrow. She'll tell you."

"If you're sure."

Jake frowned. "Of course I'm sure she'll tell you."

"If you're sure about me staying."

Something raw flashed through his eyes, but it was gone before she could give it a name. "I'm sure."

"You didn't have to come here, you know." Bryn shifted uncomfortably in her seat and glanced around the office. It was the typical doctor's office with pastel pictures of flowers hanging on beige walls, toys for the children to play with, and old magazines.

Evelyn had come home the day before, glad to hear that Bryn was staying and promptly declared Gary Stephens a good enough doctor to see Bryn for an impromptu appointment.

"What was I supposed to do? Stay at home?"

Bryn glanced around the office, überaware that the rest of the ladies were staring at her and Jake. One woman even sent them a little wave. "And why is everyone staring at me?"

"Small town and they know you"—he seemed to catch

himself—"don't live here. Everybody knows everybody in Cattle Creek."

"So they know you, but not me, and they are trying to figure out why we're here together."

"Something like that."

"Should I tell them I'm your long lost cousin?"

Jake shook his head. "It wouldn't work anyway."

"Bryn Talbot?" the nurse called from the doorway leading to the exam rooms.

Bryn stood. "Are you coming or staying?"

The look he gave her was so pained she almost laughed and cried at the same time. "What do you want me to do?"

"That's up to you, cowboy."

He looked so uncomfortable sitting there in a pink upholstered chair that she thought for a minute that he just might go back with her. Then he shook his head. "I'll just stay here, if that's okay with you."

She had been going at this alone for the last seventeen weeks. What was one more? "I'll see you in a bit, then."

He swallowed hard and nodded. She thought perhaps he was about to change his mind, then the door shut behind her and the opportunity was lost.

The nurse looked at the papers on her clipboard, then flipped the top page over. "So you're here visiting?"

"That's right."

The woman nodded and motioned for Bryn to step into a small open door space with a scale, a chair, and not much else. "Let's get your weight."

The time of reckoning was near. Bryn stepped on the scale and closed her eyes. She didn't need to see it to know that she had gained a lot of weight.

"And you're seventeen weeks, is that right?"

"Yes."

"You haven't had your glucose test yet, correct?"

"No."

"Hmm," the nurse said. "The doctor may want to have you do that. When are you going back home?"

"I'm not sure."

"You're staying with the Langstons, is that right?" There was a gleam in her eye that belied any medical interest. This was pure small-town gossip at its finest.

"That's right."

The nurse led her down a short hallway and into a small exam room. "The doctor will be in soon."

Bryn thanked her and eased on the exam table.

She didn't have long to wait before the doctor knocked on the door. He was younger than she had expected, maybe even around Jake's age. His sandy blond hair was cut neat and short, and his blue eyes held a kind light.

"Welcome to Cattle Creek, Miss Talbot."

"Thank you."

He sat down on the stool with wheels and rolled toward her, chart in hand. "And you're only seventeen weeks?" He cast a dubious look at her midsection.

"I know." Bryn gave a small chuckle. "No matter how closely I watch my weight, I seem to be getting fatter and fatter."

"Uh-huh." He clicked the end of his pen and made a note on her chart. "That can be from a number of things. You could just be carrying a big baby." He stood and set her chart on the nearby counter. "I see you haven't had your glucose test yet."

"I'm going to do that as soon as I get home."

He nodded. "Let's have a listen," he said. "Lie back."

Bryn did as he asked, feeling all the more like a beached whale. If she was this big now, how was she ever going to make it to forty weeks? She would be the size of a house!

The doctor lifted her shirt and pressed his stethoscope to her belly. He moved it around, listening intently. He even adjusted the earpieces. "Huh," he said.

He removed the device and wrapped it around his neck.

"Have you had any other testing since you found out you were pregnant?"

She shook her head.

"Not an ultrasound or an amniocentesis?"

"No. Nothing like that. Is everything okay?"

"Everything seems fine, but I do want to do an ultrasound today. You want to go get Jake? I assume that—" He waved a hand in the air, an expressive gesture than meant nothing and everything all at the same time.

Bryn nodded and pushed herself off the exam table. Her knees were shaking and her mouth dry as she went back out into the waiting area. "The doctor said you should come back."

He stood and plopped his hat onto his head, then followed her back down the hallway and into the same room as before. Someone had pushed a portable ultrasound machine into the room. Just the sight of it made Bryn feel a little sick. Was something wrong and they weren't telling her?

"Go ahead and hop up on the table," Dr. Gary said.

Bryn did as he asked while Jake hovered nearby. He looked as worried as she felt. But in no time at all, the doctor had the lights dimmed and the test started.

The slushy thump of the baby's heartbeat filled the room.

"You hear that?" Dr. Gary asked.

Tears rose into Bryn's eyes. "Yes." She looked to Jake. He swallowed hard and gave a quick nod. He might not have ever wanted this baby. But he was clearly moved.

The doctor moved the wand about on her belly. Pressing here and running over a spot more than once. "Just trying to get a clear picture and . . . there it is."

Bryn turned to look at the screen. "The baby?"

Dr. Gary smiled. "The other baby."

"I don't understand." The screen looked like a lava lamp with bad antennae reception.

"Twins," he said. "That's why you've gained so much weight. You're having twins."

* * *

"I don't understand."

Bryn's words came to him like he was underwater. They floated to him, waving on the current of thoughts.

"It's pretty simple. There are two babies."

Bryn shook her head while Jake stood there. Stupidly.

"But how can that be?" she asked. "I've already heard her heartbeat."

"Babies are clever, and sometimes they like to trick us. Just when we think we have it all figured out, they throw us a curveball."

Bryn stared at the monitor. The doctor had stopped the actual ultrasound, having found what he had set out to find, but the image was still there. Jake followed her gaze. Two little forms. Each distinct. Two babies. Twins.

He pushed himself off the wall, just then realizing that he had used it for support. "Isn't that dangerous?"

Gary chose his words carefully. Jake could almost see him mulling over each one. "It can be, but it doesn't have to be."

"It can be?" His stomach knotted. "What do we do? She needs to be safe."

"The usual things. Diet, exercise, prenatal care."

"I feel fine," Bryn said, but Jake didn't know if she was informing the doctor or reassuring him. "In fact, I feel really good."

Gary nodded and turned back to Bryn. Suddenly Jake felt left out of the entire pregnancy. He couldn't let her leave Texas. He couldn't let her take his baby—his *babies*—away.

"You have vitamins, right?"

She had barely gotten into his truck and shut the door before he started asking her questions.

"Yes, I have vitamins."

"The prenatal kind?"

"Straight from the pharmacy."

"What's that other stuff you're supposed to take? Are you taking that?"

"Not sure."

"Folic acid. That's the stuff."

They had reached a red light, and Bryn laid one hand on his arm. "Jake, I'm fine."

"But—"

"No buts. We're having twins. Allow yourself to enjoy the news and quit worrying."

"Twins." He whispered. He still wore that stunned look, and she wanted nothing more than to change it from worry to wonder.

She could reach over and smooth away the wrinkles, but what about his heart? That would be harder to change.

A horn honked behind them. The light had turned green while they sat there and stared at each other.

Jake gave a small wave and started the truck into motion.

All the way back to the ranch she could tell that he was trying to come to terms. She was a little shocked herself. She had come to terms with being a single mom. She was okay with that. But a single mom of one baby. Now there were two.

She rubbed one hand down her belly and tried her best to calm her pounding heart. This was a blessing, a *double* blessing, and she would look at it as such. But still, *adjust* was no longer the word for what she had to do.

Jake pulled the truck in front of the ranch but made no move to get out. She was certain he was trying to come up with the words to go inside and tell his family the news.

Or rather his mother and grandmother.

"Have you told Wesley at all?"

He shook his head. "I thought we might tell her together."

That surprised her. Why would they tell her as a couple if she was going to be gone in a few days? She hadn't exactly set a day of departure, preferring to leave it open. She wanted to stay. Get to know everyone a little better. And now . . . well, now they had even more to work out.

"Tonight?"

"What's wrong with right now?"

Bryn blinked. "O-okay. Don't you want to tell your mother first?"

"I got an idea. Why don't we tell whoever we come to first?"

"Sounds fine to me." She let herself out of the truck, sliding to the ground just as Jake came around to help her.

"You shouldn't be trying to get out by yourself."

She shook her head. "I'll do it by myself as long as I'm still able. Lord knows there's going to be a time real soon when I may be stuck in there till the baby comes."

"Babies," he corrected.

"Right."

Together they walked to the front door of the ranch house. It opened while they were still on the porch, and Wesley flung herself toward Jake. "Daddy! Daddy! You were gone forever. Where'd you go? One of the kittens got stuck up in the barn loft and Joe Dan had to crawl up there and get him down. I don't know who was madder, Joe Dan or the cat. Where were you?"

He hugged her close, then allowed her to slip to the ground. "I had to take Miss Bryn to the doctor."

Wesley squinted her eyes and looked up at Bryn. "Why? Are you sick?"

She wasn't sure what to say, but thankfully Jake stepped in. He took Wesley's hand and led her into the house.

"That's exactly what I want to talk to you about. How about we discuss it over a bowl of ice cream?"

"Bubble gum?" she asked. "That's my favorite." She skipped on ahead.

"Bubble gum?" Bryn asked.

Jake shuddered. "It's bright blue and terrible. But I have a secret stash of vanilla with chocolate syrup if you're interested."

She should say no, but he'd just hit upon her one weakness. "I'm more than interested. Lead the way, cowboy."

Wesley had already gotten the bubble gum ice cream out of the bottom freezer by the time Jake and Bryn managed to get to the kitchen.

"Go sit down," he said, motioning for Wesley to head to the table. "You too."

It had been so long since anyone had waited on her that Bryn didn't protest. She obediently walked to the kitchen table with Wesley, sliding onto the bench opposite her while she waited for Jake to serve up their ice cream.

It wasn't long before he joined them at the table.

"Is it good?" he asked.

Wesley nodded her head while Bryn showed her appreciation by licking every speck of chocolate off the spoon.

Jake caught her, his green eyes ablaze, ice cream forgotten.

Bryn blushed and ducked her head. She hadn't meant for the action to appear sexual but she was afraid that was the only way to take it. And that meant . . .

Their night together flashed through her mind. Soft sighs and hot kisses. Had it been as special as she remembered? Or was it merely a trick of time mixed with a little too much to drink?

And then there was that kiss in his office . . .

"Do you remember asking me about getting a little brother or sister?" Jake asked. His voice was so nonchalant Bryn looked around to see who he was talking to.

"Yes, sir. And you said you'd rather have a dozen more kittens. Joe Dan told me that a dozen is twelve. So do I get twelve more kittens?"

Bryn winced. Nothing like laying it out in the open.

To her amazement, Jake turned an unnatural shade of red. "Well, what would you say if I told you that I'd changed my mind about a little brother or sister?"

It took only a moment for his words to register with Wesley. "Really?" she breathed. "Really? Oh, really?" She stood up on the bench and flung her arms around his neck. She left a blue streak of ice cream on his face as she kissed his cheek.

"When are we going to get it?" Her immediate joy burned out fast in the light of melting ice cream. Wesley sat back down next to her father and started to eat with renewed gusto.

"We'll have to wait a few more months. Probably four. Maybe sometime around Christmas. Maybe a little after."

"Is that going to be my only present?" Her brown eyes were enormous in her elfin face. Bryn couldn't tell if she was horrified or delighted.

"I'm sure we can swing a couple more things. Maybe even a second baby."

"Two babies? Like the Brenner twins."

Bryn had no idea who the Brenner twins were, but it seemed Jake did.

"Yes, except these will be the Langston twins." Just the name made Bryn think about all the trouble two little cowboy brothers could get into. With the size of Cattle Creek, she knew they would be the talk of the town. Just like their daddy and their uncles before them.

"And who are you going to get these babies with?" Smart kid. She had already figured out there needed to be a mommy and a daddy even if she didn't have one.

"Miss Bryn."

Wesley turned her eyes on Bryn. "Can the babies have purple hair too?"

"Oh, no," Jake said. "I don't know what color their hair will be, but I do know that it won't be purple."

"Okay." Her expression went from elation to crestfallen,

then morphed to thoughtful. "Are you having the babies, then going away? That's what happened to my mom."

A lump the size of Texas formed in her throat and Bryn choked on her answer. But she would be home in Georgia long before the babies came.

She cleared her throat. "I surely hope not," she finally managed.

Chapter Eight

Jake caught Bryn's gaze and held it. He knew what she was thinking. She was going back to Georgia in just a few days. That was if he couldn't stop her.

"Ice cream time?" his mother asked. She came into the kitchen, Grandma Esther following close behind.

He answered without taking his eyes off Bryn. "We're celebrating."

His mother moved to the fridge and pulled out a bottle of water. "Doctor's appointment go okay?"

"You could say that," Jake murmured.

"It's twins," Bryn finally said.

His mother's stunned look was priceless.

"Like the Brenner twins," Wesley chirped. "And their hair won't be purple."

Evelyn eased down on the bench next to him.

"Well, I'll be." Grandma Esther shook her head. "That is something."

He could almost see his mother gearing up in her argument for them to get married, but thankfully she didn't say a word. If Jake couldn't convince Bryn, he didn't want his mother adding to the situation.

"This calls for a celebration," Evelyn said.

"Agreed," Grandma Esther followed. "I'll make a cake."

"Jake, call Seth and Jessie," his mother continued. "Too bad Chase can't be here."

His mother still held on to the fantasy that Chase had left on good terms and might walk back in the door at any minute. The saddest part of all was how she couldn't see his shortcomings. But it had been that way so long everyone was pretty much used to it by now.

"You don't have to go to any trouble." Bryn finally broke eye contact and turned to his mother.

"Nonsense. This is special." Grandma Esther had already made her way to the fridge and had laid out the butter to soften.

"What's your favorite meal, Bryn? Let's feed those babies something special."

And just like that, Jake lost control of the situation.

You need any help with those?" Seth sauntered up, pointing his beer bottle toward the steaks sizzling nicely on the grill.

"I got it." Jake lowered the lid on the large charcoal grill and turned toward his brother. "But I could use one of those." He indicated the beer.

Seth handed him the bottle from his other hand. Jake took a grateful swig. Beer he could handle, but anything harder . . . Memories and whiskey were a bad combination. He learned that the hard way after Cecelia. And if it hadn't been for Seth, he might still be lost in a bottle. But his brother had sobered him up, pointed out that he had a newborn baby who needed him, and that it was time to snap out of it. For that, Jake would be forever grateful.

"You okay?" Seth asked.

Jake nodded. "Yeah. Of course." But was he? He looked over to where Bryn stood talking to Jessie and his mother. Grandma Esther was still inside putting the finishing touches on the cake while Wesley was hiding out in her playhouse.

Bryn was glowing with the news. Or was it just a side effect of her pregnancy? He knew better. She seemed almost happy that she was having twins. Things didn't seem to ruffle her. And he was ruffled. More than ruffled. Bryn, on the other hand . . . She patted her belly and laughed at something Jessie was saying.

Jake worried about Jessie. He had known her since she was little and with a house full of boys, she became like a sister to them all. She had suffered a miscarriage not so long ago and had fallen into a deep depression afterward, almost leaving Cattle Creek and everyone behind. Jake worried how she would take the news. Like Jake and Bryn, Jessie and Seth's pregnancy had been unplanned, but that didn't make it any less important.

"Twins," Seth said with an incredulous shake of his head. "That's pretty special."

"Bryn's pretty special." The words were out of his mouth before he had a chance to call them back.

Seth looked toward his wife and Bryn and gave a quick nod. "Yeah."

He could ask his brother what he meant by that, or he could change the subject. "How's Jessie feeling?"

"She's good," Seth said. "Healing."

"Have you heard from Chase?"

He shook his head. "You?"

"No. But he won't stay mad long. He never does." But Chase had been upset for months now, with no signs of change coming.

"Jacob Dwight," Grandma Esther called. "Quit that yakking and get those steaks up before they're too done to eat."

Seth gave a shrug, and Jake went to pull the steaks from the grill.

"Seth, get over here and help me bring the rest of the food out here."

"Yes, Grandma."

Grandma Esther enlisted everyone's help, and by the time Jake got the steaks over to the large outdoor table, everyone was seated and ready to eat.

"Let's go tomorrow," Jessie said, obviously continuing a conversation that had started before everyone sat down.

"Go where?" Seth asked.

"I asked Bryn to go shopping and to lunch."

"I need some more clothes, if I'm staying for a while."

She was staying?

"If that's okay."

"Of course it's okay," Evelyn said.

"You can stay as long as you like," his grandmother added.

"Thank you." Bryn shot them a sweet smile. "I seem to be gaining weight by the second."

"You look amazing," Jessie said. "And it'll be fun. I'll show you the town."

"What are you going to do after that five minutes is up?" Seth quipped.

Everyone laughed as Jake felt a pang of something he couldn't name. Remorse, maybe. He should have offered to take Bryn into town. But she had a car. And she seemed fiercely independent. He hadn't thought that she might want someone to go with her.

He needed to be more attentive. Especially if he had any hope of getting her to stay longer. And he needed her to stay longer. For the babies, of course. And no more reason than that.

"The car."

Jake spun around as she came up behind him. She hadn't meant to take him by surprise, but she had to say something to him to let him know she was there. He was standing on the back patio, staring out at the ranch with Kota at his side. "What?"

"Your lie," she explained. "Remember?"

Kota padded over, nudging his nose against her hand in a plea for attention.

She gave the dog a quick scratch behind the ear as she waited for Jake's answer.

"Right. So, how'd you figure that out?"

She smiled as Kota sat next to her as if guarding her. "Well, you have a five-year-old daughter and I've seen how you are with her. So I'm sure you get your toenails painted on a regular basis. I don't know about the teacher. But I have a feeling your first car was a truck."

He chuckled. "I wanted a Firebird, but Dad said no way. I couldn't make any money with a sports car. What about you?"

"My first car was a Volkswagen Golf."

He made a face.

"I agree."

"And you still drive one?"

"Hey. That's a Beetle, not a Golf."

"And that's totally different."

"Of course it is. That is my dream car. I've wanted one for as long as I can remember."

He nodded. "What are you going to do when the babies come?"

She hadn't given that a great deal of thought. She had mulled over double cribs, double stroller, double everything, but she hadn't thought about a small car, two babies, and two car seats. "I'll just buy a new car."

"And give up your dream car?"

"They're a little more important, don't you think?"

"Of course." For a moment there he looked like he was about to say something else, then he gave a small shake of his head. "Your turn."

"What?"

"It's your turn in our game."

So they were still playing. Or was he changing the subject? She couldn't be sure. "Let's see . . . I drank my first glass of Kool-Aid when I was in college, I always wanted to be on the cheer squad but never made it, and I would rather spend Saturday night reading romance novels instead of going to the movies."

"Romance novels?" Jake gave her a pained frown.

"What's wrong with romance novels?"

"I dunno." He shrugged. "Aren't they sort of cheesy?"

"Have you ever read one?"

"I can't say that I have."

"Then how can you pass judgment?"

"Well, look at the covers. All that skin and kissing."

"What's wrong with skin and kissing?" Wait, this conversation was not going according to plan.

He took a step toward her, his expression unreadable. Maybe not. Maybe she didn't want to examine his expression since it mirrored her own.

"Nothing," he whispered, though the words were almost snatched away on the cool night wind.

"Jake, I—"

"Jake I what?"

But she didn't have the answer for that. So she made something up. "I need to go inside."

"Why?" He took another step closer.

"Because . . ." She sucked in a deep breath as he came closer still. "Because if I stay out here, I think you'll end up kissing me."

"Probably." The rough note in his voice made her heart skip a beat.

"That's a bad idea, Jake."

"I think it's a good idea. Aren't you here so we can get to know each other better?"

She would not retreat. She would not retreat. "That didn't include kissing."

"Why not? There's obviously something between us and if it leads to something more, why is that a bad thing?"

Because she couldn't stay here. Because she wasn't a part of his life. Because she lived in Georgia and a leopard couldn't change her spots and she didn't belong here. But she couldn't say any of those things as he ran the back of his fingers across her cheek.

She shivered and told herself it was the night breeze stirring the strands of her hair against her neck that caused the reaction, but it was him. All him.

"Jake, I—"

"We'll never know if you don't give us a chance, Bryn."

"A chance," she breathed. Was that really so much to ask? Not when he was so warm and solid. Not when he smelled so good and felt so steady beneath her fingers. Everything in her life had been turmoil for the last two years. Steady was incredibly appealing.

He lowered his head and pressed his lips to hers. He gave her plenty of time to say no, to push him away, but she didn't. She couldn't. All she could do was slide her arms around his neck and hold on as he took their kiss to the next level.

She was only vaguely aware of her stomach bumping into his as he pulled her closer. He must not have minded her extra girth. Or maybe it was just a good thing she wasn't self-conscious of it. How could she be when she wanted these babies more than she wanted her next breath. They were the future, her future. Jake's future.

She felt an unfamiliar nudge at her knees and briefly registered that Kota was trying to step between them. It seemed the dog had more sense than she had.

"Down boy," Jake growled, his lips hovering a breath above hers.

Kota released a small whine, but did his master's bidding, leaving Jake to take over the kiss once again.

They fit so perfectly together, she and Jake. Even with her altered shape it seemed as if they were two parts of a whole. His arms slid lower and gathered her closer still. She couldn't get enough of his kiss. It was like water to a dying man, wine to an alcoholic, the nectar of the gods and a bunch of other pitiful metaphors that flitted through her mind and away again in the wake of his kiss. He filled her senses, filled her to the top. She was spilling over with something she couldn't give a name to. Not yet anyway.

She wanted to be closer to him, to spend the night in his arms. To never let him go. But she knew. This was the hormones talking. She had heard of pregnancy doing that, making normal women sex freaks. She had to keep that in mind. It wasn't Jake. Even as luscious as he was. It was just the hormones, and she would do well to remember in the future.

She was treading a fine line, but she couldn't stop herself. Didn't want to, really. How easy it would be to fall in love with Jake. Marry him. Spend the rest of her life pretending that they were the perfect family. They might even convince themselves for a while that everything was amazing, but she would always know the truth: he had married her because she was pregnant. And that just wasn't right for anyone involved.

But right now, in this moment, she could enjoy his hands on her body, his mouth ravaging hers, and blame it on hormones and the like. But what about tomorrow in the light of day? Would she hate herself for being so weak? And would she regret being with him once again when the future held nothing for them except shared visitation rights?

Reluctantly she pulled herself from his embrace. It might have been the hardest thing she had ever done voluntarily.

"Good night, Jake."

He watched her hurry back into the house and forced himself not to go after her. Pressuring her wouldn't make things any better. Kota whined and lay down, propping his chin on the top of his paws.

"I know how you feel, buddy."

This was something she had to realize on her own. That she needed to stay in Texas. That they needed to make a family. It could work. Why not? The attraction was there. They were having babies together. Wesley adored her. All the makings for a perfect family were in place. So why couldn't she see it?

Damn! Nights like tonight made him wish he'd never stopped drinking the hard stuff. But whiskey wouldn't take the edge off his desire for her. Or get rid of his raging hard-on. The first night he'd spent with her had taught him that. And the hard liquor would just make things fuzzy, and whenever Bryn was around his thoughts were indistinct enough.

Actually that wasn't entirely true. His thoughts were crisp and clean, but they were all about pulling her close and never letting her go. He hadn't allowed himself to feel that way about anyone in a long, long time. Cecelia had been his last love. He'd met her when he'd gotten his master's, a city girl from Houston and a West Texas rancher. It was an ill-fated match from the start, but they had tried. Oh, how they had tried.

He pushed those thoughts from his mind. He wasn't traveling down that road tonight.

"Jake, are you out here?" Grandma Esther came out of the house, still wearing her clothes from dinner.

Kota jumped back to attention.

"It's getting late, Grandma. You should be getting ready for bed."

"Don't sass me, young man. I just saw Bryn running through the house looking like the devil was on her heels. What'd you do to her?"

He'd kissed her like there was no tomorrow, because maybe for them there wasn't. He'd tried to talk to her about staying in Texas and raising babies, but mostly he'd just kissed her. But he couldn't tell his grandmother that. "Nothing."

"Now you and I both know that isn't true. And whatever you did or said, you better go make it right."

"Yes, ma'am." His intention had been to go back into the house, head in the general direction of Bryn's room, then abandon the idea.

His grandma must have figured that out. She followed him all the way to Bryn's room and stood behind him, overseeing his every move. What choice did he have but to knock and wait?

"Jake." She seemed breathless as she pulled open the door.

"I came to make sure you're all right." He cut his eyes to the side trying to let her know that his grandmother was just out of view. This was almost as bad as the time he asked Danielle Maynard to the seventh-grade dance and his grandmother had come along, hiding just out of sight and feeding him unwanted lines like some crazed Cyrano de Bergerac.

"I'm fine." But she looked tired. Not physically, but emotionally. He couldn't say that he blamed her. It had been a trying week. And she had been dealing with all the stress and surprises a lot longer than he had.

He cut his gaze to the side once again.

"Do you have something in your eye?" she asked.

He smiled and repeated the motion. "No. Can I come in?"

"I don't think that's a good idea."

"Please, Bryn." He cut his gaze to the side once more, and she finally understood that something else was afoot.

"Okay, fine." She stepped to one side to allow Jake the space to enter.

His grandmother patted him on the back encouragingly. "Attaboy."

At least Bryn waited until the door was shut behind him before crossing her arms and staring him down.

"You want to tell me what that was all about?" With her arms folded like that, her belly looked all the bigger. He reached toward her wanting to feel the curve, touch the place where his babies rested. But he stopped himself, shoving his hands into his pockets instead.

"Grandma Esther can be a little meddling."

"And she's trying to push us together?"

"Something like that."

She raised one brow and waited for him to continue.

"She saw you come through the house and decided I had done something to upset you. She wanted me to come in here and make sure you're okay."

"And she followed you here?"

Jake nodded.

"I'm okay." She seemed to relax a little and dropped her arms at her sides.

He shot her a sheepish grin. "I'm a little afraid to leave."

"You don't think she's out there waiting for you?"

"I wouldn't put it past her. She takes her great-grandchildren very seriously."

Bryn shook her head. "No, no, no, you can't stay here."

"Just for a little bit."

"Jake, really. This is ridiculous."

He made his way over to the door and pressed his ear against it. He couldn't hear anything, but that didn't mean she wasn't out there silently waiting.

Of course she could have already headed to bed. But he wasn't willing to chance it. And . . . okay, he admitted it. It gave him the perfect excuse to stay with Bryn a little while longer.

And what? Sit panting at her feet hoping for a couple of scraps of her attention like Kota?

He was being overly dramatic, but it beat facing the truth. The more time he spent with Bryn, the more time he wanted to spend with her. And that was something he didn't want. He would marry her if only she agreed, but he didn't want to love her. Love got messy. He had fallen for a city girl once, and he didn't plan on doing it again. But somehow whenever Bryn was near, he forgot all those rules he had set for himself.

"Trust me. I know." He turned around and rested against the door as he stalled.

"I'm sure you do. But you can't stay here. I don't want you here."

"Are you afraid of me?"

She shook her head. "When you kiss me, I lose my direction. I forget about things I need to remember. Always."

"Like what?" he quietly asked.

"Like the fact that I don't belong here. This isn't my family. I live in Georgia. And—"

"And what?"

She shook her head. "You should leave."

But he didn't want to.

"So which one is it?" he asked, grasping onto the first thought he had to prolong their time together. "Which one is your lie?"

"I thought the object of the game was to guess."

"Okay." He straightened to his full height and rubbed his chin. "Every girl in Cattle Creek wants to be a cheerleader, so that one's got to be a truth. And you've already defended romance novels."

"I did?"

"Pretty much." He took an involuntary step in her direction. She pulled him to her like metal to a magnet. "And I certainly hope that you had Kool-Aid before you were in college. So that's my guess."

"Final answer?" she quipped.

He gave a quick nod. "Final answer."

"Nope. I never wanted to be a cheerleader."

"Really?"

"I was all about art class."

"And you never drank Kool-Aid?"

"Science nerd parents." She took ahold of his arm and led him back to the bedroom door.

"Right," he said.

"Good night, Jake."

He shook his head. "What if Grandma Esther is still out there?"

"It's a chance you're going to have to take."

"Hold on." He dug in his heels, using his superior size to hold his ground. "Don't I get a turn?"

She dipped her chin in a quick nod. "Okay, then. Go."

He thought about it a minute. "My favorite color is yellow. I love barbeque ribs, and I don't own any type of shoes but boots."

"You aren't even trying." She maneuvered him toward the door once again.

"Let me go through there, at least." He pointed toward the bathroom door.

She stumbled a bit as if she had forgotten that their rooms connected, then caught herself and redirected him. "Fine, as long as you leave."

Next thing he knew, he was halfway through the bathroom door. "Wait. So that means you really do read romance novels?" It was a pitiful attempt to distract her and as he had known all along, it didn't work.

"Good night, Jake."

"But—"

She closed the door on his words.

He stared at the stained wood. When had he lost his charm? Wasn't he the fifteenth most eligible bachelor in Texas?

He raised his hand to the knob, but didn't make contact before she spoke.

"And don't even think about using this door again."

Chapter Nine

Bryn stepped out on the porch around ten the following morning. She refused to look over at the corral and see if Jake was among the cowboys working there. Well, she didn't need to. She knew he was there. Saw him right off. And the sight of him in those loverly Wranglers and scarred chaps was burned into her memory forever. So that wasn't really the problem. She just didn't want to give him the satisfaction of having her stare at him like a lovesick schoolgirl.

Jessie honked as she pulled her dark blue Jeep into the driveway. A cloud of dust followed behind her as she waved enthusiastically at Bryn.

Bryn returned the wave, thankful to be getting off the ranch for a while. The place was starting to get to her, starting to feel like more than it should. If she had any fortitude at all, she would pack her car today and head out first thing in the morning, but instead she was headed into small Cattle Creek to shop for new maternity clothes.

She adjusted the shoulder strap and headed toward the

passenger's side of Jessie's SUV. "Hey," she said after Jessie rolled down the window. Thankfully the dust cloud dissipated and the air was clear once again. "Are you sure you're up for this?"

"Shopping?" Jessie shrugged. "I have to admit that I'm not one for shopping all the time, but occasionally it's fun to get out and browse the stores."

"I mean shopping for maternity clothes."

Her gray eyes clouded over for just a moment, then cleared once again. "I can't say it'll be easy, but I can't hide from pregnant women forever."

"Or we could just go get some lunch and forget shopping." She could go into town tomorrow and get a couple of things.

Jessie smiled. "Whatever you want, I'm game. But don't you need some clothes?"

Getting more clothes meant staying longer, and after last night, she really needed to get herself on back to Georgia. "I could use a couple of packs of underwear."

"I know just where to get those." She cocked her head to one side. "Get in. Let's go."

"It's so different here," Bryn said as they drove toward town.

"Different how?"

"It's . . . rugged," she finally said.

Jessie gave a quick shrug. "I've never been anyplace else. I wouldn't know."

"Never?"

"Never."

Bryn decided not to press. She really hadn't been out of Georgia much. Especially after her parents died. Not until she had to keep her promise to Emery. Not until she decided to follow Rick to Austin and hook up with a sexy cowboy rancher.

"Tex-Mex okay?" Jessie asked as they neared the outskirts of the town.

"Sounds good to me."

Jessie pulled the Jeep into the parking lot of a tiled-roof adobe-looking building. THE CANTINA was painted across the front in large, old-school cursive lettering. Next to that was a wrought iron basket of silk flowers that was both cheesy and welcoming at the same time.

The inside was more of the same. Mexican blankets tacked to the faux-adobe walls, more silk flowers, and brightly painted clay statues of lizards, frogs, and the like.

"What's good?" Bryn asked after they were seated and handed menus.

"Everything." Jessie glanced up from her menu. "But the enchiladas are my favorite."

"Sounds terrific."

The waitress came back bearing a tray with waters, little bowls of salsa, and a large basket of chips. Bryn and Jessie placed their orders and the waitress was gone again.

"So," Jessie said, suddenly seeming uncomfortable. "You and Jake."

Bryn nodded and punched down the ice with her straw.

"I've known Jake since I was seven years old. He's like a brother to me."

"I could tell that you were very close," Bryn murmured, unsure of what to say and a little unsure of where this was going. She had an idea though.

"I don't know what the future might bring, but I see how he looks at you when he thinks no one is looking."

She had?

"And if you hurt him . . ." She trailed off with a shake of her head. "Just don't."

Jessie had to be mistaken. Bryn could never break Jake's heart. He would never let her close enough. Anyone could see that he was still hung up over his late wife. It was Bryn's heart that was in danger.

"I would never hurt him."

Jessie gave her a sweet, understanding smile. "Just see that you don't."

* * *

Once Jessie seemed to get it out of her system, her "you better not hurt Jake" speech, Bryn enjoyed the sassy redhead. One thing she could honestly say about Jessie Langston, she was forthright and down-to-earth. Okay, that was two things, but they both fit her to a T.

"Are you sure you don't want to look at clothes?" Jessie asked as they eased down Main Street.

Cattle Creek was the quintessential small Texas town. Everything about it screamed "come in and sit a spell." Bryn had been raised in the city and had always lived in one big metropolis or another. But this . . . she was pretty sure that if a person looked up *charming* in the dictionary, a picture of Cattle Creek wouldn't be far down the page.

Brick storefronts that looked as if they had been there since the turn of the century, the twentieth century. Lampposts she was certain were turned on each night. Hanging flowers and striped awnings. Who had hanging flowers in this heat? Cattle Creek, that was who.

"It's quiet here," she said.

Jessie shook her head. "Only if you're not from here."

Bryn didn't have a chance to ask what she meant by that before Jessie pulled her SUV into the parking lot of the Dollar General.

"They won't be silk, but they'll keep your fanny covered until you can get back home." She slid from the truck, then stopped. "You are going back to Georgia, right?"

Bryn nodded. Every day she stayed in Cattle Creek, the farther away Georgia seemed. She had to get back before she forgot herself and where she was from. "In a day or two." Maybe a week.

"Is Georgia nice?" Jessie asked as they walked inside. She pointed her over to the small clothing section.

"It's green." Bryn said. "I live in Atlanta. It's big and . . ." Big. That was the only word she could think of to describe her hometown. There were so many great things about the city and she couldn't think of one.

"Seth would love having a baseball team that close." Jessie smiled. "That man loves his baseball."

"I thought football was king in Texas."

Jessie laughed. "It is, but Seth says baseball is a gentleman's sport."

She had only talked with the sheriff of Page County twice, but she could see him saying that, as if she had heard it firsthand. Seth Langston was a gentleman cowboy, no doubt about it.

And what was Jake? More of the same. Except sexy. Yet she didn't know if he liked baseball or not. She had been there over a week, and she still didn't feel like she knew that much about him.

"I don't see any maternity panties," Jessie mused as they perused the wall of packaged undies.

"I guess I'll just have to get some regular ones, just a bigger size." It wasn't like she'd be wearing them for long.

Her cell phone chimed, alerting her to a new text message. She fished it out of her purse. Jake. She couldn't stop her smile, then it froze as she immediately wondered if something was wrong. She thumbed open her messages.

> I'm something of a cat person. I've never been to the movies alone. I hope you have two girls.

She stared at the screen a full five seconds trying to figure out what he was talking about.

"Is something wrong?" Jessie asked.

"I don't think so." She typed What? into the phone and hit send, still staring at it as she waited for his reply.

> Our game. It's my turn right?

> Right, she responded with a laugh.

Tonight you tell me which one is the lie.

This wasn't two lies and a truth, which was exactly what it looked like. She was fairly certain he wasn't a cat person and maybe he had been to the movies alone, maybe not. But her having two girls . . . ? That didn't seem like Jake at all.

"I tell you, it's a crying shame."

Bryn looked up from replying to Jake. She might not have ever paid any attention to the voice and the woman it belonged to except Jessie stiffened like she'd been shellacked into a stick.

"First Seth and now Jake."

They were talking about the Langstons. How many Seths and Jakes could there be in a town the size of Cattle Creek?

"Did you see her?"

Bryn caught Jessie's eye. Jess shook her head.

"Well, at least we know she truly is pregnant."

"Right, unlike Miss McAllen, who managed to trap Seth and get him off the market."

"But Jake . . ." Bryn could almost hear the woman shake her head. "He was still grieving over poor Cecelia. He deserves so much better than that."

"That's it," Bryn mouthed to Jessie. She started down the aisle, set on rounding the corner and giving someone a piece of her mind.

Jessie grabbed her arm. "They're not worth it," she said loud enough for half the store to hear. "Let's go. We need to get back to the ranch. Seth will be home later, and I'm making tacos. He just loves when I make tacos. If you know what I mean."

"I don't think I do," Bryn muttered, but allowed Jessie to pull her toward the checkout counter. "Why do you put up with that?"

But Jessie shook her head. "Outside."

Bryn paid for her package of boring beige granny panties just as a couple of women came into view. Bryn didn't have to be told to know they were the gossips.

But instead of charging after them, she took her change and together, she and Jessie headed for the door.

"Who are they?" she asked once they were back out in the parking lot.

"Sissy Callahan and Lindy Shoemake. They went to school with me and Chase."

"Why do they care about why you and Seth got married?"

Jessie beeped the alarm on the Jeep and climbed inside. She waited for Bryn to hoist herself up before starting the truck. "Seth has been one of the most eligible bachelors in Cattle Creek for a long time." She cranked the Jeep, then adjusted the air against the dry Texas heat.

"But Jake was in the magazine."

Jessie grinned. "Yeah, I did that."

Bryn shook her head. "I'm confused."

"There's nothing to be confused about. Sissy hates me from way back and Lindy was hoping to lure Seth down the aisle herself."

"So why do you let them talk about you that way?" She buckled her seat belt as Jessie reversed, then pulled out into the street.

"That's just small-town talk."

"But—"

She shook her head. "They can talk about me all they want these days. I used to let it bother me, but I don't anymore."

"What changed?"

Jessie held up her left hand for Bryn to see. "I married him. I have the greatest husband in all of Cattle Creek. And I know he loves me. They can talk about me all they want and nothing will change that."

"Wait . . ." Bryn shifted in her seat to get a better view of Jessie. "That's what's on the water tower. 'Seth loves Jessie' and then a big heart."

Her grin widened. "He painted that the day I almost left town."

"Almost?"

"Would you leave town if the man you loved painted the water tower for you?"

Bryn shook her head. "No. I don't think I would."

Once again Jake was flying through the air. He landed on the ground with a hard thud. Dust flew up around him as Joe Dan chuckled.

"I do believe you have lost your touch, my friend." He reached out a hand to help Jake back to his feet.

"Bull," Jake muttered, but he was beginning to think the same thing. Except he knew better. He wasn't losing it; he was distracted. By a curvy woman with a purple streak in her hair and a penchant for embroidered tops.

He hadn't been able to concentrate since Bryn left that morning. He'd lost count of the times he'd been thrown.

He would never be as good as his mother or his brother Mav at calming horses, but he was better by far than he was showing today. Then again, he was going to have a serious talk with his mama about the string of ponies she'd brought back from Tyler. They were wild-eyed bucking creatures and not a one of them showed signs of strong breeding. She was usually so meticulous in her purchases that these five horses had him wondering what was distracting his mother. At least he knew what was taking up all his thoughts.

A cloud of dust rose in the distance. Bryn! She was home!

He shook his head as Jessie's Jeep came into view. She might be back from town, but she had made it clear that the Diamond would never be her home.

Come walk with me." They had no sooner got up from the supper table than Jake reached out a hand toward her.

"I want to go too," Wesley added, dancing up and down with excitement.

Evelyn looked from her to Jake, then reached out a hand toward Wesley. "Why don't you come help me in the kitchen? I have a special dessert for little girls who help with the dishes."

Did she know something Bryn didn't?

"I think I should stay and help clean up."

Jake shook his head. "Come walk with me," he repeated.

Bryn swallowed back her trepidation and followed him out of the house.

"Where are we going?" she asked.

He gave her another of those one-arm shrugs she had come to adore. "Nowhere special. I guess down to the creek."

"There's a creek?"

He chuckled. "Why do you suppose they call it Cattle Creek?" He whistled and Kota trotted up next to them. Even though Jake had called, the dog stayed close to Bryn's side.

"I don't know." She laughed. "Didn't I read somewhere that Big Lake, Texas, has no lake?"

"They have one sometimes."

"What about this creek of yours?" she asked.

He held open the gate and allowed her and Kota to go in before shutting it behind them. "We have the creek all the time," he said drily.

Bryn stepped over a metal piece that looked like rotisserie bars planted in the ground. There wasn't much space between them but enough that she treaded across them cautiously.

"What's that?" she asked, pointing to the metal in the ground.

"It's a cattle guard," he said. "The cattle don't like them so we put them up sometimes in place of a gate. That way they'll stay inside."

"They don't like them?" she asked.

"They won't walk across them. I think they're afraid they might get their feet stuck in the spaces between, so they just don't go across them at all."

"I've never heard such a thing." She smiled in awe.

"City girl."

Once the gate was shut, they started walking through the scruffy pasture. The land here was rugged. That was the only way to describe it, but it had a beauty all its own. There were a few cactuses and still there were wildflowers as if the desert and the lush green of the Hill Country couldn't figure out which one belonged there more. Every so often Kota spied something of interest and went to investigate, but he always returned to Bryn's side. She liked having a dog. Maybe she would get one when she got back home.

Or maybe not. All too soon she would have more companionship than she could shake a stick at.

"If that wasn't true, I might take offense," she said.

"But it is true."

She nodded.

"Did you have a good time in town today?"

Bryn opened her mouth to tell him about the two girls in the Dollar General, but decided against it. "Yeah," she said. "A real good time."

"You didn't buy very much."

"I don't need very much." It was the truth. But he raised a dubious brow.

She knew the difference between things and valuables. There was one lesson losing Emery had taught her. Most things were just that . . . things. She didn't want for much, and with smart purchases and good investments, she wouldn't have to do much for the rest of her life. But that didn't mean she was unappreciative of the things she had.

"Are you saying I'm high maintenance?"

"I'm not the one with purple in my hair."

She reached up and touched that lock or at least the general vicinity where she knew Rick placed it. "That was my hairdresser's doing." She let Rick have free rein with her hair. The purple had been meant to cheer her up. After all, purple was Emery's favorite color. But a lock of hair didn't bring her sister back.

"Did you figure out the lie?"

She hadn't had very much time to think about it. "Well, I already know you're not much of a cat person."

They walked along a small path with brush on either side. She could see the crop of trees up ahead and figured that they were close to the creek.

"How do you know that?"

She shot him a look.

"Ah," he said. "Wesley. I guess I'm not very good at this game."

"The lies have to be believable." She chuckled. "But I think you lied in this one twice."

"Should I be offended by that?"

"Did you mean it?"

"Yes. I've never been to the movies by myself."

"No. About having girls."

Wasn't it every man's dream to have sons to carry on his name?

"Yeah." The one word was soft on the evening air. Bryn stumbled, but he caught her elbow and helped her straighten.

"Careful," he murmured.

"I'm being careful. Just don't drop bombshells like that."

"What's wrong with wanting girls?"

She studied him in the waning light. The sun wasn't down yet, but it would be down soon. She had a feeling they might be walking back to the house in the dark. But she knew better than to be afraid. Not with Jake at her side.

"You're a good girl's daddy, aren't you?"

They broke through the small growth of trees to a clear, flowing creek.

"I don't know about being a good girl's daddy, but I like having a daughter. I enjoy her."

Bryn had seen it too many times to count, how he acted and reacted with Wesley.

"So, no. I don't mind if they are both girls. I'm sure my mother doesn't either."

"After five boys, I can only imagine." Bryn ran a protective hand down her belly, the action more instinctive than conscious. "I just want them healthy."

It seemed as if Emery's name floated on the breeze around them, but neither one of them said it. Emery had meant everything to Bryn and she had lost her. These babies were a second chance, and they both knew it.

"This creek," he said, picking up a rock and tossing it into the water, "was one of the last good stops before getting into Mexico. Drovers brought the cattle here to water them."

"So this became Cattle Creek," Bryn said.

"You got it."

Bryn raised her arms overhead and stretched a bit, enjoying the coolness of the evening after the heat of the day. That was one thing about prairie-desert, it cooled off nicely in the evening. At least it did for her. Someone like Jake might not notice the big change, and as far as she knew he had lived here his whole life.

"It's so beautiful here," she said.

He looked around as if seeing the land he worked for the very first time. "Yeah," he said. "It is."

Bryn looked at the clear creek, the wild vegetation growing on its banks, the few sparse trees and hardy scrub, the sky coming down and touching earth. "I wish I brought my sketchbook."

"You should've gotten one while you were in town today."

She shook her head with a smile. "No, I left it in my room. I never go anywhere without a sketchbook."

He shot her a funny look. She wasn't sure if it was disbelief or wonderment. "Why? I mean, I guess you draw?"

Yeah, you could say that. "I get inspiration from the world around me for my jewelry." She shook her head. "Once Emery got sick, it became harder and harder to find that inspiration." She gave a self-deprecating chuckle. "Okay, so it's been nonexistent. I haven't designed anything since she got sick. It was as if she was my muse, and everything about creativity was wrapped up in her. When she fell ill, it just went away."

"But you want to draw here."

Bryn looked around at the ruggedly beautiful, hardy landscape that was West Texas. "Yeah. I draw. But I haven't designed anything. That part of me is still quiet."

"And what will you do if that part never comes back?"

She shook her head. "I can't let myself think about it. It's bad enough not to have the desire, but to think about never doing it again . . . ?"

"You design jewelry?"

She held out one arm, showing off the cuff bracelet she wore. It was hammered silver and looked more like something off a knight's armor than modern-day jewelry. Antiqued and soldered with intricate designs, it was a one-of-a-kind piece. And definitely showed the level of her craftsmanship.

He took her arm in one hand and turned it side to side as if looking at the bracelet from all angles. "You made this?"

"Yes."

"It's exquisite." He glanced up, his gaze snagging hers. His green eyes were bottomless, unreadable. "Beautiful," he murmured. But she had a feeling they were no longer talking about the bracelet.

"Jake," she whispered. The words to tell him to stop wouldn't come.

He used his hold on her to pull her forward. He was going to kiss her again. Why did it seem like every time they were alone, the kissing began? Or maybe this was a warning to not be alone again. She couldn't keep this up with him. She was going home soon. And if she gave into him again, if she let him show her what loving him meant, she might just lose her heart to him. And that was one thing she couldn't afford to give up.

He leaned in, brushed his lips so softly across hers. Then he took a step back. "I, uh . . . wanted to tell you I took tomorrow off."

He couldn't have surprised her more if he told her he was becoming a drag queen. "What?"

"I took the day off."

"I didn't think ranchers did that."

"Well, this is sort of a special occasion. Joe Dan can take care of things for a bit."

"Why are you doing this?"

There went that one-shoulder shrug. "Wesley starts school day after tomorrow. You keep saying you're leaving. I thought it would be a good opportunity to take some time and spend it with the two of you."

She shook her head.

"Why not?"

Because that was too much like family time, and that was one thing she couldn't allow herself where he was concerned. They might be having a family get-together, but they would never *be* a family together. "You should spend that time with Wesley."

"I will. And with you. I thought we might go swimming."

"I don't have a suit."

"Then swim in shorts or naked. I don't care. Just spend the day with me tomorrow."

"Naked?" It was better by far to concentrate on that than him asking her to spend time with him, like he really wanted her to. Like there was more—could be more—between them than the babies they created.

"Okay, maybe not naked." His eyes darkened when he said the word. And she thought for a moment he might want to talk about it some more. But thankfully he dropped it. "But you don't need your own suit. I know we have some in the mudroom. That is, if you don't mind wearing a castoff."

It was her perfect opportunity to tell him no. To get out

of this ridiculous plan to spend tomorrow together like a family. “Jake, I—”

“Say yes,” he said. Then swooped in for another kiss. Unlike the first one, this one was filled with tangled tongues and heavy breathing. When he lifted his head, how could she say anything but yes?

“Okay,” she breathed. “I’ll swim with you tomorrow.”

He smiled, his teeth flashing in the last rays of the Texas sun. The sky she could see through the trees was painted purple and orange in hues like she had never seen before. All at once she wanted to capture that moment and keep it in a bottle, keep it so once she returned to Georgia she could pull it out whenever she missed him and have it to experience all over again.

He brushed back a strand of hair from her face and tucked it behind her ear. “Just one more thing,” he said. “Can I touch your belly?”

She nearly laughed. Had it not been for the serious light in his eyes, she might have. She had shared so much with this man, at least physically. He had just kissed her till her head swam and her knees buckled, but he was reluctant to touch the spot where his children nestled inside of her.

Without a word, she reached for his hand and pressed it to her abdomen.

Chapter Ten

Why couldn't he remember doing this very same thing with Cecelia? He had to have at some point, or maybe they had been too busy being polite to one another that it hadn't come up.

"Can you feel them moving yet?" He wanted to just go on touching her forever. It was a strange feeling.

She shook her head. "The book says that since I'm active I probably rock them to sleep. So they sleep all day and stay awake at night."

"So you're telling me that you have spoiled them already?"

She laughed, and he was certain his life would be good and complete if she just kept doing that. "I guess so. Though if that's the case they're probably kicking me all night long."

He moved his hands, trying to get a feel for where they were, trying to see if they would kick. He was filled with awe. He'd kept his distance as much as possible, doing his best to not think about babies. Especially not when he pulled her into his arms. But the longer she stayed, the more evident her pregnancy became, and the more he realized he couldn't ignore it much longer.

Fear knifed through him, hot and cold. She was having babies, two of them, his. He had done everything in his power to talk her into staying. It was wrong of him, so very wrong.

He cleared his throat and took a step back, away from her. His hands fell to his sides. He coughed again. "I guess I should get the appointment now," he said. "With the attorney, I mean."

Some emotion flitted across her face. Fear? Worry? Some form of trepidation? He wasn't sure. "I suppose so," she murmured. Suddenly, there was a wall between them, one that hadn't been there a few moments before.

Because he mentioned attorneys? It was necessary. As long as she refused to marry him, refused to come to Texas, insisted on staying in Georgia, they would need someone to help them hash it out.

He reached a hand out toward her, the gesture of assistance in good faith. "Come on," he said. "Let's go back." He whistled for Kota and the moment was gone.

Just after lunch the following day, Jake turned the ranch over to Joe Dan and donned his swim trunks. Bryn could see how excited Wesley was at the thought of spending the afternoon with her father. Bryn had to admit she was a little excited as well, and it had nothing to do with how Jake looked bare chested and barefoot standing on the edge of the pool preparing to dive in. That was just a perk.

He had seemed to be avoiding her the entire time she had been here. Even with their ongoing game of two truths and a lie, he seemed to avoid her for the majority of the day, only letting his guard down and talking to her, spending time with her, at night. This was different. But this meant she would definitely need to go home soon, especially with all the talk of going to the attorney's office and hashing out whatever visitation arrangement they came to.

She waded up the steps and sat down on the edge of the pool, her feet still dangling in the water.

"Daddy! Daddy! Teach me how to dive." Wesley bounced on her toes as she threw the pool toys into the water. They sank immediately as they were designed to do.

Jake looked as if he was about to protest, then he glanced over to where Bryn sat. She smiled hoping he got the hint. Today was just as much for Wesley as it was for her. Maybe even more so since she started school the next day. This was her last day of summer before kindergarten.

"Okay," he agreed. He dove into the pool, his lean body slicing the water perfectly. He surfaced a few feet into the pool and slung his hair back out of his eyes. "Come on." He motioned for Wesley to jump into the water. She did so but without the grace and confidence of her father. But one day, Bryn knew the young girl would blossom with that same confidence and grace. It was there, simmering just below the surface waiting for its time to be revealed.

And you won't be here for it.

She ignored that little voice and shaded her eyes as Jake began to show Wesley the finer points of diving. He was a good dad, and for that she was grateful. She might have been uncertain at the beginning, needing time to get to know him before trusting that he would care for the twins, but these last few days was just her dragging her feet, pretending she needed to know him more before she went home. Yes, she would have to send her children here for more than one vacation, of that she was certain. She didn't like the thought of being separated from them, but there was no doubt that Jake would care for them, love them, and cherish them just the way he did Wesley. But the big question was, could she take care of two children all by herself?

She would have to hire a full-time nanny in order to care for them. More than a full-time nanny, a live-in nanny. And though she hadn't had to worry about money in a long, long time, she wasn't sure that sort of expense was in the budget.

And child support? Jake might be willing to pay his part in raising their twins, but how could she ask for money for a live-in nanny when so many times he had invited her to stay? When so many people here would help her love and care for those babies around the clock?

"Bryn!" Wesley waved to get her attention. "Did you see? Did you see me?"

"I'm sorry, baby. Can you do it again?"

Wesley grinned. "Of course I can." And there was that confidence.

Bryn watched, paying attention this time as Wesley dove to the bottom of the pool and picked up two of the pool toys before resurfacing.

Bryn clapped her hands and cheered. "That's quite an accomplishment."

"Can you do it?"

"Once upon a time," she said rubbing a hand over her belly.

Jake laughed. "I thought water made a person more buoyant." He had a point. And had just called her out for avoiding spending too much time with him, or maybe it was too much time in close proximity. The gauntlet had been tossed down. She couldn't let the challenge go by.

She pushed herself off the pool's edge and back into the water. It felt cool against her sun-warmed limbs as she waded out where the two of them were. Jake had one arm around Wesley, holding her up in the deeper water.

"I have an idea," Wesley said. She clapped her hands in glee. "Let's have a race."

Bryn was just about to shake her head when Jake reached out a hand toward Wesley. "You're on," he said.

But the young girl shook her head. "Not me. You two."

Bryn was definitely out of this one, but that gleam of challenge sparkled in Jake's green eyes once again.

"Are you chicken?"

Was she? Hell, no. But she was supposed to be avoiding him, now wasn't she? Wasn't that the plan? Enjoy the day but keep her distance so she kept her heart when she went home?

As if they didn't belong to her, she watched her hands reach out and grab Jake's. His fingers wrapped around hers and sealed the deal.

"What are the rules?" Bryn asked.

Wesley wiggled out of her dad's hold and swam to the ladder. She climbed out and started gathering up more pool toys and tossing them in. "I say the one with the most toys wins."

"Only one at a time," Bryn said, eyeing Jake. She could already see his competitive streak rising to the top and could imagine him holding his breath grabbing as many toys as he could before surfacing again. That wasn't quite sporting.

"You want it to be more of a relay race?" he asked.

"I guess," she said. "You have to dive down, get a ring, bring it back up, and put it on the edge of the pool. Then dive down again."

"Why do you want to make it harder?"

"Make it harder to cheat," Bryn countered.

Jake shrugged. "Have it your way."

"Bryn, you put your toys here and, Dad, you use the other side. That way we can keep them separate. All right?" Wesley finished tossing all the toys back into the water. She eyed them, hands on her hips. "Are you ready?"

"As I'll ever be," Bryn grumbled. From beside her, Jake laughed.

"On your marks."

"You're going down," Jake muttered without looking at her.

"Get set."

"In your dreams," Bryn countered.

"Go!"

How had she gotten talked into this? Bryn dove down, grabbed a toy, and resurfaced, tossing it to her edge of the pool. She barely registered that Jake had done the same before diving back down to find another. There had to be fifty toys on the bottom of the pool. They would both be exhausted by the time they found them all. But something in that competitive light in Jake's eyes made her want to win, just this once.

Toy after toy hit the pool skirt as the two of them dove beneath the water. Bryn felt like she had a good handle on the situation but checked to see how many toys Jake had on his side.

They resurfaced at the same time. She caught his gaze, then looked into the water to find the next toy she was going after. It took a second to locate it because there was only one.

He saw it the same time she did. They looked at each other and their gazes locked. He laughed and dove beneath the water. He was a split second faster than she was, but she had proximity on her side. She snatched the ring and pushed to the surface.

She tossed it onto the side with the rest of her toys as Wesley counted.

Bryn looked to Jake. "Can she count?"

The proud dad grinned. "High enough."

Wesley jumped up and down on the edge of the pool. "Dad, you got twenty-two, and, Bryn, you got twenty-three! Bryn wins," she cried. "Hey, that rhymes."

Jake chuckled as Grandma Esther came out of the house bearing a tray with drinks and snacks.

"I say the winner gets a kiss." His grandmother set the tray on one of the pool side tables.

Before Bryn could even blink, Jake hauled her to him. Their limbs tangled in the water as he swooped in and captured her mouth with his. It was more than a kiss of victory and less of a kiss that they might share had they been alone, but Bryn was still grateful they were in the water. Otherwise her legs might have given way underneath her.

Jake broke the kiss, but retained his hold on her.

"But you didn't win," she weakly protested.

Jake laughed. "Oh, yes, I did."

Are you sure about this?" Bryn looked dubiously at the four-wheeler.

"I want to show you the ranch," Jake said. "If you can't ride horses, I figure this is the next best thing. It's what we use when we go ride fences or need to get out pretty quick."

Bryn shook her head sadly. "My image of the cowboy has just been shot to hell."

Jake laughed. "Don't worry. I ride a horse often enough. But an ATV can be replaced a lot easier than a trained horse can."

"Good point."

"It is easy to ride," Jake said. "If you've ever ridden any type of motorcycle, it's the same concept." He explained the high points of gearshifts and gas lines and that sort of thing, then handed Bryn a helmet. "We'll take it slow. I don't want you to get hurt."

"Thanks for the vote of confidence."

He shook his head and trailed his fingers along the curve of her stomach. "That's precious cargo you're carrying."

Bryn shook her hair back and donned the helmet, unwilling to dwell on his touch. Last night something had shifted between them. He seemed unable to keep his hands to himself and she was drawn further away. She was leaving soon. She needed to keep her distance. She needed to keep her heart.

"Come on, Wesley," Jake called. Wesley came out of the barn carrying the half-grown black kitten she loved. She promptly dropped it to the ground. It scampered away, and Bryn suppressed her chuckle. That girl loved cats.

"Where's my helmet?" Wesley asked. Jake held it up, and Wesley ran to him. She donned it and climbed on the back of his ATV, and they were off.

Kota ran alongside them for a bit, then grew tired of the game and ambled back toward the house.

Bryn stalled only a couple of times, but soon got the hang of the gears and the gas. She started to enjoy the ride, the fine hum of the machine beneath her. She had to admit though, it couldn't compare to riding a horse. Though it had been years and years since she'd been on one.

The land was beautiful and stretched on forever until it touched the sky in the distance. In Georgia there were trees upon trees and only they got to meet the sky, but here it was all about the land. Jake motioned for her to follow him and Bryn did as he asked, running up onto a small plateau. It was odd, this formation that seemed to sit in the middle of the tabletop, but it wasn't so steep that they couldn't ride the ATVs up one side. They parked and got off. Bryn took off her helmet as Jake and Wesley did the same. He pointed toward the distance. "Over there," he started, "that's Reagan County." He turned back the other direction and pointed. "And over there is Hill Country."

"It's amazing," Bryn said. "How much of this do you own?"

He looked down at her and laughed. "All of it."

"All of it?"

"All of what you can see."

"How many acres is that?"

"About two hundred and fifty thousand."

She had no idea.

"We don't use all of it for cattle though. Like where you're standing right now is part of the conservation project. I lease some of it out for hunting in the winter and sometimes the college in San Angelo comes over. We let them do some studies here."

It seemed there was a lot more to modern ranching than she realized.

"Let's go back down," he said. He donned his helmet and together they rode back down the small incline. He parked to one side and got off. "The creek is just over here."

They walked side by side, with Wesley skipping ahead picking up rocks and kicking at this and that as she went along.

Kota sniffed his way behind Wesley. Bryn hadn't seen the dog catch up to them, but she wasn't surprised. It was as if anytime she were outside, he needed to be there to guard her.

In that instant, they felt so much like a family that it brought tears to Bryn's eyes. She missed her family so much, but she never had this. It'd always been her and Emery going here and there, to plays and musicals or out to get a treat at their favorite sidewalk café. Emery had been her everything and now that she was gone, there was a gaping hole in Bryn's heart. She was doing what she could to patch it back together, but she knew it would never be the same.

She glanced out over the rugged landscape, so different than Georgia. Emery would've loved it. She would have loved riding on a four-wheeler across the dusty desert land. She would've loved the horses and the kittens, Kota, and everything else the Langstons had.

They came to the edge of the creek and Jake stopped. "Are you okay?"

Bryn raised a hand to her cheek, only then realizing that she was crying. "I'm fine."

But the tears kept coming.

"You don't look fine."

Bryn laughed through her tears. "Thanks."

She didn't have a tissue so she dashed them away with the back of her fingers and sniffed. "I'm okay, really."

He studied her intently, and Bryn wanted to duck her head lest he discover all her secrets.

"I was just thinking how Emery would have loved it here."

Wesley made her way to the bank and began throwing the rocks she had collected into the clear water. From the outside her childhood looked picture-perfect, and suddenly Bryn wanted that for the twins, more than she wanted anything else in the world.

"I'm sorry," he said quietly.

Bryn nodded. "Me too." She shook her head and tried to pull herself together. "But you have to move on. Everybody's lost somebody. I mean, you lost your wife."

His green eyes darkened until they were unreadable. "I don't like to talk about her."

And just like that a cloud descended on their beautiful, clear day.

Of course he didn't want to talk about her. He was still in love with her. And that was just one of the many reasons why Bryn couldn't marry him. Why she couldn't stay in Texas. And why she could never be a part of the Langston family.

"Wesley," Jake called. "Come on. Let's go back to the house."

They rode back in silence. No talking, just the noise of the engine between them. Bryn tried to tell herself that it was that noise that kept any conversation at bay, but she knew that she had treaded on sacred ground. She could tell by the hard line of Jake's jaw, by the severe angle of his shoulders, and by those handsome lips pressed together in a thin, unattractive line.

As soon as they got back to the barn, Wesley went in to play with the kittens, but Jake brought her out.

"Tomorrow's the first day of school," he said. "Perhaps you'd forgotten?"

"I ain't forgot."

"You haven't forgotten," Jake corrected. "So that means we need to get your stuff ready. It's a big day. We need to pick out what you want to wear to school. We need to get your notebooks and pencils in your backpack."

They started toward the house, and Bryn trailed behind like a lost puppy. It was better this way. At least now she could leave without such guilt on her shoulders. She would wait until Jake left with Wesley to go to school tomorrow, and she would head out. It was past time for her to go. They could let the lawyers work it out themselves.

Wesley grabbed her dad's hand and turned around to Bryn. "Will you help me pick out clothes?"

Bryn stumbled a bit, so surprised by Wesley's request. "I—"

"Miss Bryn has grown-up stuff to do right now." Jake didn't bother to turn and look at her.

Wesley started walking backward beside him. "Please, Miss Bryn, please come help me pick out clothes. You always look so pretty. I like to dress myself but . . ." She shook her head. "Sometimes the adults say I look . . ." She craned her neck to peer up at her father. "What was that word?"

"Eclectic," Jake said.

"Please, Miss Bryn. I don't know what that word means, but I have a feeling it's not very good."

"Wesley," Jake warned.

Bryn chuckled. How could she say no? "Jake, I don't mind."

A stern nod was his only response.

Bryn spent the rest of the afternoon helping Wesley get ready for school. They picked out a denim overall jumper and a comfortable T-shirt with scalloped edges to go underneath. Since Wesley was intent on wearing her cowboy boots, Bryn took a damp washrag and wiped the dust off them. She'd have to see if maybe Jake wanted to shine them up a bit, but she had a feeling that cowgirls didn't care about such things. Even on a big day like the first day of kindergarten.

"How do you want to wear your hair?" Bryn asked.

"Can I get purple in it?"

"No." Jake's voice was adamant.

Bryn shot him a glaring look, then turned back to Wesley. "How about we do something like that when you're older?"

"How much older?" Wesley asked.

"No," Jake reiterated.

Then an idea occurred to Bryn. "Jake," she said low enough her voice carried but not so loud that Wesley could hear. "I used to dye Emery's hair with Kool-Aid. It doesn't damage the hair and it washes out in just a few days. You have grape Kool-Aid in the kitchen. We could do purple."

Jake frowned. "You colored your sister's hair with Kool-Aid?"

Bryn laughed. "Can we do it or not?"

She could almost see the internal struggle of the father who wanted to give his child everything and the conservative cowboy who thought purple hair was completely out of the question.

"It'll be washed out by next week. Just the ends." She could see him breaking down. "What's the harm?" For a moment she thought he would tell her exactly what the harm was in having a chunk of purple hair and going to school at Cattle Creek Elementary, but instead he snapped the magazine he was reading shut and glared at her. "Fine."

"Why are you so angry with me?"

He shook his head. "I'm not angry at all." But it was the biggest lie she had ever heard.

Bryn had to put Wesley's hair in a ponytail for supper to keep her from swinging it across her shoulders and possibly getting it in her food. She loved the purple and couldn't wait to get to school and show everybody tomorrow. But in the meantime Bryn was afraid she was going to drag it through her chicken casserole before everything was said and done.

"Come on, tater," Jake said, reaching out a hand to Wesley after the table had been cleared. "It's time for a bath and bed."

Wesley looked aghast. "You can't wash my hair!" Her hands flew to her newly Kool-Aid-dyed tresses.

"You can do what I used to do when I was your age and

put your hair up in a bun on the top of your head. Then you can have your bath without getting your hair wet."

"A hot dog bun or a hamburger bun?"

Bryn laughed. "It's a type of hairstyle. Come on. I'll show you."

She took Wesley into the bathroom and put her hair up, then turned her over to Jake.

"No," Wesley hollered as Bryn started to leave the bathroom. "I want you to give me my bath."

A look passed between Jake and Bryn. She had been so worried about losing her own heart that she hadn't given a thought to the most precious heart there. Wesley's.

Bryn tried to let him know that she was sorry. But she hadn't meant to encroach on father-daughter time. This wasn't her place. This wasn't her family. This wasn't her child to raise, to give baths.

Definitely. She was leaving tomorrow.

Jake came back in the bathroom as Wesley got out of the tub. "Are you ready for a bedtime story?" he asked.

It'd been the hardest thing he had ever done, walking out and allowing someone else to give his daughter a bath. For five years she'd been in his total care, if he didn't count those first three weeks after her birth where he spent all of his time at the bottom of a bottle. To this day he still wasn't sure who took care of her during that rocky time, though he was positive his mother and grandmother had made sure she didn't want for anything. Since then, he had taken his daddy duties very seriously, and it was painful to walk out and hand them over to someone else.

"Miss Bryn, will you read me a story?" Wesley asked.

Bryn seemed as shocked as he was hurt. "I'm sure your dad would like to read you a story tonight."

"He reads me a story every night. And tonight I want you." Wesley pouted. She put her arms around Bryn's neck and refused to let the woman leave. What choice did she have but to lift her up and take her into her bedroom right across the hall?

"I'll make a deal with you," Bryn said. "I'll help you pick out your pajamas, then you let your dad read your story and I'll see you in the morning before you go to school."

"No deal," Wesley said. "I want you to read me the story and you to pick out my pajamas. Dad can stay, but you need to do it."

Each one of her words was a stab to the heart. She didn't mean to hurt him, but that was what daughters did when they grew up, when they became independent and started to know their own minds. But one thing was evident to Jake: Wesley missed a woman's touch. Even with his mother and his grandmother around, he knew it wasn't the same. She had never even known her and yet she missed her mother.

"Go ahead," Jake said. His voice sounded thin and rusty. If he noticed it, he was sure Bryn did too, but she didn't say anything and for that he was grateful. He stayed just long enough for Bryn to get Wesley into her pajamas, take her hair down from the bun they had decided to call a Wesley bun, and brush it out for the evening. He still couldn't believe that he let her dye the ends purple with Kool-Aid of all things. He supposed that just went to show what a big old softy he was down deep inside. Anybody who thought cowboys were tough never looked at their hearts.

Once Wesley was in her pj's and had crawled into bed, Jake kissed her on the forehead and got a hug and a kiss on the cheek in return. "Good night," he said, then closed the door behind him as he left.

Bryn let herself out of Wesley's room, shutting the door quietly behind her and leaning against it. The nightlight was on and the little girl, soon to be a big kindergartner, was ready to go to sleep. She had been kissed good night and tucked in, all the other wonderful things that children needed.

It was perhaps the sweetest and the hardest thing she had ever done. And she felt for Jake. She could see in his eyes the hurt and the daddy betrayal that he had endured to be thrown over for a virtual stranger. But that would only happen one time. Bryn was leaving tomorrow, no doubt about it. Getting out of Texas, going back to where she belonged, and allowing the Langstons to continue their lives without her. Because truly she had no place there, even as badly as she wanted it. She wasn't one of their family.

With a sigh she pushed herself off the door and started toward her own bedroom. She would pack tonight, get all her things together, then in the morning, after she got Wesley off to school—with Jake, of course—she would haul her stuff out to the car and head back to Georgia. She was almost nineteen weeks pregnant. If she waited much longer, she would be stuck here for the rest of the pregnancy. Time to get out now.

She let herself into her room and closed the door behind her, turning around and nearly jumping out of her skin when she saw Jake lounging on her bed, looking as if he'd been there half the night.

Chapter Eleven

"What are you doing here?"

Jake pushed himself upright as if it was the most natural thing in the world for him to be sprawled across her bed at eight thirty at night. "Did you get her all tucked in?"

Bryn nodded but stayed right where she was. Jake might not realize the intimacy of their positions, but she did. Or maybe that was because she had fantasies about this very scenario every time she closed her eyes.

"Thanks, that was . . ." He shook his head. "That was hard. I don't have to share her very often."

"I'm sorry. This is a special time, and I'm making a mess of it for you."

He frowned. "Why would you say that?"

"Because it's true. You should have this time with her without me around and—" She broke off as he stood.

"Having you around has made this more special for her. I didn't realize until tonight, but she misses her mother." He nodded his head and waved away the words that he thought she might say. "I know. She never knew her, but she's smart.

She sees other kids, the kids here on the ranch. And she knows that her life is different."

He came a bit closer and she caught the scent of his aftershave. His hair smelled clean and fresh. He must have taken a shower before coming in here, even if the scent of leather and horse still clung to him. Somehow it was a lethal combination. At least to her heart.

"I'm leaving tomorrow," she blurted out. "I'll stay until you leave to take Wesley to school, then after that, I'm going home. I need to go home."

When had he gotten so close to her? Close enough that he could reach out and touch her? She took a step back. He followed, so she held her ground.

"Why?" he asked, his voice barely above a whisper. "I thought you wanted to get to know everyone better."

"I do." She shook her head. "I did. I have. Now it's time to go."

"Bryn . . ."

Don't come any closer. She wanted to scream the words, keep him at arm's length, but he seemed to pull her in without any effort.

"You don't have to leave, you know."

"I do." Some argument. Her words were barely above a whisper. All two of them. "Jake, I—"

"What's in Georgia?" he asked. "You have anything like this there?"

He leaned in. Bryn closed her eyes and waited for the touch of his lips on hers. It came, as soft as butterfly wings. Yet strong enough to make her knees buckle.

He tasted like toothpaste, coffee, and all good things. And heaven help her, she never wanted that kiss to stop. But it had to, if she was going to get out with her heart intact.

But oh, how easy it would be to cave to the desires washing over her. Give in to the pleasure of the now and not worry about any of the consequences. But what then? After she had fallen completely in love with Jake? How would she ever get her heart back? Would she even want it?

He lifted his head, his green eyes shining into hers. She hoped their twins had his eyes, those beautiful bottle green eyes that saw everything, missed nothing, and loved without end.

It was the perfect time to protest, to tell him that she had made up her mind. She was leaving first thing. But he tilted his head the other direction and started kissing her again and the words were lost.

Then she realized. She was too late. She was already in love with Jake Langston. She had been fooling herself to believe that she hadn't been for quite some time. Maybe even the first time she had seen him swing Wesley into his arms as if she was the most precious thing in the world.

"Do you ever wonder about that night?" Jake asked as he trailed little kisses down the side of Bryn's neck. She clutched his arms to keep herself upright.

"What about it?" Whose breathless voice was that?

"If it was really as good as I remember."

"Yes," she admitted. The night in her dreams was beyond compare, but she knew the Jake in her arms could beat it any day. Nothing could top the real thing.

The warmth of his skin beneath her fingers, the softness of his kisses, the strength in his size. He was everything she could want and more. But what was the harm in a little experiment, especially since her heart already belonged to him.

"Make love to me, Jake."

He captured her lips in a soul-stirring kiss.

"I thought you would never ask."

He retained his hold on her, yet turned her around, reversing their positions so he could walk her backward toward that big bed.

Her legs bumped into the mattress, but she remained

upright as she clutched his shirt, trying to undo the buttons as he continued to kiss her. She pulled his shirttail from his jeans and ran her hands across his abdomen and around his back as he sucked in a breath.

Could she affect him that way? With just a simple touch? The thought was heady.

He pulled her shirt over her head and tossed it aside. His hands clasped her shoulders, ran down her arms, as he continued to devour her with his eyes. Almost as potent as his kiss was that green gaze that seemed to take in every detail, overlooking flaws and making her feel like the most precious thing on earth.

She didn't hide herself from his gaze. She wasn't embarrassed or uncomfortable by her growing girth. The babies were too special for her to regret her altered shape.

She tossed her hair back and met his gaze. Then she saw no censure there, no love. Only desire. And for now that would have to do. She reached for the button on his jeans as he snaked one arm around her and lifted her onto the bed.

With deft fingers he undid the back hook of her bra, releasing her swollen breasts. The hormones had made them full and sensitive and they spilled eagerly toward his touch.

She closed her eyes and ran her fingers through his hair as he captured one nipple in a soft kiss.

"Do you remember this?" He blew over the wetness his mouth had left behind, and Bryn shivered.

"Yes." She remembered all that and more.

He gave the other breast similar treatment as his fingers skimmed down her side to the elastic waistband of her shorts.

"Sexy," he murmured as he tugged on the elastic.

Bryn braced her hands to give him better access. "Don't make fun," she scolded.

"Oh, I'm not."

And he proved it by skimming away the denim and

cupping her. Moisture pooled in her lower regions and she squirmed against the barrier of her panties, seeking a more intimate touch.

He laughed as she reared against him. "Slow down, sweetness. We have all night."

And they did. They had all night to enjoy each other. They had all night to reacquaint themselves with the other's body, mind, soul. They had all night to rediscover those oh-so-sensitive places that made the other sigh or cry out. They had all night, but in the morning . . .

Bryn pushed that thought away. She could enjoy the here and the now. She would worry about tomorrow, tomorrow.

"Kiss me," she commanded.

He did as she asked without question. Kissing her until her toes curled and her fingers tingled so badly she could barely work the zipper of his jeans. She needed this. She needed him. She needed that human connection. It had been denied her so long, and she had fallen victim to it that night in Austin. Just as she would fall victim to it here, tonight, with Jake once again.

She pushed his jeans from his hips and he shimmied out of them, rolling off to one side naked. Gloriously naked.

She wanted to touch him everywhere at once. All that warm skin. Hard as steel. Soft as velvet. Dusted with hair. The man's body was a myriad of tactile pleasures, and she wanted to experience each and every one.

She slipped her hands between them, cupping him in her palm, loving the little involuntary jump as she touched him.

He rained little kisses across her shoulders, the tops of her breasts, down one arm as she continued to caress him.

He hooked his fingers in the side seam of her panties and tugged.

"I hate to say this, but you need to stop that." The confidence in his voice sounded shaky and rough. "If I'm going to make it through," he coughed, "without an accident, you need to stop."

"Oh," Bryn exclaimed. She hadn't realized that she had been rubbing him with her thumb, squeezing with the other hand, just enjoying the feel of holding him once again.

Jake tugged on her underwear. They tangled in her legs, but she didn't care as he ran one finger down that sweetest crease. She was ready for him. She didn't need to feel his caress against her slick folds to know that she was ready. She had been ready since she pulled into his driveway and he frowned at her. She'd been ready since she decided to come here. Since the dawn of time.

"Jake," she gasped as he slid one finger inside her. It was wonderful, exquisite, and not enough. She needed him, all of him.

"Hold on, sweetness. Let's make sure you're ready."

"I'm ready."

He kissed her then, deep and true, slid one hand from her buttocks down to her knees, lifting her leg over his side.

"This might be a little tricky."

"Tricky?" she asked.

He ran a hand between them, over her belly and lower until he could position himself to enter her.

They were side by side, one of her legs draped over his waist. It felt so good to be in his arms once more, but the position was awkward, not allowing her to take him all like she wanted.

She tried to sink lower, tried to take him deeper, but she shook her head. "This isn't enough. I need you." Oh, how she needed him.

He adjusted them once again. It was a little better, but still not enough. "I don't want to hurt you. I'm too heavy for you."

"I need you," she repeated. She squirmed against him once more.

He groaned. "Yes," he said. "We need more. Do you think you could handle being on top?"

"Yes," she gasped. "Please."

He rolled to his back, taking her with him, but holding her hips to keep her at a distance.

"It will be . . . deeper," he groaned as she sank onto him.

He filled her completely, sending shards of pleasure throughout her body. Not an orgasm, just the pleasure of him fully inside her. It was strong and powerful, a connection she had never felt before, a connection she never wanted to end.

She rose up, then down once again, and the ripples of pleasure became more, waves that washed her halfway to heaven. Wave after wave crashed her against him until she thought she might die from the pleasure of it all.

"Wait," he panted, holding her still for a moment. She wanted to move. She wanted to see this through to the end, she wanted to love him with no bounds, with no limitations; nothing stood between them now. Not the past, not the embarrassment of the one-night stand, nothing.

She rocked against him, and he grabbed her hips, slowing her pace. It was fantastic and frustrating at the same time. She wanted to toss her head and love him like there was no tomorrow, because really there wasn't. There was only now, and this desire between them.

Jake leaned up and captured her lips with his. He kissed her as he set their pace, somewhere between heaven and driving her crazy.

He lay back and she went with him, unwilling to break any connection they shared.

"Let go," she whispered against his lips.

He shook his head. "I don't want to hurt you."

"You're not going to hurt me," she promised. "Let go."

He released her hips and she crashed into him. He filled her so completely, so perfectly, tears filled her eyes.

She moved against him, loving him with every ounce of her being. Mind and body. He clutched her hips, his fingers digging into the flesh as he found his release.

He rolled her to one side and tucked her into the crook of his arm.

"Jake, I—"

He shushed her, rubbing one hand down her arm, their legs intertwined, her body still pulsing from her last release.

But it was okay. She didn't know what she was going to say anyway.

Sometime in the night, Jake woke. He reached out a hand and found her there, sleeping beside him. His beautiful Bryn. He scooted closer, turning onto his side as he spooned against her.

She was so amazing to him. Not once seeming self-conscious of her pregnant body. He found it beautiful, even doubly so that she seemed to enjoy it so much.

She was as different than Cecelia as night and day. Cecelia had hated every minute of being pregnant. She had hated her swollen ankles, the sickness, not being able to eat her favorite foods. She had hated the clothes, the weight gain, and being so far away from her parents. At the time he felt that he had done everything he could to make her happy, but the truth was clear now. He could have done more. He wasn't sure what. But more. Something.

And maybe if he had . . .

He pushed the thought away. He couldn't go down that road tonight. Not when he had Bryn in his bed. Or rather he was in hers.

He snaked an arm around her waist and gathered her closer to him.

Something jumped and fluttered under his arm. Then again.

Was that . . . ?

He pressed his hand against that jump, realizing only then that it was one of the twins, awake and kicking.

He couldn't take his hand from that spot. He leaned in

close to her ear and planted a kiss there. "Bryn, honey, wake up. Bryn."

She stirred, and he gave her another kiss. Long and sweet.

"What's wrong?" she asked, as if he woke her every night with a stirring kiss.

"Nothing. Here." He took her hand in his and pressed it to that fluttering spot on her belly.

Her eyes flew open, the sleep gone in an instant. "Is that . . . ?" she asked. Her eyes filled with tears and damn if his didn't as well. He couldn't help it. There was life there. Beautiful, kicking life.

She turned in his arms, and he gathered her close. Kissing her lips, her cheeks, the arch of her brows. He was still scared, terrified even that something would go wrong. But somehow he trusted that everything was going to turn out just fine. At least he could tell himself that for a time.

But the kiss of happiness soon turned to the kiss of gentle passion.

He wanted her again. And again. Maybe forever. They would be good together if only she would stay. He could show her how wonderful life could be between the two of them.

He kissed his way from lips to shoulders to breasts and below. A new determination filled him. He would love, touch, caress, and claim every inch of her until she screamed his name in the night, until she could say nothing but yes.

He would show her that the night in Austin and earlier, here in this very room, weren't isolated incidents but how every time, every day could be for them.

And tomorrow morning when they got up, he would somehow convince her that she may be a Georgia girl, but she belonged in Texas, right by his side.

Chapter Twelve

Bryn woke the following morning feeling languid, a little sore, and completely satisfied. She stretched out an arm hoping to find Jake next to her, but she knew better. He had a rancher's internal timing and had most likely risen before the sun.

She just hoped she hadn't missed Wesley's first day of school.

The thought had no sooner formed in her mind than her bedroom door burst open and Wesley came flying in. "Bryn, Bryn," she cried as she flung herself onto the bed next to her.

Bryn looked up as Jake appeared in the doorway, looking like every woman's fantasy in a pair of well-worn Wranglers. "I'm sorry," he mouthed, easing into the room behind his daughter.

Bryn was thankful that she got up in the night and put on a T-shirt. At least she was decent for Wesley's early morning visit.

"Are you coming out to see me get on the bus?" Wesley asked.

Jake frowned. "I thought I was taking you to school. It is the first day and all."

Wesley sat up importantly and tossed her purple-tipped ponytail over one shoulder. Bryn briefly wondered who had fixed her hair, and decided that it was an equal toss-up between Wesley or Jake himself. Her ponytail was a little askew, a little messy, and somehow so perfectly Wesley. "Daddy, I'm a big girl. I want to ride the bus with the other ranch kids."

If it hadn't been so sad, Bryn might have laughed at the stricken look on Jake's face. "But I thought . . . We talked about this already."

"You don't need to take me to get me ready for the first day. We already did all that. Now I just need to go to school." *And I don't need you for that* was left off and Bryn was grateful. She didn't think Jake could handle that much independence in one day.

He caught her gaze, his eyes searching for help. But Bryn had already been through this cry for individuality with Emery. It was heartbreaking when a child broke free to stretch their legs a little further than the parents were ready for. And as much as she would love to, she couldn't take any of that pain from Jake.

"So are you?" Wesley bounced up and down. "Are you going to come out and see me get on the bus?"

Bryn nodded. "Let me get dressed and I'll be right there. Sound good?"

Wesley bounded off the bed, nodding her head as she did so. Bryn was surprised she didn't fall over from all the counteracting motions. "Don't take too long. The bus will be here in a few minutes, and he doesn't like to wait."

"Give me ten and I'll be out to wait with you."

Bryn started for the bathroom as Jake turned Wesley to the front door. "What am I going to do?" he hissed under his breath.

Bryn gave him a sad smile. "You're going to let her catch the bus."

* * *

Ten minutes later she skidded to a halt in the kitchen. Jake was at the stove flipping pancakes while Wesley sat drumming her fingers and swinging her feet at the kitchen table. Bryn barely had time to register the domestic scene. "I thought the bus was going to be here soon." She'd been worried she was going to miss Wesley's big school bus debut.

Jake had turned. "We have plenty of time for breakfast. The bus won't be here for another half hour."

And that was what Bryn got from listening to a five-year-old. "Do you want some help with that?"

Jake tossed a grin over one shoulder. "You can get us some juice."

Bryn moved to the refrigerator to get out the juice. "Where's Grandma Esther? Doesn't she usually make breakfast?"

He frowned. "She's not feeling well this morning."

"I hope nothing's wrong." Bryn poured three glasses of juice and took them to the table.

Wesley glanced up at her with impatient eyes. "This is taking forever."

Bryn laughed. "Just give it a couple years, sweetie. You'll change your mind soon enough."

Jake shot her a look. "Wesley's going to love school, right, tater?"

"I won't if I don't get there," she grumbled.

Jake set the platter of pancakes on the table. "You have plenty of time," he reassured her.

Bryn took up Wesley's plate and fork. "How many do you want? One or two?"

"Just one." She continued to swing her legs, her head bobbing up and down with the force of her motions. She was nervous as could be and ready to get the day started. Bryn glanced to Jake. It looked as if he was going to throw up at any minute. Poor guy!

"Eat," she told him. "It'll make you feel better."

Jake forked a couple of pancakes from the stack and passed it to Bryn, who did the same. They slathered them in butter and syrup, then bowed their heads as Wesley said grace.

"Amen." Bryn lifted her head.

Wesley forked up her entire pancake and shoveled it into her mouth. Then she looked to her father. "Hurry up so I don't miss the bus."

At least that was what Bryn thought she said. It was hard to tell with so much food in her mouth at the time.

"Wesley Jane," Jake admonished. "It's okay to be excited, but it's not okay to be rude."

Wesley ducked her head and somehow managed to swallow the big bite of pancake. "Yes, sir."

"Don't worry," Bryn said. "We'll make sure you get to the bus on time. Okay? Just trust us."

Wesley turned those enormous brown eyes to Bryn's. Lord how she loved this child. "That's all I have to do? Trust you?"

"A couple of hugs and kisses every now and then wouldn't hurt either." Bryn smiled.

Wesley flung her arms around Bryn's neck and kissed her on the cheek. "You can have a hug when I get home from school."

Bryn laughed. "I'll be counting on it."

I can't do this." Jake leaned close where only she could hear. About twelve kids stood in front of the big house waiting on the school bus to come down the lane.

Bryn had discovered that a ways over there was a housing addition for the married men who lived on the ranch. *Housing* was a poor choice of words considering they were beautiful ranch-style homes, three bedrooms, two baths with a garage and a common swimming pool. It seemed being an employee of the Diamond had its perks. But after Jake told her how many acres they owned and all the work they did with conservation and the universities, why should she expect any different?

"I don't think you have much choice," she returned.

"Sure I do. I can homeschool her and keep her with me till she's thirty."

Bryn shot him a sympathetic smile. "It gets easier."

He gave a stern nod. "I certainly hope so, because it couldn't get much harder."

The words no sooner left his mouth than the kids started jumping up and down. In the distance a big yellow school bus lumbered down the road. The driver honked his horn and the kids begin to cheer.

"Oh, boy," Jake muttered.

Bryn slipped her hand into his and squeezed. He glanced at her, and she did her best to tell him without words that it was going to be okay. He gave a small nod, but a muscle in his jaw jumped. She could almost hear his teeth grinding together. She squeezed his hand again. The cheers grew louder as the school bus came closer, then pulled to a stop in front of the house. The bus driver opened the door and leaned toward it. "My name is Gus, and I'm driving the bus," he said.

The children laughed and cheered.

"If you want to go to school with me, you have to say your name before you find your seat. Ready? Go."

One by one the ranch children climbed up the bus steps, said their name to Gus, and found a seat for the ride.

Bryn's heart thumped heavily in her chest as Wesley stepped forward for her turn. One of the steps was so steep she almost didn't make it but somehow managed to pull herself up.

"Wesley Langston," she said.

Gus nodded. He was quite a character with pork chop sideburns dyed royal blue to match the school colors.

"Nice to meet you, Wesley. I like your hair."

She grinned, then glanced back at Bryn and gave her a thumbs-up. She turned back to Gus. "Thank you. I like your hairs too."

Only two more children were left to get on the bus. Bryn watched as Wesley made her way toward the back and sat down in the seat, scooting over to the windows so she could wave.

Bryn and Jake both waggled their fingers at her, but Bryn was having a hard time holding back her tears.

"She looks so little sitting there."

Jake started forward. "I'm going to get her."

Bryn laid a hand on his arm, somehow holding him in place. "No. You're not. She has to do this. Just be thankful she's not clinging to you sobbing that she wants to go back home."

"Is that what Emery did?"

Bryn shook her head. "But there is always one."

"Tell me she's going to be okay."

"She's going to be okay," Bryn parroted.

He squeezed her hand as the bus engine revved. Then it pulled away carrying Wesley and the other kids to school. Parents waved. Bryn did her best to hold back her tears.

"Come on." Jake tugged her away. At first Bryn thought they were going back into the house, but he switched gears going around the side of the building that could loosely be called a garage.

"What are you doing?"

He took a set of keys off the pegboard on the wall and got in one of the trucks. "We're following her."

"Jake," Bryn started in protest, but he shook his head.

"Either ride with me or stay here, but I'm following her to school."

With a smile and a shake of her head, Bryn opened the door to the truck and climbed in beside him.

"They can't have gotten far," Jake said as he pulled onto the road.

"Yeah, but she'll recognize the truck if she looks out the back. You need to stay as far away as possible."

"Right." He looked so serious and intense that Bryn couldn't stop her laughter.

"What's so funny?"

She shook her head. "You."

"I hardly think this is funny at all."

"You may have only made it to fifteen on the top bachelor list," Bryn started. "But you're number one Dad of the Year to me."

He leaned over and bussed her lips. "Good morning."

Bryn felt the small kiss all the way to her toes. "I think you've already said that."

"Maybe, but definitely not properly."

She turned a bit in her seat, the belt rubbing against her belly. "Just what is a proper good morning?"

The smile he sent her was just short of wicked. "I'll show you when we get back home."

A pang of desire zinged through her. "I'm holding you to it." Bryn glanced back at the road. The school bus was just up ahead and looked as if it was making another stop. "You'd better hold back before she sees us."

"She won't see us. She's too busy talking to Tori Davidson, Ol' Buck's great-granddaughter. She's in the second grade, and I'm sure right now Wesley is bragging about her purple hair." He shot Bryn a look. "By the way, how did you talk me into that?"

Bryn smiled and shook her head. "I will never reveal my secrets."

Jake slowed the truck as the school bus made a right turn. If Bryn remembered right, they were halfway to town now. "How far are you going?"

"All the way. I want to see her walk in the building."

Bryn couldn't say she blamed him. She would feel better today knowing that Wesley had made it to school safely.

"Does she know how to get to her classroom?" Bryn asked.

Jake growled under his breath. "Someone will show her the way," he said. But she had a feeling he was convincing himself more than answering her.

"Independent little thing, isn't she?"

"I blame myself."

Bryn laid a hand on his arm as he pulled in behind the bus. "It's not a bad trait to have."

Jake looked down to where Bryn's fingers rested on his arm, then back up to the kids getting off the bus in front of them. If luck was on his side, Wesley would be so engrossed in talking to friends and being a big kindergartner that she wouldn't notice the ranch truck behind her.

"There she is," he said, nodding toward the familiar pink backpack bobbing through the crowd.

Bryn took her hand from his arm, and Jake did his best not to feel bereft at the absence of her touch.

They sat in the parking lot and watched that backpack as it wove through the crowd and into the schoolhouse. It was a typical elementary school, sprawling brick with royal blue trim to match the high school Longhorns mascot. A playground sat off to one side with slides, swings, and merry-go-rounds along with a variety of other toys for kids to burn off energy during the day. All in all, it was a good school, and he prayed they would take care of his little girl.

"Someone will show her the way," he muttered under his breath. "Someone will show her the way."

"I think it's time to go," Bryn said.

She was right. But he had to be certain that Wesley wasn't going to pop back out and need something. Who knew fatherhood would be this difficult? Why did no one warn a guy how painful it could be? Even those day-to-day victories could squeeze a heart until it bled.

"I guess you're right." He made no move to put the truck in gear.

"Grandma Esther is still in bed and your mom doesn't come home till sometime later today. . . ." Bryn leaned a little closer to him. Close enough that she could whisper in his ear. "That means we have the house all to ourselves for . . . When's the next time you have to do something today?"

He sighed. "I'm a rancher. I have stuff to do all day."

She kissed the side of his face somewhere between his short sideburns and the curve of his ear. Jake shivered. "Well, then I guess we have the house for as long as you'll stay in there with me."

He wanted to stay in there all day and lose himself in Bryn. Forget that his little girl was growing up, forget the chores, the paperwork, the breeding schedule. Forget it all, and just bury himself in her. Not worry about a blessed thing.

He shoved the truck into gear and started to back out. Someone honked as he barely missed the car next to him. He braked and waved at the person in apology, then turned back to Bryn. "I think you're trying to distract me."

She smiled. "I think it worked."

Somehow Jake managed to drive the speed limit, or maybe just a little above, all the way back to the Diamond. It'd been a hell of a day so far, and he needed therapy. Therapy by way of Bryn.

He came around the truck to her side, helping her down despite her protests that she could do it. What was it with the women in his life going all independent on him? Then he grabbed her hand and hustled her inside.

Without releasing her, he shut the door behind him and started toward the bedrooms.

"Don't you think we should check on Grandma Esther?"

Damn it! She was right.

Retaining a hold on her wrist, he marched them into the living room. His grandmother was lounging on the couch watching the soap opera she DVRed daily, a large bowl of pistachios in her lap. She sat up straight when she saw them. "Jake. How good you're home."

"How are you feeling, Grandma?"

She placed the bowl on the table and patted her hair, then her stomach. "Oh, I'm better, I guess. Much better."

Bryn shot him a look, her lips twitching with a suppressed smile.

Grandma Esther had been faking. But why?

"As long as you're better we're going to uhum . . ."

"Work on some things." Bryn finished for him.

Could she have come up with a more lame excuse?

Grandma Esther winked. "You do that. And if Joe Dan and the boys come looking for you, I'll tell them you're"—she smiled lasciviously—"busy."

Jake laughed. "Sounds like a plan."

"I don't think I've ever been this embarrassed." Bryn said as Jake led the way to her room. He opened the door and swung her inside, then shut it behind them. He leaned against it and smiled. "Why? Because my grandmother knows what we're doing?"

Heat rose into her cheeks and she knew she had to be the color of an overripe tomato. "Yes! You don't find that the least bit embarrassing?"

"I'm used to it. You forget I grew up around her. She's been this way my whole life."

"I can't imagine."

"Come here." He jerked his head. "You're too far away."

"I don't know that I can do this." She shook her head. "I mean, who's to say she's not outside right now telling your entire crew what you're in here doing?"

Jake pushed himself off the door. Evidently he'd grown tired of waiting for her to change her mind. "And that would bother you too?"

She shook her head. "I'm not used to having this many people around."

"I see. I suppose it could be a bit daunting," he said. He grabbed her hand and pressed it to his chest where his heart beat beneath the hard muscle and warm skin. "But it's nothing no one else out there hasn't done before."

"Not the point."

He held her hand in place with one of his and took her other fingers and raised them to his lips.

"In a large household the best thing to do is ignore everybody as much as possible."

He used his hold on her to tug her a little closer to him. Suddenly the air was thick with wanting. "Isn't that sort of counterproductive to having a big family? Ignoring the family?"

He smiled and pulled her closer still. "I don't make the rules."

Bryn melted when his lips touched hers. How could one kiss be so perfect? How could everything about loving Jake be so perfect?

But it isn't.

She pushed those thoughts away and instead wrapped her arms around his neck and held on. The situation might not be perfect, but there was nothing wrong with this kiss.

His lips teased, searched, his tongue rediscovered, enticed, until she thought she might self-combust. He ran his hands down her sides, holding her to him. He skimmed her belly with the backs of his fingers and palmed that round curve.

"Are they asleep?" he asked.

"I think so."

"Good," he said. "They don't need to be awake for this."

After Jake reluctantly went back to work, Bryn donned her borrowed swimsuit, grabbed a large floppy hat and her sketch pad, then went out to the pool.

The house was quiet without Wesley around. And Bryn found herself missing the little girl more and more. Evelyn was gone once again with strict instructions from Jake that if she'd brought back any more horses like she did the last time, she better not come back at all.

Evelyn had just smiled at his threat and patted him on the cheek. "Mother knows best," was all she said before climbing in her large pickup truck and heading out of town. Grandma Esther had gone in to Cattle Creek to the senior center for cards and water aerobics, which left Bryn with more time alone than she'd had in a while.

But time alone on the ranch was different than time alone at her house in Georgia. Plus something about the beautiful landscape around her had her sketching more and more things. They had mixed with Wesley's current hair obsession and had Bryn thinking about jewelry in a different way.

Her fingers flew over the paper, adding a curve here and another piece there. The thoughts stacked up on each other, one on top of the other. She could use copper and add turquoise and other natural stones. Hammering and embossing everyday hair pieces. But she would want CZ chips and a sterling silver wire to render a daintier, more intricate look for those special occasions.

She hadn't been aware of how long she'd sat there sketching until she heard the unfamiliar engine coming toward the house. The school bus! Wesley was home.

Bryn closed her sketch pad, set it to the side, and slipped on her shoes and a cover-up. She didn't know where Jake was. He wouldn't want to miss this. She'd left her phone poolside and would miss it if she went back to call him. With any luck, he'd heard the school bus as well and was on his way to watch his daughter disembark for the first time. All of the ranch kids unloaded, and the ones who lived in housing started toward home.

"Miss Bryn! Miss Bryn!" Wesley ran toward her, those little girl legs pumping furiously, her excitement almost palpable. "Look what I did today! Look what I did today!" She had a paper in her hand, overlarge and slightly rough as if made from pulp.

"Teacher told us to draw a picture of our family. Look at mine!" She danced in place as she handed the drawing to Bryn.

Tears filled her eyes as she gazed at the artwork. It was crude of course and in crayon with bulky stick figures, but it was perhaps the most beautiful thing she'd ever seen.

Wesley hopped from one foot to the other as she waited for Bryn's assessment. "See? There's daddy and me and you and Grandma Esther and Nana and the babies." Her face turned serious for just a moment. "I know they're not here yet, but they will be and that'll make our family even bigger."

Tears clogged her throat. "That's right. They will be here, and our family will be that much larger." But were they a family? These last couple of days it sure felt like it. Or was she just fooling herself?

"I see you got your cat in here," Bryn said.

"Of course. And look there in the background. That really small thing? That's Joe Dan."

"Why is he so little?" Bryn asked.

"It's far away. He's working."

Bryn suppressed her laugh. She didn't want Wesley to think she was making fun of her. "I see. It's a very good picture, Wesley."

She bobbed her head. "Thank you." Then she sucked in

a deep breath as if gearing up for her next big announcement. "And everybody thought my hair was so cool and I told them about you and how you had purple in your hair and how we were having babies and I wasn't getting any more kittens and Miss Stringer said that was good."

Ms. Stringer. The now-grown-up teacher that Jake had crushed on. "So would you say your first day was amazing?"

Wesley nodded in an exaggerated motion that sent her chin from her chest pointing straight in the air. "Amazing," she said.

Bryn leaned down and gave the girl a quick hug. "I'm so glad."

"Can we put my picture on the refrigerator?" Wesley asked.

Once again emotion clogged Bryn's throat. "Of course." They may not be a family the way Wesley interpreted family. But they would always be connected through the twins. The twins would always be her half siblings and even the distance between Texas and Georgia couldn't change that.

Together they walked to the house.

"Would you like a snack?" Bryn asked as they went inside the cool interior of the house.

"We had snacks before we left school."

Bryn was only slightly disappointed. That was one of her most favorite times, when Emery got off the bus and they had a snack together. Not that Bryn needed to eat again. "Would you like to join me in the pool?"

Wesley's hands flew to her hair. "Oh no. I don't want my purple to wash out."

"When I said it would wash out, I meant that we wouldn't have to do anything to make it come out, but it won't come out immediately. Do you understand that?"

"I think so. No. Not really."

"What I mean is you can get your hair wet and you can even wash it and it'll be a couple of days before the purple comes out of your hair."

Wesley shook her head. "But I don't want the purple to come out of my hair."

Bryn nodded. "I understand that. But do you know what happens when it washes out?"

"What?" Wesley asked wide-eyed.

"We do it again."

"Do you think Daddy will let me?"

Bryn nodded. "I do."

"Okay, then." Wesley skipped from the kitchen and started down the hallway toward her bedroom. "Let's go swimming."

Jake checked the time on his cell phone and cursed under his breath. That was the hardest part about ranching: there was a schedule, but the schedule shifted regularly, the unknown was always around the corner. He had planned to be back at the house in time to see Wesley get off the school bus. But those plans disappeared in a heartbeat on the back of a runaway stallion. If Bryn hadn't been at the house, his poor baby would've gotten off the bus by herself. His mother and his grandmother were both gone. It made him wonder what he was going to do when Bryn left.

As if that was the real problem with her leaving.

The only hope he held was the longer she stayed, the easier it would be to talk her into staying forever. They got along good enough. And she seemed happy here, though he figured she'd be happy just about anywhere she was. She was just that kind of person.

He took off his hat, slapped it against his thigh, and settled it back on his head. A shrill squeal rent the air. His heart skipped a beat. He couldn't tell if it was hurt or joy. He stopped and listened again. He was only a couple hundred yards from the house. Close enough to see it, but not close enough to do anything if something were wrong. He heard hollering and squeals once again, then a big splash.

Wesley was home, and it sounded like she was in the swimming pool with Bryn. He smiled thinking of the two of them playing together like a mother and daughter should.

He didn't need to remind himself that Bryn was not Wesley's biological mother. She was a wonderful mother to her regardless. So good in fact, he'd been talked into letting her dye her hair purple. He still shook his head over that one. Perhaps where the two of them were concerned, he was just a soft touch.

He hastened his footsteps, anxious to see his two girls. He meant what he said. He wouldn't mind having two more. A whole bevy of girls with pink hair bows everywhere and soft, rose-print pajamas. All the girlie stuff might bother some men, but it just made him feel more masculine. The sight of Bryn in one of her cute little dresses, her hair pinned up off of her neck, and her toenails painted a sweet shade of cherry red just made him feel like thumping his chest. It was crazy, he knew. But that was how it felt all the same. More masculine, more of a man, because of the women around him.

He got to the edge of the yard and stopped. Bryn was sitting poolside, a big floppy hat on her head and her long legs stretched out in front of her. The curve of her belly seemed to grow more prominent every day. Just the sight of it filled him with longing, desire, and fatherly pride. It was a weird combination. But that was how she made him feel: more of a man, more of a dad, more of a lover.

"Watch me! Watch me!" Wesley bounced on the diving board to get Bryn's full attention.

"I'm watching."

Wesley backed up. "I'm going to take a running go at it."

"I don't think that's a good idea, Wes. Go to the end and jump off like you've been doing."

"I got this," said his independent daughter. She started running, and Jake's heart skipped a beat.

Even Bryn knew something was about to happen. Wesley wasn't even to the end of the board before Bryn was on her feet.

Wesley jumped too soon, hit the diving board, and screamed.

Chapter Thirteen

Bryn was in the water before Jake even moved. She had the sputtering, crying Wesley out of the water and on the side of the pool.

"Ow, ow, ow!" she cried, holding her side.

Jake spurred into action. "Are you okay?"

"Daddy!" She raised her arms, her sobs intensifying.

"Oh, honey." He patted her back soothingly.

"I'm sorry, Jake." Tears rose into her eyes. "I tried to stop her."

"I know." He tried to tell her with those two little words that everything was okay while he still comforted his crying daughter.

Jake could honestly say that he made it through Wesley's first week of school. He wasn't sure how he pulled off such a feat, but he had his suspicions. Bryn.

She was like a ray of sunshine he never knew was missing. For so long he had lived his life, existing to make it through the next day. Oh, he'd enjoyed his daughter, his mother, his brothers, his grandmother, but Bryn made everything seem just a little brighter. It was cheesy and trite, he knew. But that was the truth all the same. With Bryn at his side he felt he could accomplish almost anything. Anything but keeping her in Texas.

He stepped out of the shower and dried himself off, then finished the rest of his bathroom rituals. Grandma Esther was making Wesley's favorite supper, venison tacos with all the trimmings.

After her accident at the pool, she had cried a bit, then together he and Bryn had cared for her scraped side. Jake knew that kind of injury could really hurt, but his daughter was a Langston. She was tough as nails. So she'd sucked it up and went about the rest of her day, lesson learned.

But Lord help him, he wasn't sure if he was going to survive her play for independence. Perhaps it was her age or the fact that she was going to be a big sister, but she seemed more of a daredevil these days than ever before. Thank God for Bryn.

He donned clean clothes, ran his fingers through his still-damp hair, and headed for the kitchen. It seemed like every burner on the stove was going with something or another. Queso in one pan, taco meat in another. Refried beans and Mexican corn.

"Looks good, Grandma." Jake grabbed a chip out of the bag on the counter and dipped it into the queso.

"No snacking until dinner."

Jake stopped. He propped his hands on his hips and grinned at her. "You know, you've been saying that my whole life. And I still don't know what it means. No snacking until dinner?"

Grandma Esther pointed a finger at him, her expression stern. "Don't sass me, boy. You know good and darn well what I mean. Now get on out of here if you're not going to cook."

Jake raised his hands in surrender and backed out of the kitchen. He received a poke on the rear end for his efforts.

"Watch where you're going, Daddy." Wesley skipped around him and entered that sacred domain called the kitchen. "Be careful in there. Grandma Esther is on the warpath."

"I heard that," his grandmother returned.

"You're headed the wrong direction, cowboy."

Bryn.

"You do not want to go in there." He grabbed her hand and pulled her out onto the patio.

"Why not?"

As easy as falling off a horse, he twirled her around and into his arms. "Because I'm not in there and you can be out here with me."

She tilted her head back, raising her lips at just the right angle for kissing. "And are there any benefits to being out here with you?"

"Don't you know it." He leaned in for a long, sweet kiss. How long had it been since he'd gotten to kiss her? Forever it seemed. This morning when he woke her hours before the dawn and made love to her like tomorrow might not ever come.

A discreet cough sounded behind them. Jake turned but refused to let her go. He had her in his arms and that was exactly where he wanted to keep her.

"Am I interrupting something?" his mother asked. Stupid question. She knew damn well she was. But he figured she had been kicked out of the kitchen too and was looking for someplace to wait out the time before dinner.

"Not at all," he lied. Reluctantly, he took his arms from around Bryn, feeling a chill as her warmth moved away from him.

Yeah, smart guy. What are you going to do when she goes back to Georgia?

He was going to do everything in his power to keep that

from happening. He pushed that thought away and sat on one of the patio couches, pulling Bryn down next to him.

"Are you okay?" Bryn asked.

"I'm fine." His mother waved the question away with one flick of a hand. "Just tired."

Jake's attention jerked back to his mother once again. It seemed as though whenever Bryn was around, she was all he could think about. But his mother . . . she did look tired. But that wasn't quite the point. She admitted the weakness and that was what surprised him.

"If you need to go lay down . . . ," he started.

She shook her head. "I'll be fine. By the way," his mother started, "I'm leaving for Houston tomorrow."

"Are you sure you're up for that?" Bryn asked. "You've been traveling a lot lately."

"What's in Houston? A horse show?" Jake asked.

"Of course." His mother's tone suggested that clearly nothing else would take her to Houston.

"I agree with Bryn. You sure you're up for this?"

"I've already committed to going. I'll sleep on the plane."

"Not driving?" Jake asked. "What if you find something you want to buy? Don't you want to have a trailer there?"

She gave a delicate shrug. "I'll either rent one or come back and get it. So much easier and quicker to fly out there. That way I'll be here for the rest of Bryn's visit."

If Jake had anything to say about it, Bryn's visit would never end. But until he got her to commit to staying, he knew the possibility of her going back to Georgia was always in the air.

All through supper, Bryn watched Evelyn. Something was up. But she didn't know what. There was something haunting in the look around her eyes. But Bryn couldn't place why it looked so familiar.

"And then Denny Anderson sat down right next to him and wouldn't let him get up until he apologized to Ruby," Wesley said, relating the story of her bus riding adventures. "Can we make cookies?"

"Tater, I think Grandma Esther is tired. She's not going to want to make cookies this late. Not after making all these tacos for you."

"I'll make cookies with you," Bryn said.

Jake shook his head. "You've got to be tired too."

"I feel wonderful actually. But thanks for asking." She turned to Wesley. "What kind of cookies do you want to bake?"

"Chocolate chip is my favorite."

"Mine too."

"Only one problem though. We have to make sure we have chocolate chips."

"I'll go see." Wesley pushed back from the table, her chair scraping against the floor.

"Stay right where you are, Miss Tater," Jake said. "Finish your dinner before you go anywhere."

"We can check in a bit," Bryn said. "Now mind your daddy and eat supper."

The words spilled from her mouth so naturally that Bryn almost didn't recognize them for what they were. Motherly advice. She had fallen back into mothering so very easily. She had wondered how much of it was the twins and her hormone levels, but it seemed so natural to back up Jake's statement with Wesley.

She shook her head at herself. She didn't need to be mothering Wesley. As much as she cared for the child, loved her even, Bryn had to go home soon. She might come back from time to time to visit with the twins, especially when they were smaller, but there would come a time when Wesley would probably not be a part of her life. The thought made her so incredibly sad that tears sprang into her eyes.

"Are you okay?" Jake asked.

"I just got some pepper in my eye." But it was a lie, and they both knew it.

Jake had no more than taken his last bite of supper when his phone rang. He pulled it out of his pocket knowing it couldn't be good news. Joe Dan had a problem in the south pasture. Something had gotten ahold of one of the cows. Most probably a coyote. They needed him to come down and take a look at it.

So Jake hopped on the four-wheeler and headed out to find Joe Dan and the injured calf.

It was completely dark by the time he got back to the house. He parked his four-wheeler in the equipment barn and started for the back porch. He could see them through the window as he approached the house. His daughter and this woman who had come to mean so much to him these last couple of weeks. Strange, but he could count the days since he couldn't remember her name and now he wasn't certain what he was going to do when she left.

He stopped and watched them. Someone had opened the big French doors, and the smell of peanut butter cookies wafted out to him. On the air with that delicious aroma was the sound of '70s rock 'n' roll from the oldies station. Aerosmith sang about sweet emotion as Bryn slid another batch of cookies into the oven.

"I want to eat one now," Wesley said.

"They're still too hot," Bryn warned. "Let them cool a bit more and we can eat one in a minute with a big glass of milk, okay?"

"What do we do while they cool?" Wesley asked. Jake could hear the whine in her voice. "This part of baking cookies is no fun."

"Au contraire," Bryn said.

"What does that mean?" Wesley asked.

"It's French," Bryn explained. "It means 'on the contrary.'"

"I don't think I know what that means either," Wesley said.

Bryn laughed and the sound carried to him and made him think of a spring breeze across the meadow. Maybe he was losing his mind. Or perhaps he should go to the doctor. He'd never had such thoughts about anything in his life.

"It means that it can be the most fun time while baking cookies if you make it that way."

Wesley tilted her head at a thoughtful angle. "How?"

Bryn laughed again. And the sound was so infectious that Jake nearly laughed out loud along with her.

"By dancing."

Wesley pressed her lips together, clearly not convinced. "What does dancing have to do with cookies?"

"Nothing," Bryn said. "Except they are both things that I like."

"I don't think I know how to dance," Wesley said.

"Then you're in luck." Bryn hoisted Wesley down from the chair. "I'm a great dancer."

Jake watched mesmerized as Bryn clasped Wesley's hands in her own and started moving to the beat. His heart clutched in his chest, and he wasn't sure if it was from joy or trepidation. What was he going to do when she left? What were they going to do?

He shook his head. He wasn't going to think about that right now. Not when the night was cool, his daughter was happy, and he could watch Bryn dance.

She should've been cumbersome, maybe a little awkward, but she was all grace. Being pregnant seemed to suit her. And it brought out every beautiful and womanly aspect of her body and soul.

She was the most incredible person he'd ever met. Sweet, loving, innovative. Who else could manage to get Wesley to change her mind from chocolate chip cookies to peanut butter? And all because they probably had no chocolate chips. But he had a feeling that tomorrow there would be some in the pantry for the next time Wesley wanted cookies. That was Bryn. Making the most out of life. Avoiding even the small disappointments because life was short. Something they both knew from experience.

He leaned against the porch post and watched them dance, these two important women in his life. He knew he could stand there and watch them forever.

Then the timer dinged. "The cookies are ready!" Wesley dropped Bryn's hands and ran toward the oven. The moment of their dance was gone. But it would be in Jake's memory forever.

One day turned into a week and a week into a month. Bryn had gone shopping in San Angelo with Esther and Jessie. Made chocolate chip cookies and danced with Wesley. Evelyn was off once again, and Bryn wondered how often she was at home. Of course, Evelyn had a very lucrative and prestigious horse business, but she needed to know for the babies. Would Evelyn be there to help care for them the times when they came to visit the Diamond? It was a valid question but one she hadn't got up the gumption to ask.

On one of their shopping trips, Bryn had even bought a pair of cowboy boots and a straw hat with turned-up sides. She loved how the hat made her feel so very Texan. But she refused to buy maternity jeans. *Refused.* Instead she wore her boots and hat with dresses, even as the weather turned cooler.

"All I'm saying is if you're coming home, you better do it quick. What are you now, twenty-five weeks?"

Bryn shifted on the bed and adjusted the screen so she could see Rick better. "Twenty-four."

"Lord, girl! Look at that belly."

Bryn rubbed her stomach affectionately. "It's something, huh."

"Can you even get in your car?"

The truth of the matter was she hadn't tried. She hadn't driven her car in weeks, preferring instead to ride with Jake to town in his big ol' ranch truck. Everything she did was centered on him. Not that she was complaining.

"I'm not ready to come home yet." There, she said it.

"Are you planning on staying there?"

"I don't know, Rick. I just know that I'm not ready to leave."

"Or live in your big empty house."

She opened her mouth to deny it, but it would do no good. They both knew it was the truth. "We're still working things out here."

It was the truth. Sort of. After the initial talk of finding attorneys to help them figure out what sort of visitation schedule they would have for the twins, the subject had just dropped. She wasn't eager to go through such negotiations. She couldn't imagine that they would be hateful or that Jake would turn derogatory, but the thought was stressful just the same. It was an uncomfortable situation, to carve up a year so each of them would have time with the babies. They still had to figure out what to do after they were born. She wasn't shipping them to Texas when they were three weeks old. That was not happening.

"All I'm saying is you need to make up your mind. If you don't get home soon, you're not going to be able to travel. My sister—"

Bryn nodded politely as Rick launched into his story about his sister who, when she was pregnant, traveled to Europe, couldn't get back, and was forced to have her baby in a foreign city. Bryn had heard the story too many times to count but she wasn't in France. She was in Texas.

And then there was the decision of Christmas. Maybe it would be better if she stayed there. The doctor had said the babies could come early, maybe even before Christmas. And if that was the case . . .

She had come to like Dr. Gary, as everyone called him. The moniker kept him separate from his father Dr. Stephens in the way only small towns could differentiate. If she stayed and the babies were early, they could be there for Christmas with the Langstons, but she and Jake had done nothing to get a room ready for the new arrivals. They'd just been floating along, enjoying their time together, and forgetting the responsibilities that came with the morning. Perhaps it was time they worked a few things out.

"I don't know," Bryn said again. "I'll talk to Jake about it."

Rick raised one brow, the one without the piercing. "Tonight?"

Leave it to him to see through her ruse. "Tonight."

Bryn was sitting in the chair in her room when the bathroom door creaked open just after ten. Jake eased the door closed behind him, turning around and frowning when he saw her out of bed. She hadn't even changed into her pajamas yet.

"We need to talk."

He shook his head as if those were the last words he wanted to hear. "That's never a good thing to say."

"You know it's true."

"Can I have a kiss first?"

He looked so boyishly cute, grinning at her that way as if a kiss was the only reason he came in tonight. Somehow she managed to shake her head. "We need to talk," she repeated. A dumb thing to say twice, but she couldn't think of anything else.

"Okay. What about?"

"About us."

"What about us?"

Bryn hoisted herself to her feet. The action wasn't nearly as dramatic as she would have hoped. "Jake, don't be obtuse. You know what we need to talk about."

"So marry me."

She growled and threw her hands in the air. "I cannot marry you."

"You don't want to marry me."

She hated the hurt that flashed through his eyes. He didn't get it. He just didn't understand. Want had nothing to do with this.

"I can't marry you, Jake." Not and manage to keep herself. She would lose herself in Jake and his beautiful family. And she wasn't sure she could deal with that. Not when he still grieved for his wife.

"So you're just going home. Is that what you're saying?"

She hurt him, most likely his pride and not his feelings, but she still hated it all the same. "I . . . I thought I might stay for a while longer. You know . . . Thanksgiving is coming up."

His head jerked up, his eyes locking with hers. "You want to stay here for Thanksgiving?"

"If that's okay. If you'll have me."

He stared at her for a moment.

"I mean, look at me. I'm not even sure if I can fit into my car anymore."

Jake laughed, a sound so genuine and true she felt the tension leave her body. "Most people worry about getting into their pants. You worry about getting into your car."

Bryn chuckled along with him. "I don't want to overstay my welcome but . . ." The rest of her words eluded her. *But I like it here. But I love you. But I would stay if only I knew we could have a chance at a real relationship.* None of those things she could say.

"Of course you can stay." He shook his head. "You can stay as long as you want. Longer even." He took a step toward her, clasped her arms at the elbows, and pulled her near. "Forever." He lowered his head and kissed her. Bryn melted with the first brush of his lips. Forever. If only that were an option.

* * *

"A Halloween carnival?" Bryn looked at the paper Wesley handed her. The orange missive was bordered with jack-o'-lanterns and black cats.

"They have it every year and this year I'm big enough to go!"

Bryn didn't ask why they didn't go in years past. From the list of events it seemed that almost any age could participate. Then again it was a school function.

"Please talk Daddy into it."

"Why wouldn't he want to go?"

Wesley shook her head sadly. "He'll say you're too tired. Or you need to rest. Or the babies wouldn't like it."

True enough, Jake fretted over her like no other. Being pregnant had energized her, given her a new drive, a new outlook on life. The babies were her second chance, her second wind, a new hope. But considering how he lost his first wife, she tried to be patient and understanding. "Of course we'll go. And of course Daddy is coming with us."

"Going with you where?" Jake sauntered into the kitchen, looking like a dream in dusty chaps and an equally dusty shirt. His hat had a dent on one side that wasn't there yesterday. She could only assume that someone or something had stepped on it recently.

"To the Halloween carnival at the school."

He took a bottle of water from the refrigerator and turned back to face them. "I don't know." He opened the lid and drank deeply. "I don't think you should be on your feet a lot."

Wesley bounced on her toes, her ponytail swinging from side to side. The purple had given way to orange tips to match the season for the spookiest night of the year.

"PleaseDaddypleaseDaddypleaseDaddy!"

Jake looked over and caught Bryn's gaze. Wesley was so busy jumping up and down she wasn't paying attention to the two of them.

"Please, Daddy," Bryn mouthed over the top of Wesley's head.

Jake laughed. "How can I say no to that?"

Does she even know what a zombie is?" Jake asked.

He set the alarm on the truck and grabbed Bryn's hand, interlacing their fingers.

"She's in school. She'll be exposed to all kinds of things now. Get ready for it."

Jake shook his head as Wesley ran ahead of them. Her costume for the Halloween carnival? A zombie cowgirl.

Thankfully, Bryn had toned down Wesley's makeup requests. She wasn't quite as scary looking as the picture, which was a plus as far as he was concerned. Bryn took an old T-shirt and ripped the sleeves and dirtied it with black face powder. She found a purple novelty cowboy hat to complete the outfit. She cut a hole in the crown and made it truly zombie worthy. It certainly wasn't the ripped jeans. Those were in fashion. Or so he was told.

"Just think, you could've come as the zombie cowgirl's daddy."

"I thought that's what I was."

Bryn shook her head and laughed. "Sorry, I said that wrong. You could have come as the cowgirl's zombie daddy."

Jake looked down at his starched Western shirt and meticulously creased Wranglers. "Not on your life."

"Spoilsport."

"Like your costume is better." She was wearing a flannel shirt and baggy jeans, exaggerated freckles painted on her cheeks. She looked like a rotund country bumpkin.

"Just wait."

They handed their tickets to the man at the door. Just inside the building, Bryn tied the tails of her shirt under her breasts and pushed the waistband of her pants down under her belly. Sometime while he was getting ready, she had painted her stomach orange with curved vertical lines.

"What . . . ?"

Then she cupped her hands under her belly. He laughed. Now she looked like a country bumpkin carrying a pumpkin.

She grinned at him, completely at ease with her large stomach protruding out in front of her and painted for the occasion.

It was one of those things he lo—admired about her. Yes, admired.

The moment between them ended as she turned to Wesley. "What do you want to do first?"

"Games! Games! Games!" His zombie cowgirl jumped up and down, her excitement spilling over to everyone around her.

"Okay! Okay! Okay!" His pumpkin-toting country farmer laughed.

They headed toward the hallway containing the classrooms where the games had been set up. What was a cowboy to do but follow behind them?

I wanna do the cake walk now." Wesley danced around Bryn's legs, like a fairy-sprite zombie cowgirl in a purple cowboy hat.

"Okay." Bryn took her hand and led her up onto the wooden stage. The cake walk was being held behind the thick royal blue curtains that had seen better days. The pattern for the walk had been mapped out on the floor using painters' tape.

"This is how it works," Wesley said as she walked up to the ticket taker and handed her two tickets.

"What about your daddy?"

Wesley looked back to where her father stood at the edge of the stage holding the evening's winnings. Two stuffed bears and a unicorn, a bag of cotton candy, a pennant for the Cattle Creek Longhorns, and a snake that was part molded plastic, part Slinky. "He's okay. He likes holding the stuff."

Jake laughed, and Bryn joined in. Wesley's enthusiasm was infectious, her joy contagious.

"This is what you do." Wesley grabbed Bryn's hand and led her to the numbered squares. "Find a square and when the music starts, you walk. When it stops, you stop. Got it?"

Bryn smiled down at her. "I got it."

The cheerleader volunteer who had also taken their tickets started the music player, and "Farmer in the Dell" filled the room. Wesley hopped from one foot to the other, being careful to completely step in each square. She looked back every so often to make sure Bryn understood the directions.

They made three trips around the square before the cheerleader stopped the music. Wesley hopped to the square in front of her, then back one before the number was called.

"Six," the cheerleader said as she looked around at all of the participants.

No one was on the six.

"Can we go again?" Wesley asked. "Pleasepleaseplease!"

Around and around they went once again. Number seven was the winner. Neither Bryn nor Wesley was on the number seven. The tween boy with flaming red hair and a cowlick that pushed his hair in two different directions off his freckled forehead picked the chocolate layer cake with a cherry on the top. The exact cake Bryn had been eying on every trip around.

"Again!" Wesley danced in place.

Bryn looked over to where Jake patiently waited. They shared a smile of kindred spirits who knew they weren't getting out of there until the girl got a cake.

They went around a couple more times before thankfully, Wesley landed on lucky number four.

"Look, Daddy! I won!"

Bryn took the cake Wesley chose from the table and started toward Jake. Tonight had been fun, but she was starting to wear down. She was going to sleep like a baby tonight.

"You okay?" Jake asked as she came near. He took the cake from her and she pushed her bangs back from her face.

"It's just been a long day."

"What's next?" Wesley asked.

Jake turned from Bryn and focused his attention on Wesley. "One more room and it's time to go."

"Awh . . ."

"One more. Choose wisely."

"The haunted house."

Jake threw back his head and groaned. "Anything but that."

"Dad-dy."

"I'm not sure you're ready to go in there."

"I am," she said. "I'm practically growed up. I learned how to dive this summer, and I can read and ride fences."

She might have been around the child for only a couple of months, but she could see that Wesley was gearing up to dig in her heels and hold her ground.

"I'll take her in," Bryn said. "That is, if you think she can handle it."

"Of course I can handle it. I'm five and a half now."

Jake leaned in close. She inhaled the sexy scent of him, leather, citrus, and horse. It was a potent combination. "It's going to be filled with cold spaghetti and peeled grapes."

"I think I'll be all right." She breathed in deep.

"You don't have to."

She laid a hand on his arm, loving the warmth of him beneath her fingers. "I don't mind."

Side by side, Bryn and Jake made their way to the library, which now served as the haunted house. Wesley skipped ahead in that typical Wesley fashion that Bryn had come to love.

She waited for them by the ticket taker, another CCHS cheerleader.

"Are you sure about this?" Bryn asked her young companion.

Wesley nodded, her ponytail bobbing with the motion.

"I could ask you the same thing," Jake whispered in her ear.

Bryn shivered, but not from fear.

"Okay," Bryn said. "Grab my hand and don't be scared."

Wesley did as she asked, but shot her a one-eyed squint. "That's the whole point of a haunted house, Miss Bryn. You're supposed to be scared." She shook her head as if to say *What could a kid do with adults?* then together they walked inside.

Just as Jake had warned, the haunted house was filled with bowls of peeled grapes and cold spaghetti and every monster imaginable.

"Don't be scared," Wesley said, squeezing Bryn's hand tighter.

"I'm okay. Are you okay?" Bryn had the feeling the house was a little scarier than Wesley had anticipated. She scooted closer to Bryn's legs, squeezing her hand even tighter.

"I'm okay," she said as the vampire hissed at them from a corner.

"All right, not much longer now."

The words had no sooner left her mouth than the werewolf jumped out in front of them. It was obviously a high school boy in a wolf man costume, but it was Wesley's undoing. She screamed and buried in her face in the side of Bryn's belly.

"My friends said this wouldn't be scary," Wesley cried.

The wolf man retreated, and Bryn tried to pry Wesley from her side.

"He's gone now," Bryn said. "And you know they're just pretend, right?"

Wesley sniffed and wiped away her tears. "Right," she said. "But I don't want to be in here anymore."

"Good enough. We just have to get to the end," Bryn said. They shouldn't have let her come in. Bryn should've been more adamant about not bringing her inside. But hindsight and all that.

"I can't walk." Wesley crossed her arms and closed her eyes against the sights of the haunted house all around her.

"I need for you to, Wesley. In order to get out of here, we have to walk."

"What if something gets me?"

The people coming up behind them muttered and went around. Bryn wanted to pull Wesley to one side, but that was where the monsters were. So they stood in the middle of the walkway.

"Nothing's going to get you. Not as long as you're with me." If only it was that easy. Bryn shoved that thought away. "Just take my hand and let's walk out of here."

Wesley shook her head. "Carry me."

"I can't carry you. You're too heavy."

"I am not. I can't walk out of here, Miss Bryn. Please carry me!"

Bryn was slammed with all the failure she'd had with Emery. She'd tried her best, but she had been young when she gained custody of her sister. It wasn't Bryn's fault that Emery got leukemia and died, but she still felt that she had failed her on that level. She hadn't done enough to save her. Yet here was Wesley, and she could save her from the monsters in the haunted house. What choice did she have?

"Here. Grab hold of my neck."

Wesley wrapped her little arms around Bryn's neck. She stood balancing her weight with her extra baby girth. Wesley wasn't very heavy, but it was quite a way back to the door of the haunted house. But she could do it. Wesley buried her face in Bryn's neck as the sounds went on around them.

"Shhh," Bryn whispered in Wesley's ear. "It's all okay.

It's just pretend." She was already tired and each footstep felt like she was walking in peanut butter with Wesley clinging to her for dear life.

She wasn't sure how she could take another step as she came through the exit doors. Her eyes immediately searched out Jake. He was standing off to the side, a concerned frown marring his handsome features.

"You have to get down now, Wesley."

A searing pain started on one side of her belly and streaked across to the other. She inhaled sharply. Wesley slid to the ground.

"Daddy!" Wesley ran and threw herself at her father. Despite all the things he held in his arms, he managed to scoop her up as well.

"You were right. I shouldn't've gone in there."

He shushed her and kissed the top of her head. Bryn stood, paralyzed in pain, sucking in as much air as she could.

"What's wrong?"

She pressed a hand to her side and shook her head. "It'll go away in a second."

"What'll go away in a second?"

"Nothing."

"If it's nothing, how can it go away?"

Bryn managed to get enough air into her lungs. She straightened, then took one step forward. A stitch started at her side. "Just a pain."

"A pain?"

"It's probably just Braxton Hicks. Nothing to worry about."

"You shouldn't have carried her out. She's too big for that."

"Trust me." Bryn tried to smile. "I know that now." She tried to take another step, but her muscles seemed locked in place.

"That's it. I'm calling 9-1-1. There's got to be an ambulance around here somewhere."

Bryn clutched his arm. "Don't you dare call an ambulance. I'll be fine. I probably just need some potassium."

He stared at her for a full minute. "You're as pale as a ghost and your face is all pinched, and you think eating a banana will help?"

"I'm fine, Jake. I promise."

A muscle in his jaw jerked. He was worried. She couldn't blame him, not after everything he'd been through. But she was fine.

"Why don't you take Wesley and all the stuff out to the truck and then come back and get me. Just let me rest a minute. I'll be fine."

Jake looked as if he was about to protest. "Okay, but on one condition. If you can't walk when I get back, then you have to go to the hospital."

Bryn sighed. "Fine. You can call an ambulance if I can't walk when you get back." But she would be okay. All she needed was ten minutes to rest.

Chapter Fourteen

"What the hell is Braxton Hicks?" Jake asked on the way home. He still couldn't believe he let her talk him out of taking her to the hospital. His palms were sweaty, his mouth dry.

"They're practice contractions."

"Practice?"

He didn't remember that from Cecilia's pregnancy. But at the time he had been wrapped up in other matters. Like holding his marriage together and running a ranch and maybe a little bit of just himself. But he'd been younger then and things were different.

"I'm telling you, I'm fine. I promise you, I'm fine. I love these babies too. And I wouldn't do anything to jeopardize their health and well-being."

He tried to relax. Her words were the truth as much as he hated to admit it. He knew she wouldn't do anything to harm the babies she carried. Yet it was so hard . . .

"Is it time for you to be practicing?" he asked.

She smiled. "Babies do what they do. At least that's what

all the books say. But Braxton Hicks can start at any time in the third trimester. And if it wasn't Braxton Hicks, then it had to have just been a muscle cramp."

"Wait. Now it's not Braxton Hicks but muscle cramps? Do you even know what this was? I'm driving to the hospital."

"No! Jake, please. Everything's going to be okay." She scooted a little closer to him. As close as she could with the captain's chairs in the front of his truck. She laid one hand against his leg. Her touch was warm and comforting. And he wanted to believe her. He wanted to believe everything was okay. There were times like this when he wasn't sure he would get through this pregnancy without having a heart attack. That would be just what they needed: all four of them in the hospital. And Wesley at home running the ranch. The thought brought a smile to his lips.

"That's better," Bryn said.

She turned to look at the backseat, where Wesley rode with all of her carnival winnings including the coconut cake.

"Did you have a good time tonight?"

Jake glanced at Wesley in the rearview mirror. She nodded, though her expression remained solemn. Or maybe it was just the shadows of the truck that made it look that way.

"Are you and the babies going to be okay?"

"Of course we are."

"I didn't mean to hurt you."

His daughter was near tears.

"You didn't hurt me," Bryn said. "Or the babies. But from now on, I don't think I can carry you. So you've got to be a big girl and walk on your own."

"Even in a haunted house?" Wesley asked.

Bryn nodded. "Even in a haunted house. Sorry, chickadee. That's just the way it has to be for now."

"I guess."

"Where's the big-sister smile?" Bryn asked. Whether it was the word *big* or the word *sister*, Jake wasn't sure, but Wesley perked up and gave Bryn an ultrabright smile.

"There's my girl." Bryn reached back and patted Wesley on the leg, then turned to face front.

"You're good with her," Jake said.

"Try not to scare her again."

"I'm serious. You really are good with her."

"I've had some practice." Five years of it, to be exact. Though she wasn't sure that last year counted for much of anything. It'd been too filled with doctors' appointments and hospital visits and chemo treatments and a ton of other sad, depressing ordeals that she never cared to remember.

Jake pulled the truck in front of the house and everybody got out. He helped Wesley down as Bryn started reaching for stuffed animals and other treasures.

"I'll get that," Jake said.

"Jake, they're stuffed animals. They're not heavy."

"I'll get them anyway. You go lay down on your left side, or your right side or whatever you're supposed to do to make sure you're okay."

For a minute he thought she might protest, then she gave a quick nod, handed over the unicorn, and started for the door. He stood there a moment and watched the two most important women in his life walk into the house. Then he scooped up the coconut cake and followed behind them.

"No," Jake said. He grasped Bryn's fingers, removing her hand from such a sensitive place and laying it on his chest instead. "Not tonight. You should rest."

"I told you. I'm fine."

He raised her fingers to his lips and kissed each one in turn. "I know what you said. But I think we should wait. At least until we have another doctor's appointment or something."

"Or I have the babies?"

"Maybe."

She rose up on her elbow and glared down at him. "It's

one thing for you to be concerned, but it's another for you to go completely off the deep end."

"I'm just being safe."

"I don't want you worrying."

Too late for that. "Of course I worry."

"Well, don't." She leaned in and kissed him. She tasted like apples and Halloween candy and every good thing in life.

"Bryn," he groaned as she lifted her head.

"Yes?"

"Tomorrow night," he promised. Tomorrow night he would love her like there was no tomorrow. But for now . . . "Just let me hold you."

She turned in his arms, snuggling her back against his chest and her bottom against parts of him that didn't know how worried his brain was. He wrapped his arms around her and pulled her even closer. He buried his nose in the curve of her neck, his arms around her thick middle.

She sighed against him and for that moment everything seemed right in the world. But there was so much still left unsaid. So much they hadn't worked out yet.

He had been dragging his feet about getting an attorney involved. She had been talking about staying through Christmas, yet an agreement would still need to be reached. But attorneys, custody, and visitation rights, those were things he didn't want to deal with. Not yet anyway, but they loomed before him, whether he liked it or not.

I got us an appointment."

Bryn sat with her back against Jake while a billion stars twinkled overhead. It'd been a week since Halloween and her first contraction. It'd taken four days and a trip to the doctor's office before Jake was finally convinced that everything was A-OK with the twins. But that didn't mean he spent the dark hours in his room. He slept with her every night, simply holding her in his arms. Bryn had never felt so cherished. Every day that she stayed in Texas she was that much closer to never wanting to go home again.

"An appointment where?" She tilted her head back so she could look at his face. He sat in the chaise lounge while she rested against him, snuggled between his thighs. Kota lay at their feet, chin on his paws, though Bryn knew he watched her every move. The cattle dog had taken to following Bryn wherever she went. Bryn wasn't sure if the dog was extremely clever or picking up on Jake's stress, but the pooch knew Bryn might need her and stayed close just in case.

"With an attorney."

She sighed. She'd known all along it was going to come to this. Two people who shared children couldn't live in two different states without a legal agreement. It was just a sign of the times. But the news made her heart thump heavily in her chest. Everything had been so beautiful between them. Why did they have to have a legal agreement at all?

But just because they came to a legal agreement didn't mean everything was going to be ruined. In fact, it might be liberating to know where they stood with each other, what was coming in the future, and how they planned to work it out so the twins would spend adequate time in Texas as well as Georgia.

She pushed herself up and turned so she could see his face. "Tell me everything's going to be okay," she said.

"Everything's going to be okay," he parroted. He held his drink up so she could sip from the straw. Lemonade on a cool Texas night. Didn't get much better than that. And it was getting cooler and cooler. Before long there might even be some snow.

"When is it? The appointment?"

"Next week. Thursday."

"Thursday," she repeated. After that there was only a week until Thanksgiving and then two more months until the babies were expected. Twins were notorious for coming early. They could come any time after the first of December. She would need to go home right after Thanksgiving or risk the chance of not going home at all.

Would that be so bad?

No, she decided. It wouldn't be bad at all. But . . . how long before she realized that she didn't really belong in Texas? How long before she had outstayed her welcome?

"Did you mean what you said? About staying through Thanksgiving?"

She nodded. "Absolutely." She studied his face, looking for any sign of deception or insincerity. She saw none.

"You wouldn't have to go home then . . . not if you didn't want to. I mean, the babies will be coming soon, right? Maybe you should stay a bit longer. Through Christmas or maybe even the first of the year."

"Are you saying you want me to stay here through the first of the year?"

"It was just an idea."

Staying in Texas would mean not having to set her foot down about who got first Christmas with the babies—assuming that they came beforehand. And she wouldn't have to go home now. She wouldn't have to worry about snow and travel time or whether she was too big to fit behind the wheel of her car. Staying through Christmas would take a lot of weight off her shoulders.

"If that offer is still open . . . ," she started.

Jake swallowed hard. "You mean that?"

She nodded.

"That offer's definitely still open."

She smiled as he swooped in and captured a kiss. The idea seemed to fill him with joy. And passion. His hands were everywhere at once, his lips seeking, searching, devouring. He seemed to not be able to get enough of her. And as far as she was concerned, that was all right too.

* * *

So, what's this all about?" Jake looked from his mother to his grandmother, who shrugged. Dinner had been served, the dishes washed and put away, and Bryn was reading Wesley a bedtime story. His mother had asked if she could talk to him. He and Grandma Esther were sitting on the couch in his mother's office. As usual his mother was braced behind her overlarge desk.

"This isn't easy for me to say." She looked down at nothing, then back at him. "I've been lying to you."

He gave a quick nod, ignoring the pang of trepidation that sliced through him. "Okay. About what?"

"I haven't been going to any horse shows."

He wasn't sure what to make of that. His mother was a horsewoman through and through, and if she hadn't been going to any horse shows lately . . . "Then where have you been going?"

"MD Anderson." The name of the cancer hospital fell between them like a bag of dirty laundry. His heart stilled in his chest. But just because . . . that didn't mean . . .

"Why—" He cleared his throat. "Why have you been going there?" It was a stupid question, but the only one he could think to ask. MD Anderson had treated her six years ago when she had discovered she had breast cancer. But after three surgeries, countless rounds of chemo and radiation, and lots of prayers, Evelyn Langston was cancer-free. There was only one reason she would return to MD Anderson.

"The cancer's back."

"Oh, Evie." Grandma Esther pushed to her feet and went around the desk to pull Evelyn into her arms.

Jake felt as if he were made of stone. He could only sit there, his mother's words echoing around in his head.

The cancer's back.

How could the cancer be back?

The cancer's back.

Why was the cancer back?

The cancer's back.

Why? How?

"What do we do now?" Grandma Esther asked.

His mother stood and came around the desk, leaning against it as she stood in front of him. "Jake?"

Finally, he raised his gaze to meet hers.

"Are you okay?"

He smiled and swallowed hard. "Yes," he croaked. But the word was a lie. How could he be okay?

"What are the doctors saying?" Grandma Esther asked.

"Well, I've been going through treatments, and they seem hopeful. But it spread, so it's going to be a tough battle."

If anybody was up for a tough battle, it was his mother. But he didn't want her to have to fight. He didn't want to have to worry about her. For so many years, for so many days, he'd worried about her. When did the worry stop?

"But I wanted you to know," she said. "It's been hard to keep it to myself."

Jake shook his head. "Why didn't you tell us?"

"At first, I didn't want you to worry until I knew something. After that, I just couldn't find a good time. It's not exactly fun news to hand out." She gave him an encouraging smile, then leaned in and grabbed his hands in her own. She squeezed them and gazed into his eyes, much like she had when he was little. "It's going to be okay, Jake." But he wished he had her faith.

The bathroom door creaked open, and Bryn sat up in bed. "Jake? Is that you?" Unlike all the nights before, Jake had gone to his room mumbling something about a headache and brushing his lips across her cheek before disappearing out of sight. She could tell something was wrong. Yet it wasn't her business. She might be staying here through the first of the year, but she was an extended houseguest.

The baby mama. And not truly a member of the Langston family.

He shut the door quietly behind him and padded to the bed on bare feet. He climbed in beside her, not saying a word as he scooped her into his arms and pulled her close.

"Jake?" she whispered. "Say something. You're scaring me." Something was wrong. Something was terribly wrong.

He shook his head, burying his nose in the crook of her neck. Tears wet her skin and the bodice of her nightgown.

She lost track of how long they lay that way, him cradled in her arms. He had one hand splayed across her belly as if seeking out the new life that nestled there. Then he pushed himself up and kissed her. Tears still wet his cheeks as he deepened their kiss.

Bryn braced her hands on his shoulders and held him away from her. As fantastic as it was to have his lips on hers, she had to hear what was wrong first. "Will you tell me?"

For a moment he didn't breathe. Then he exhaled heavily and rolled onto his back, pulling her half on top of him as he did so. His arms were around her, her head tucked under his chin.

"It's Mama," he said. "The cancer is back."

Bryn pushed herself up so she could look into those marvelous green eyes. "Oh, Jake. I'm sorry."

He nodded, swallowed hard. "She's been going to treatment. Not to the horse shows. That's why she hasn't been around much."

"And that's good, right?"

He gave a small shrug.

"But she has to fight."

Memories flooded her, one on top of the other. All those countless nights in the hospital with Emery. All the pain, all the suffering. Emery had suffered. She had suffered. Cancer was a terrible enemy. It was an evil thief that robbed people of their lives, took parents from children and children from parents. It was a horrible, horrible thing. And it had to be fought at all costs.

"She's a fighter," Bryn said, scooping up all the pain and memories and storing them away. Right now she had to be strong, for Jake. Emery was gone, but Evelyn could still win this battle. "She beat it before, right?"

Jake nodded.

"Then she'll beat it again." Bryn said the words with more confidence than she felt. But she had to. They couldn't let cancer get the upper hand. They couldn't even say those words aloud. The only way to fight was to fight with all their hearts. And she knew that was what Evelyn would do.

"Come here." Jake pulled her up, closer to him. "I need you." The words were strangled, nearly choked as they worked their way out of him.

"You have me."

He kissed her then, rolling her onto her back and running his hands over every inch of her he could reach. He loved her slow and gentle, fast and intense, then like he could never get enough. He entered her slow, showing her without words how much he cherished her, how much it meant for the two of them to be together. Then the passion took over and the need for mindless whirling desire. Again and again and again. Over and over until the friction was so much she felt as if she might explode from it all. And then she did. Into a million sparkling pieces. She felt like she would never be whole again. But it was okay, because in that moment she was the happiest she had ever been in her life.

Jake stilled above her. His teeth clenched, his expression strained as if trying to hold back. Trying to prolong that pleasure just a little more. Then it broke. He groaned and collapsed on top of her. Then he rolled them to one side. His nose was buried in the hair just behind her ear as he planted little kisses all on her neck. "I love you," he murmured. "I love you. I love you. I love you." And those three special words pounded out a tempo that matched the breathless speed of her heart.

This feels strange," Bryn said as Jake opened the truck and helped her to the sidewalk.

"Why?"

Bryn looked up at the building before them. Harley Green, attorney at law. The office was down at the end of Main Street next to the library and kitty-corner from the empty lot on Tenth. The building looked worn, as if the bricks had been used to make something else before brought here and set up as a law office. An American flag flapped in the breeze out front. Bryn pulled her jacket a little tighter around her, suddenly chilled. "Most times when people need an attorney they're at odds with each other. Yet here we are coming together, riding in the same truck." She shook her head. "It just seems strange."

He held the door open for her and waited for her to step inside. "I'm trying to circumvent all that," Jake said. "We get everything settled now and we don't have to worry about all these details later."

It was a good plan, most likely an unnecessary plan. And maybe that was what felt so strange about it. Bryn hadn't planned anything in the last couple of years. When Emery got sick, their time was spent between doctors' appointments and doing everything in her power to help her remember what it meant to live. After Emery died, Bryn had drifted, not planning much at all, not even dinner. Yes, that had to be what it was.

Jake hadn't mentioned his confession of the night before. But she hadn't wanted to bring it up herself. He had been hurting last night, worried about his mother and her fight against an unfair killer. But still . . .

Bryn basked in the knowledge. She took that moment and tied it up with a yellow bow and put it in a box for special keeping. Jake loved her. She was staying through Christmas. And maybe beyond. Life was good.

The law offices of Harley Green were exactly what she suspected from a Cattle Creek attorney. The building itself looked as if at one time it had been a café or maybe even a variety store. Two large plate glass windows flanked the glass doors like one would see at a restaurant. There was a large front office with a cheap laminate desk and stained, olive green carpet. Framed pictures of waterfalls and creeks dotted the pine-paneled walls. A bell over the door signaled their entrance.

The woman behind the desk had to be a hundred and fifty if she was a day. But bright, sparkling eyes squinted at them from all the wrinkles.

"Jake," she greeted. "So good to see you. I'll let Harley know you're here." She used the phone to alert him, then looked back to Jake. "So how's your mama?"

Jake took his hat off and twirled it in his hands. Was he nervous? "She's fine, Miss Emma. Thank you for asking."

The phone buzzed. She looked down at it, then back up to Jake. "Harley says go on in. You tell her I asked about her, okay?"

Jake gave a small nod. "I will." With a hand at the small of her back, he guided Bryn toward the cheap wooden door in front of them. He gave a small knock, then opened it for Bryn to proceed inside.

The interior office was more of the same as the outside reception area. Cheap pine paneling, plastic plants, and framed pictures of various outdoor scenes. It might not be modern or up-to-date, but it was clean. And that said something.

"Jake Langston." The man stood and reached out a hand to shake.

Jake took it in his own. "Harley."

"Good to see you." He turned his gaze to Bryn. "And you must be Bryn."

She shook his hand as well. "Nice to meet you."

Harley returned to his seat and shuffled through the papers on his desk. "Okay, then. Let's get down to business, shall we?" He shuffled a few more papers and pulled the file from the top drawer. Suddenly the good-old-boy demeanor became all business. "Jake, I looked into a few things like you asked me. And I drew up something I think will be satisfactory. We can make changes as necessary." He turned to Bryn. "I've got everyone a copy here so we can follow along."

Wait. Jake had contacted him before?

"I'm not sure I understand."

"Well, that's why we're going over it," Harley said. His words were neither condescending nor sarcastic. But Bryn had the feeling she was way out of her league.

She pressed a hand to her side against the cramp that was starting there. She tried to take in a good breath. The bigger the babies got, the harder it was for her to breathe at times. And in times like this . . . well, anxiety was not her friend.

"Are you okay?" Jake's concerned voice brought her attention around to him. Those green eyes searched her face for signs of distress. They seemed so loving and caring, so why did she feel out of sorts all of the sudden?

"I'm fine, just a little cramped."

"A cramp?"

"I'm fine, Jake." But she pushed herself up to sit a little straighter in the seat. She needed all the air she could get for this one.

Harley handed them the documents. It had to be fifteen pages long. What did they have to discuss that would require fifteen pages, single spaced?

"As you can see, the main parts that we're here to talk about today are visitation and custody."

Custody? The word seared through her like a knife through butter.

She stopped. She was overreacting. It was just a word. One people used when they shared children.

She lowered her gaze to the paper in her hands. Scanning it and trying to decipher the legalese.

And primary custody will remain with Jake Langston.

Chapter Fifteen

Her blood ran cold in her veins. Her hands trembled. She swallowed hard and looked to Jake. He seemed to be reading as if it were nothing more important than the sports section of the Sunday paper.

She looked back to the document she held. Maybe she read it wrong. Yes! That was what she did. She read it wrong. She skipped a line. She needed to get glasses. She . . .

"You want custody?" The words were spoken so softly that she wasn't even sure she'd said them out loud.

She cut her gaze over to Jake. He was looking at Harley as if somehow the attorney could explain better than he could.

"Look at me," she said. Still her voice was deathly quiet. It seemed to come from a place inside her that she never knew existed.

"Bryn, just hear me out."

"I can't hear you out. You've never even talked to me about this."

"I'm just trying to look out for the babies."

"You're trying to look out for yourself." She wanted to jump to her feet in indignation, but she was a little too round for that these days. She managed to hoist herself up out of the broken spring chair and turned on him. "You never once even hinted that you wanted custody. Then I come here, and you throw that bomb on me? What kind of game are you playing, Jake?"

He remained seated, which was just fine with her. She might not be superior in many ways, but with him sitting down, she had height on him.

"You said so yourself," he said. "You don't have a job. You don't have any family. How are you going to take care of two babies all by yourself?"

"I'll hire a nanny."

"Aside from the money that would cost, don't you think it would be better if the kids were taken care of by their family?"

"Like your mother and your grandmother?" She wished she had something bad to say about that, but there was nothing. Grandma Esther would love these babies beyond measure. Evelyn too. They would do everything in their power to take care of the twins. But if the babies were with Jake, that meant they weren't with her. "Why are you trying to take my babies from me?"

He stood, suddenly taking away her advantage. "I've tried to get you to marry me. I've tried to get you to stay here. I've done everything in my power—"

"So that's what all this has been about. All your late-night sneaking into my room—"

"I tried time and again to get you to marry me. I've made no secret that I want you to stay here with the babies."

"And if I wouldn't stay here with them, then you wanted them without me." How could she have been so naive?

"Ahem." Harley cleared his throat.

Jake's gaze swung from the attorney back to Bryn. "This is not the place to discuss that."

Her anger rose, something she wasn't sure was possible until it actually happened. "This is the perfect place to discuss it. You used me and manipulated me, so I would let my guard down."

He shook his head. "I don't know why you would think that."

"Because it's true!"

"Ahem." Harley cleared his throat once again.

This time they both looked at him.

"How about we discuss this like rational adults?" Harley suggested.

That wouldn't work, because there was nothing rational about it.

Bryn collapsed in an ungainly way back into her seat. Jake stared at her for a full heartbeat, then returned to his chair as well.

"I can't believe how stupid I was." Tears rose in the back of her throat as she blinked them away. She would not cry. Not now. Not in front of him. Not after the stunt he'd pulled.

Jake turned toward her and clasped her hand in his own. She jerked away. She didn't want to touch him, didn't want him touching her. That was what got them into this mess to begin with.

"Just hear me out," Jake said, his voice returning to a normal level. But even then, Bryn didn't want to hear what he had to say. Anything else would just be a lie. Or how could she determine if everything he told her up to this point was a lie?

"There's nothing to hear, Jake. I will not give you custody of these babies. In fact, I'm going back to Georgia, and they're going with me."

Driving back to the ranch with Jake was sheer torture. If there was any other way for her to get back there without him, she would've jumped on it in a heartbeat. But she was stuck. Another reason why it was time for her to go home. She had been such a fool. She had thought she'd found something in Jake that she had never found in anyone else. How blind could one person be? She had fallen for his lines and sweet kisses . . .

She shook her head trying to dislodge those thoughts. Dwelling on it was not going to change one thing. She just needed to pull herself up and get herself back on track.

"Bryn, please, listen to me."

"There's nothing to listen to, Jake. Those papers said everything. But don't expect me to sign them."

"I don't know why you're so angry."

She turned in her seat to face him, barely managing to keep her chin out of her lap. "You don't know why—" Men were stupid. "If I have to tell you why, then it's not worth it."

"Why are women so stubborn? I'm just trying to help you."

"I don't need your help. I have a trust fund, plenty of money, and a house that's paid for. I can take care of these babies just fine."

"That's what I'm trying to say, Bryn. Don't you think they deserve better than fine?" He pulled his truck to a stop outside the ranch house and cut the engine.

"You always talk about family. Do you think your mother will be able to help you take care of these babies? She's going through cancer treatments. That's hard on a person, Jake. Where will you be then?"

"I'll hire a nanny." He slammed out of the truck.

Bryn hurried to get herself down without his help. The last thing she wanted were his traitorous hands on her. Or maybe it was her body that was traitorous. She could be angry with him, then when he touched her she would melt like chocolate in the sun.

"Then what's the difference if I hire one?"

"You could still move here, you know. That's all I wanted."

"Oh, and marry you? Not a chance. I'm going home soon as I can." She flung open the door to the house and stepped inside. Jake was hot on her heels.

"You can't even get behind the wheel of your car."

She whirled on him then. "Oh, really? Now you're calling me fat?"

He exhaled through his nose, nearly snorting like a bull. "I think this conversation should wait until later."

She shook her head. "This conversation is never going to happen again. I'm going back to Georgia. However I have to get there."

She hated that he was right. She couldn't fit in her little Volkswagen these days. But that didn't mean she was stuck in Texas. She would call Dr. Gary tomorrow, get clearance to fly, then she was out of here.

"What is going on out here?" Evelyn came out of her office, skidding to a stop when she looked at the two of them. Bryn supposed they were a sight, both ruddy with anger.

"Would you please tell Bryn that family is important to children?"

"Will you please tell Jake that I am part of these babies' family?"

Evelyn looked from Jake to Bryn, then back again.

"And would you please tell Bryn that it's only logical that the babies stay here after they're born?"

"Would you please tell Jake that he doesn't have to worry about it because I'm taking them back to Georgia tomorrow?"

She grabbed her cell phone out of her purse and pushed past the two of them, heading toward her room. She would call Dr. Gary now. The first flight out of Texas and she was gone.

"Will you please tell Evelyn what's going on here?" His mother's look pinned him to the spot.

Jake exhaled again and felt those tense muscles start to

relax, but only a bit. "We had an appointment with the attorney today," he said. "Bryn isn't happy that I asked for custody."

His mother blinked at him. Opened her mouth to speak. Shut it again. And blinked once more. "You asked the mother of your children for custody?"

He frowned and nodded. "It's only logical. They would have the whole ranch to grow up on. They would have Wes and you and Grandma Esther. Seth and Jessie. Bryn has no one in Georgia to help her. I've asked her to marry me—*repeatedly*—and she refuses. I gave up on that and asked her to move in. She refuses. What else did you want me to do?"

"Well, I didn't think you would do *that*," his mother said.

"Why not? Women ask for custody all the time. I'm not trying to take them from her. I'm trying to protect them and raise them, take care of them. She's the one being stubborn. All she has to do is marry me and this would be over."

His mother shook her head. "Maybe you should've told her that option before you took her to the attorney's office and presented her with legal documents to the effect."

"Maybe," he muttered. He scrubbed his hands over his face and tried to get a handle on the situation. Last night, everything had been so perfect between them. Despite the devastating news that his mother's battle had begun again, he had held Bryn in his arms and told her how much he loved her.

Maybe he exaggerated the truth of it. He cared for her. A great deal. And he had hoped his confession of love would've brought about a change of heart today for her. She would look at those papers, know that he cared about her, and she would change her mind about going to Georgia ever. And yet the exact opposite had happened. "Why are women so complicated?" he asked.

"The same reason men are so stubborn."

* * *

What do you mean no?"

Sharon, the nurse at Dr. Gary's office, sighed. "Dr. Gary feels that it's not safe for you to fly."

"But the books—"

"Sweetie, the books aren't the one having twins. Now, I suppose you can go ahead and do whatever you feel like doing, but if I were you, I'd just stay put."

"I can't do that." She had to get out of here, and she needed to leave now. "Can I drive?" She wasn't sure how she was going to manage that but she had to ask.

"There are always risks. How far are you talking about?"

"Far," Bryn mumbled. "To Georgia."

"And I trust you will be traveling with someone."

"No," she managed to squeeze out.

"Hon, you don't want to risk that. You can't drive halfway across the country by yourself."

"But if someone else was driving . . ."

Sharon sighed again. "If you're just riding and you stop and rest and stretch your legs often, I don't think Dr. Gary would have any problems with that."

Bryn's shoulders slumped in relief. "Thank you," she said. Now all she had to do was convince Rick to come get her.

She thumbed through her contacts for his number, then stopped as she heard footsteps outside her door.

They paused.

Jake.

She could almost hear him breathe. Then the footsteps started up once more.

Bryn exhaled, only realizing then that she had been holding her breath.

Finding Rick's number, she called him, impatiently waiting for him to answer.

"This better be good, sister."

"I need you to come get me." Her voice caught on a sob.

"Bryn? Honey, what's wrong?"

"I need to come home and I can't drive and I can't fly. I know it's a lot to ask, but I can't stay here any longer."

"Of course."

She collapsed on the bed. "Thank you, thank you."

"Are you going to tell me what happened?"

"Not now. Maybe when you get here. And when will that be?"

Rick chuckled. "That bad, huh? Well, you're in luck. I'm in Austin."

Jake saw the car pull up and shook his head. Just what he needed. Another cowbride had come calling. It had been a while, and he thought the new had worn off the article and the visitors would stop. Now here was another one.

He waved to Joe Dan and motioned toward the car coming down the drive. "I'll be back in a bit."

Joe Dan gave him an "okay" sign, then turned back to the horse he was grooming.

Jake slapped his hat against his thigh, then settled it back on his head. His chaps flapped against the wind as he walked with purposeful strides toward the car.

But he almost stumbled when a man stepped out.

This was different.

But he kept his feet going. He was in a surly mood. He could admit that. Who wouldn't be in a bad mood after what he had been through?

He had heard Bryn packing last night. Not that he had been listening at the bathroom door that separated her room from his. He just happened to hear her. And he refused to go in and ask her what she was doing. She was damn stubborn, *damn* stubborn. But he couldn't save her from herself. He had offered her everything—*everything*—and she had thrown it back in his face. Well, let her leave. He didn't care anymore. Just flat-out didn't care.

He drew closer to the young man who stood in his driveway looking like a misplaced *GQ* model. His fitted leather jacket surely protected him from that West Texas wind. The weather was getting cooler and cooler. Wouldn't be long before winter was officially upon them.

As Jake walked he geared up exactly what he was going to say. He would be nice, but firm. Adamant, but not condescending. And he would send him on his way.

"Well, hello there." The young man eased his sunglasses down on his nose a bit as if trying to get a better look.

Jake pulled off his work gloves and shoved them into his back pocket. "I know why you're here and although your devotion is admirable, I think you should leave."

The man flashed a confused frown that turned into a Cheshire smile. "I think you've got it wrong."

Jake propped his hands on his hips and shook his head. "I don't. And it's okay. But it's not. I mean, I'm flattered and all that you saw my picture and drove all the way out here." From behind him he heard the door open. Let Grandma Esther do what she wanted with this one! "But I'm sorry. I'm not interested."

That smile remained firmly in place. "That's good to know. But I came for what's behind you."

Jake whirled around. Bryn attempted to pull her suitcase across the uneven yard. He noticed two things immediately. She was struggling, and she wasn't dressed for the cooler temperatures.

So the man in front of him had to be her best friend she was forever talking about, and he really needed to take her shopping for some new clothes.

Then what was really happening hit him. She was leaving.

He felt like he'd been kicked in the gut by a crazed stallion. Muscles clenched, time stopped, and the air left his lungs in an audible whoosh. He had known from the very beginning that she would be leaving, but he wasn't prepared to actually *see* her leaving.

"Are you going to help her, or am I going to have to?"

Damn it to hell!

Jake stomped over to where she tugged on her suitcase.

"Go away," she snarled. Like that was going to deter him.

He snatched up her case with ease and carried it back into the house.

"Jake Langston, you get back here with that."

"No, ma'am." He set her bag back inside. Then he turned and waited. He knew she wasn't going to let this pass.

And he was right.

She marched over to him, her legs stiff and her jaw clenched. "That is my suitcase," she said. Her tone was pleasant and that made it all the more dangerous.

"I'm aware."

"If you want to take it someplace, carry it over to Rick's car."

"No way."

She moved to go around him, presumably to reclaim her bag, but he was too quick, moving before her and effectively blocking her from the door.

She darted toward the other side, but he blocked her again.

"Jake," she growled.

"You promised to stay, Bryn. Through Christmas and the New Year."

"I changed my mind."

"You can't do that. So just tell your friend that you're staying here."

There was a moment, maybe two, when he thought she might completely lose it. Then she stopped, her shoulders fell, and she shook her head. She looked so utterly defeated that he almost told her she could have anything she wanted. But he couldn't do that. There was too much on the line. More than just the two of them.

"Fine," she whispered, her words spoken so softly he almost didn't hear them.

"What?" he asked.

"Fine," she said, louder this time.

"Fine what?"

"Fine, I'll stay until after the first of the year."

Relief flooded him. That was all he could ask. "Thank you."

Rick came forward and gave her a kiss on the cheek. "Good. I'm glad that's settled. And I'm glad you changed her mind; I didn't want to be the one to tell her that I wasn't taking her back to Georgia."

What do you mean you weren't going to take me back home with you? Why would you come all the way out here just to turn around and leave?"

Once Esther found out that one of Bryn's friends had stopped by, Rick had immediately been invited to stay for supper. And since it was a four-hour drive back to Austin, he was invited to spend the night.

He readily accepted, seeming to enjoy all the cowboy culture that surrounded him.

Bryn had suffered through supper—Grandma Esther had made her almost-famous creamy chicken enchiladas—with Jake glaring at her, Rick asking a hundred cowboy questions, and Wesley wanting to know more about how to make hair purple.

The only reprieve she had gotten was when Ol' Buck came to get Jake. One of Evelyn's prize mares was having trouble and they needed Jake to help deliver the new colt.

Last year Bryn would have jumped at the chance to see a horse give birth. The miracle of life and all that, but she was staring down a due date of her very own. She would experience the miracle of birth soon enough. And of course staying close to the house with Rick gave her plenty of excuses not to see Jake.

"I have eyes. I've seen the two of you together and, girl, you two are a match made in heaven."

"It was made all right, but not in heaven." In a hotel room in Austin. But that night in his arms had been pretty celestial. And every night since then . . .

"There's chemistry there, and you shouldn't deny it."

"I'm not denying anything." But chemistry was one thing and being deceived by someone you thought you could trust was another.

"Then why do you want to leave?"

She opened her mouth to respond and ended up closing it again instead.

"Come on, you can tell Papa Rick."

If she told him, then it might not sound the same. And the last thing she needed was Rick on Jake's side.

Oh, who was she trying to kid? Rick was already on Jake's side.

"He wants custody of the twins."

"Like after they're born?"

"He can't very well have custody of them until then."

"Point taken."

"And?" Bryn prodded.

"Hmmm?

"Are you going to tell me what a sorry SOB he is for wanting to take my babies from me?"

"Did he say why he wanted custody?"

"Because I don't have a job or any family. He said he could take care of them better here."

Rick looked out over the view from the Langstons' back porch. Security lights shined from the outbuildings; the sounds of cows, horses, and insects filled the air; and Kota lay at her feet, his usual place these days. "And what do you think of that?"

He was too slick to actually say the words, but his implication was clear. The ranch was a beautiful place. Who wouldn't want their babies to grow up on such a magnificent and meaningful piece of property?

The vision she had of Langston twins came to her mind.

Two little boys with their daddy's dark hair and green, green eyes. The picture was becoming clearer. They were wearing mini Wranglers and tiny cowboy boots. Little straw hats hid their fantasy faces from her view, but they captured her heart immediately.

She ran a hand over her stomach. This ranch would be a great place to grow up. But how could she give up all that she had in Georgia and come to Texas?

"I take it that's out of the question?" Rick said.

"How can you expect me to even think about the idea?"

"Because you won't marry him. You won't move here. What choice does the man have if he wants to see his kids?"

"He can—he can—" she sputtered. "I don't know. But he's not getting custody."

Rick studied her for a full minute. "Tell me, Bryn. What's keeping you in Georgia?"

Chapter Sixteen

What was keeping her in Georgia? The question echoed in her mind all through the night and into the next morning.

How could she explain? She lived in Georgia. It was her home.

And even more than that, Jake had deceived her. He had said all the right things, made all the right moves. Convinced her to love him and then wham! How could she ever trust him again? How was she going to be able to work out an agreement with him knowing what he truly wanted from her?

Then again, how could she not? They were in this together, like it or not. If he went through with filing for custody—and she had no reason to believe that he wouldn't—then she would have to fight him in court or at the very least in a lawyer's office until they worked out a plan that would suit them both. Did one even exist?

No.

What's keeping you in Georgia?

She wished she had the answer to that. Nothing and everything.

And the truth of the matter . . . the only thing keeping them from being a family was her own stubbornness. Was it worth it?

No.

The thoughts and questions swirled around her head, looking for an answer she didn't have. But maybe she did.

The questions circled once more and landed on the same answer, the answer she hated above all else. The answer that made her more vulnerable to Jake than she had ever been.

The only answer she had.

She dragged herself out of bed, dressed, and skipped brushing her teeth until she knew Jake was outside and there was no chance of running into him there. Then she headed for the kitchen and the coffee she knew to be waiting there.

She allowed herself only one cup a day and savored each sip. Today, she figured it wouldn't be near as enjoyable. Not with everything hanging over her head.

Rick was leaving, she was staying, and Jake wanted the twins for himself.

How had things gotten in such a mess?

"Then Jake came tearing out of the house wearing nothing but a towel. He ran across the pasture after Seth and chased him clear to the next county." Grandma Esther wiped her eyes as Rick chuckled.

"Tell another one, Grandma Esther." Wesley bounced in her seat.

Then they caught sight of her.

Rick straightened. Grandma Esther cleared her throat.

"Miss Bryn," Wesley cried. She slid from her bench and flung herself at Bryn.

"Good morning," Bryn murmured, returning her embrace.

"Grandma Esther was just telling family stories," Rick said.

Wesley returned to her seat, and Bryn moved to the coffeepot for her morning joe.

She poured her cup and turned back to the trio at the table. “Where’s Jake?”

“He’s out at the bunkhouse.”

Bryn nodded. At least it was safe to brush her teeth.

Chicken.

She pushed that voice away. It was self-preservation, pure and simple.

Rick stood. “Well, I guess I should be getting back to Austin.”

“So soon?” Bryn muttered.

“Don’t be mad, love.”

Bryn glared at him. “Traitor.”

Rick shot her his sweetest smile. “One day you’ll thank me.”

Bryn waited until the afternoon before she went to find Jake. Her palms were sweaty and her mouth dry as she knocked on his office door.

“Come in.”

Bryn took a hefty breath and opened the door.

Jake looked up from the papers on his desk while she stood nearby, stupidly staring at him. “Do you need something?”

“Yes.” She nodded. “I need to talk to you.”

Jake put the papers he’d been shuffling on his desk and leaned back in the big leather chair. “Oh?”

“That is the . . . is the . . .” She swallowed hard and looked up at the ceiling as if the words she needed were written there. “Why is this so hard?”

He studied her intently. “Just say whatever it is, Bryn.”

“Is that offer to get married still available?”

He stopped and the moment seemed suspended in time. Then he let out a breath and pushed to his feet. “Yes. Yes, of course." He came around the desk and took her cold hands into his. "Are you serious?"

She nodded, unable to speak around the lump in her throat. *Please let this be the right thing to do. Please let this be the right thing to do.*

She bit her lip as he continued to stare at her. His gaze was so intense she felt stripped to the bone. Then he dropped her hands as if they were on fire. "If you're sure, why do you seem so reluctant?"

"You threatening to take them from me."

"I see." He leaned back against his desk and crossed his arms. "So that's how it's going to be."

"How do you expect me to react? I'm just looking out for them."

"So am I."

"Georgia is all I've ever known."

"Texas is all I've ever known."

"You're not the one moving."

"Touché."

"I just need time to get used to the idea." She was scared, surely he could understand that.

"Of moving to Texas or marrying me?"

An uncomfortable laugh escaped her. "Both."

"No deal. Sorry. You'll have to get used to it after the fact. We're getting married as soon as possible."

Her heart gave a heavy thump in her chest. Or maybe it was excitement. She didn't really know "I'm mad at you, you know."

He nodded. "I know. You can be mad at me all you want. Just as long as you marry me."

There were entirely too many plans to make. Bryn was exhausted. Her back hurt, her feet were swollen, and she still hadn't become accustomed to the idea of leaving everything she had in Georgia and moving to Texas to marry a man she barely knew.

But you know him well enough.

She knew that he could cook a steak good enough that it didn't need steak sauce. That his eyes were the color of a deep forest after the rain. And he could take her to bed and have her begging for mercy in nothing flat. Yet, was that enough to build a marriage on? Did they really have a choice?

"Mama will be back from Houston in two days. After that, I'm sure she'll take over all the planning. Fair warning," Jake said.

Bryn looked down at the checklist she'd made for the movers. They had hired somebody to pack all her stuff in the house and put it up for sale as is. Part of her wanted to keep it just in case. But another part of her said "in for a penny, in for a pound"; wasn't that how the old saying went? Was that just an old version of "go big or go home"?

"Are you ready to go shopping?"

Bryn jerked her gaze up to meet Jake. "What?"

"Shopping," he said very slowly as if talking to someone who had trouble understanding English. "You need some clothes and a coat. Maybe some boots and definitely something to get married in."

She shook her head. She didn't want anything special. Because if she bought a new beautiful dress and matching jewelry, had her hair fixed and all that other finery, it would seem too much like a real marriage. And that wasn't the case. Not ever.

"Okay, it's like this: you can go shopping with me or you can go shopping with my mother."

"She can't go shopping, not after coming back from the chemo treatment."

"Exactly. Now get your purse, and let's go."

Bryn had expected to drive in to Cattle Creek and shop in the quaint little stores on Main Street. But once they climbed into Jake's big pickup truck, they headed for the highway. "Where are we going?"

"San Angelo. It's an hour and a half drive, but it'll be worth it in the long run. You'll have so many more choices."

That was what she needed: choices. But the one thing she wished she had a choice on, she didn't have a choice at all. Her life.

She hated her morose attitude. It was so unlike her. And though she would love to blame it on pregnancy hormones, she suspected that it had more to do with the man sitting next to her than it did anything else. He told her he loved her and then he threatened to take the twins from her. Now he was going to marry her. It just didn't make sense. Where was the real Jake? He had so many walls up around himself she didn't know if she would ever find out. And what kind of marriage would that be?

She laid her head against the window and watched the miles go by. Jake turned on the radio to a classic rock station. She'd been a little surprised. She had expected him to listen to nothing but country. But he sang along with almost every song, drumming his thumbs against the steering wheel. It was more than a little unexpected. And just went to prove there was more to her future husband than she realized. And more than he was letting her see. When would she ever get to see the real Jake?

An hour and a half later, Jake pulled his truck into the parking lot at the mall. Bryn hadn't realized how accustomed she'd become to ranch living until she got back into big-city traffic. Not that San Angelo could hold a candle to the traffic of Atlanta, but it was a sight more than Cattle Creek for sure.

They walked through the big doors and Jake fished his wallet out of his back pocket. He pulled out a credit card and handed it to Bryn. "Do whatever you want. I'll wait for you in the food court."

"Oh, no, you don't, cowboy. You wanted to come shop, so you're coming shopping."

There were only a couple of choices for maternity clothes at the Sunset Mall, and they hit every one of them.

"Don't forget a coat," Jake told her. "And try on the jeans."

"I hate the jeans." She took off the gigantic pair of maternity jeans and hung them on the hanger.

So far they picked shirts, a couple of casual dresses, and a bunch of other clothes. Jake had been a great sport. She ducked into the changing room and he'd brought her clothes consistently. Surprisingly enough, he seemed to have an eye for such things. Or maybe he just paid attention to the clothes she already owned. Then again, maybe she just didn't care. She had no qualms with anything he brought. Just whether or not it fit was the only issue she had. Except for the jeans.

"Try this." He dropped a dress over the top of the door, hanging it on her side.

"No." She shook her head even though he wasn't around. She couldn't try on that dress. It was beautiful. Pale blue chiffon with tulle over the top, it had an empire waist and looked to fall just below the knees.

"It's a something blue."

"I can't get married in that. It doesn't have any sleeves." It was perhaps the dumbest excuse she'd ever used.

"That's why you need to buy a coat."

"You can't wear a coat over a dress like that."

"I had a feeling you were going to say that. Try this." Once again he deposited something over the top of the door. This time it was a beautiful pashmina of the palest pink, embroidered with blue flowers that perfectly matched the blue of the dress.

"The saleslady said you could wear that around your shoulders. That would keep you warm enough if you were inside. And it's perfectly acceptable to wear sleeveless things in the wintertime. That's what she said anyway."

He had asked the saleslady? Just another piece of Jake she never knew about, never thought was there. At least he let her see this side of him. But what about the real Jake? The thought of it haunted her.

"And I found these." He held a pair of brown cowboy boots over the top of the door. They were beautiful. Caramel tan distressed leather with cream-colored roses stitched all across the shaft. They definitely didn't look like they belonged in a mid-price department store.

"Where did you get these?"

"Don't worry about that. Just try them on."

"I already have cowboy boots."

"Now you have two pair. Try them on."

He bought her cowboy boots?

Even as reluctant as she was, she donned the outfit. It was the most unorthodox wedding attire she'd ever seen. And somehow she loved it. The dress should've made her look like she was wearing a tent, but it didn't. And the cowboy boots should have been ridiculous paired with such a feminine dress, but they worked. The pashmina was silky-soft against her shoulders and somehow the pastel colors complemented her dark hair and eyes.

"Come out and let me see."

She stared at herself in the mirror and shook her head. "If I wear this to get married in, it's bad luck for you to see."

"Just come out. We've already had more than our share of bad luck."

She opened the door and hesitantly stepped from the dressing room. She wanted to tell him how ridiculous she felt, how unlike her the outfit was, how she couldn't wear it to get married, and a dozen other reasons why she needed to take it off immediately. But none of them would come. Maybe because all of them were lies.

"I think that'll do just fine, don't you?"

She had never been able to deny him anything. And she couldn't deny that satisfied sparkle in those green eyes. He was so competitive, such a perfectionist. He put so much effort and time into every aspect of his life. Of course he would be proud that he picked out the ensemble even with the salesperson's help.

And that light in his eyes had nothing to do with the love he confessed. She didn't trust those words. They were just words. And as much as she wanted to believe them, he backed them up the next day with a request for custody.

She pushed those thoughts away. They were moving past that to a marriage. But how was this marriage ever going to be successful with so much hanging over them? She didn't know, but she had to give it a try.

Bryn was appalled at the amount of money Jake spent at the department store. She had tried to pay, but he refused, telling her it was his treat. Even so, after the one store she was tired and just about ready to go home. Carrying around fifty pounds of extra weight wasn't the easiest thing to do. Especially not when it all stuck out in the front. It didn't help that Esther and Evelyn had her planning a wedding every spare moment of the day. Still, she couldn't deny this to either woman.

Esther Langston adored Jake and would do anything for him. She wasn't so young anymore, and who knew how many of her other grandchildren she would see married. And Evelyn . . . Bryn worried about Evelyn every day. She tried to put on a brave front, smiling though her eyes remained tired and lined. Bryn tried to talk to her about it on several occasions, but Evelyn just waved away her concern. But Bryn had seen that look on so many faces at the hospital and even though they belonged to children, the look was the same. As heartbreaking as it was, she had seen that same look on Emery's face. It was the look of fighting a losing battle.

"One more stop," Jake said.

"One more."

They headed back down the mall the way they came in, and Jake stopped at a jewelry store.

She shook her head. "Oh, no. We're not buying jewelry."

"We need rings to get married with."

"We could buy something in town. We just need wedding bands."

"There's not a store that has this selection of fine jewelry in Cattle Creek. We might could find a couple of pieces at Donna's Gifts, but nothing like you will find here. Now stop fussing."

But she couldn't let it go that easily. "Gold bands. I draw the line at gold bands."

A twentysomething salesperson hustled over when she saw them pause at the display counter. "May I help you with something today?"

Jake flashed the young woman a charming smile.

Bryn could almost see the woman melt right there on the floor. "Yes. Thank you. My fiancée and I would like to look at some wedding rings."

The young woman's gaze dropped to Bryn's expanded middle. Her eyes widened just a bit before she caught herself and smiled. "Of course. Right here in this showcase.

"This is a lovely set right here." She pulled a flashy wedding set with one big diamond and lots of little diamonds, some baguettes and others round, out of the case.

Bryn shook her head. "No. I appreciate that. We're looking for gold bands. Maybe even white gold. But nothing fancy."

The woman blinked at her as if waiting for an interpreter to tell her what she really said. "All righty, then. We have a beautiful selection of wedding bands right here."

It took only a few minutes for them to find a set of

matching gold bands. They had agreed to yellow gold over white gold. Secretly Bryn was grateful for the change. Most chose white gold these days, but since she worked in all sorts of silver metals, she was looking forward to the change.

"Are you sure you don't want to look at any sets? A beautiful diamond engagement ring?" Jake asked.

"No. First, we don't need to spend that kind of money and second . . ." She couldn't say it. She couldn't bring herself to say those words. That their marriage wasn't real. It was just for the babies. Who knew how long it was going to last? Why spend thousands of dollars on diamonds and flash when it could be over before the ring needed to be cleaned?

Jake frowned. Then he turned back to the salesclerk. "One more thing. Do you carry the silicone wedding bands?"

The woman blinked at him a moment, then nodded. She went to the back and came out bearing a tray of bands made of silicone. "Most people choose the black. Though I like the blue for something different and the gray since it looks a little like titanium."

"Black will be fine."

"Very good." They found his size, and the woman returned the tray to the back room.

"What's that for?" Bryn asked.

"Wearing a wedding band in my profession can be dangerous. This will tear. Gold won't. I'd rather lose my silicone band than my finger."

Bryn's eyes grew wide. She'd never thought about it much. Of course she never dated a rancher before either.

"Can I get you anything else?" the woman asked. "Wedding presents, engagement presents?"

For a moment Bryn thought Jake might start picking out all sorts of jewelry, then he shook his head. "No, we're good. Thank you."

The lady took them over to the counter to pay.

"Jake," Bryn whispered close to his ear. "I need to go to the bathroom."

Jake turned back to her. "Do you want to go now?"

She looked down at her belly and then back up at him. "Really?"

He chuckled. "Okay, go ahead, and I'll wait for you here, how's that?"

She nodded. "Okay. I'll come back here, right?"

He smiled. "Absolutely."

Bryn waddled out of the jewelry store and down three doors to the bathroom. It seemed she spent over half her day in one restroom or another. Sometimes she would go to the bathroom only to find out that she didn't need to go at all. It was just the babies kicking on her bladder and making her life just a little more complicated already. Lord knows how it was going to be when they actually arrived.

She finished her business, washed her hands, and headed back to the jewelry store. Jake was standing outside, a small sack in one hand. Funny how that little sack contained something so important. A symbol of their love, their . . . marriage.

"Are you ready to go?"

"I'm ready."

He smiled and she got the feeling he held a secret, though she couldn't imagine what it would be.

I thought we would just go to the justice of the peace." Bryn looked to Jake for backup, but he merely shrugged. "I mean, I'm hugely pregnant. I just don't think we should have a ceremony."

"Of course you should have a ceremony," Grandma Esther and Evelyn said at the same time.

"Wesley can be your flower girl," Grandma Esther added. "And you can invite Rick and his friend."

They continued to make out a guest list, including Seth

and Jessie, somebody named Millie, and a dozen or so other people that Bryn had never heard of. She was getting married and the only guest on her list was Rick.

She tried not to let the thought get her down. She was all alone in the world. Wasn't that why she was marrying Jake? Getting married or not, this wasn't her family. And who knew if they would ever accept her as a part of it?

But you've already accepted them.

"We should wait until the first week of December," Evelyn said. She ran one finger down the calendar blotter on her desk. They had all gathered there to discuss wedding preparations. Bryn was surprised at how bright eyed Evelyn looked, or maybe she shouldn't have been. Evelyn Langston was a fighter. Everyone knew it. Still, her hair had started to thin and she had taken to wearing a bandanna around the house.

"You don't think Chase will come home?" Grandma Esther asked.

Evelyn's eyes clouded over. She pressed her lips together and shook her head. "I don't think so, but, Jake, you'll call him, right?"

Jake nodded. "I'll try, but I can't make any promises. You know Chase."

"And I'm sure Tyler can't get away for that. But he did tell me that they are thinking about bringing his battalion home in time for Christmas."

Times like this Bryn wished she had a playbill to keep up with all the characters in Jake's family. Chase was the bull rider. That much she knew. But something happened earlier in the year between him and Seth, and Chase hadn't been heard from since. Tyler she knew was in Afghanistan and his deployment was ending soon, if she had overheard the conversation between Grandma Esther and Jake correctly. So many family members and yet her only guest would be Rick. But she wasn't going to allow herself to dwell on that.

"What do you think about that, Bryn?"

She hadn't been listening. But the whole thing was overwhelming. She was just now adjusting to the thought of having twins. The wedding? She just couldn't give herself that to worry about too.

"Whatever you think is fine with me."

Evelyn seemed to take that as a green light. She pulled out a legal pad and started making a list.

"I should have warned you about my mother." Jake's breath stirred the hair near her ear.

Bryn turned to find him sitting oh-so close to her. She must've been in a daze that she hadn't realized he was so near. "Oh?"

"She didn't get her wedding fix out with Seth and Jessie's wedding. So I'm afraid you're going to get the brunt of all that. I'm sorry."

"It's okay."

"Why don't you take a nap?"

"Why, Jake, you old flatterer. Are you saying I look tired?"

"I'm saying you look tired and pregnant."

"Not any better."

Lord, when he smiled like that she could almost forgive him anything. Including the attorney's office. But none of that would matter now. They would be here, they would be married, and custody was irrelevant. But how much easier would it be if she really knew the man she was marrying?

I'm so glad you finally came to your senses," Rick drawled across the miles when she explained to him about the wedding.

"It's not what you think." She pushed herself up onto the bed and sat cross-legged, her belly filling up the space in between. Tucking the phone between her ear and her shoulder, she ran a hand over that mound of stomach, feeling the babies tumble like they were playing. They were boys. She knew that now. None of the ultrasounds had been conclusive, but she knew. They were rough-and-tumble boys.

"It's you marrying your cowboy. That's enough."

"For all the wrong reasons."

"You're marrying because you are having two kids together. That sounds like a good enough reason for me."

"Oh, what would you know about it," she grumbled.

"I know enough." His tone suggested he held the secret.

"Okay, spill it."

"Well," he drawled. "I didn't want to intrude on your good news but . . . I'm moving to Texas."

"You're what?"

"You heard me. Rusty and I have decided to make it official."

"How official?"

"Oh, not that official. We're just getting an apartment together."

"In Austin?"

"Yeah. That's where he lives."

How could Rick do that? Just walk out of Georgia and not look back? Move in with the man he loved and not think twice? His parents lived in Georgia. His sister lived in Georgia. All of his cousins, aunts, and uncles, the entire McFadden clan lived in Georgia. Yet he could pick up and walk away without even blinking an eye. How?

True love.

For what he thought was true love. Jake hadn't said those words to her again since that night. Nor had he spent any time in her bed. Not even sleeping.

And whose fault is that?

Hers. She set the parameters. She would have to be the one to break them. But she wasn't ready yet. Not by a long shot.

"Are you happy for me?"

"Oh, yes, Rick. I'm so happy for you. Really I am. It's just . . ."

"Pregnancy hormones."

"I guess. One minute I'm happy, the next minute I'm angry. I don't know what to feel about anything anymore."

"Well, the Bryn I know would just be happy. Someone should concentrate on that."

He was right. The Bryn of old would be happy to find happiness wherever she could find it. But the Bryn of today had taken too many hits. Things hadn't come easy and she was a little tired of struggling. So was that why she decided to marry Jake?

"When will you be in Austin?"

"I'm coming back through Christmas and then after the first of the year for good." She could hear the joy in his voice, almost see him smiling across the phone line.

"The wedding is December first."

"Does that mean I have a plus-one?"

"Plus-one? You're the maid of honor."

"Terrific! I've never been one of those before. Wait. I don't have to wear a dress, do I?"

Bryn laughed. "Not unless you want to."

The rest of the week was taken up with talk of flowers, e-invites, and cake. But all wedding preparations were put on hold for Thanksgiving.

Since Texas was a lot colder than Georgia, Bryn was thankful for the clothes Jake had helped her pick out. But every one had that memory attached to it. Everything she wore reminded her of that day.

The morning started off with Wesley waking her up to watch the Thanksgiving Day parade on TV. She barely allowed Bryn to drag on her robe before pulling her into the family room and cuddling up next to her on the couch to watch the wonderful parade.

"Are you watching this, babies?" She put her mouth up to Bryn's belly and spoke as if they could hear her. Then she tilted back her head and looked at Bryn. "What are their names? I mean we can't just call them the babies, right?"

What were their names? She and Jake hadn't talked about any of that. They'd been too busy arguing over who was going to get them, where she was going to live, and now trying to get married. It was almost shameful. That was what most couples did first, name the baby, and they hadn't given it one thought.

"Your dad and I haven't talked about that yet. I guess it depends on whether there's two boys, two girls, or a boy and a girl."

Wesley seemed to think about that a minute. "I think a boy and a girl would be nice."

Bryn laughed. "Maybe, but you know we don't get to choose. Whatever's there is there. But secretly I think it's two little boys."

Wesley wrinkled up her nose. "There's plenty of boys around here. We really don't need any more of those."

Bryn suppressed her laughter. "You said it was okay if there was one boy and one girl."

She nodded. "One boy is more than plenty."

"I guess we'll know soon enough."

And hopefully they would have names for them by then. Being Thing One and Thing Two wasn't going to cut it.

After watching the parade, Bryn and Wesley joined Evelyn and Esther in the kitchen.

The table was completely covered with dinner makings, yet there wasn't a turkey in sight.

"Are we having turkey?" Bryn asked.

Esther stopped peeling sweet potatoes. "Always."

Bryn looked around the kitchen once again. "Shouldn't we have the turkey on to cook?"

"Tell her, Wes," Evelyn said. She looked a little more tired today than usual and Bryn felt for the woman. Her heart went out to her knowing that she was once again engaged in the battle of her life. And Bryn knew firsthand how easily that battle could be lost.

"Daddy's frying it," Wesley said. "That's what he does every year."

She had heard of people frying turkeys in a deep fryer, but she'd never eaten one.

"Jake fries turkeys for everybody this time of year. He's been at it since three o'clock this morning," Grandma Esther said. "He fries one for us, one for the boys at the bunkhouse, and one for Ol' Buck and his family." Bryn remembered seeing the old cowboy out in the corral. He seemed like more of a fixture than actual help on the ranch, and she figured Jake kept them around as part of his retirement. But she wasn't sure the old man knew he was retired.

"That's really sweet of him."

"My daddy's one of the good guys," Wesley said with a big grin. She had managed to pry the lid off the bowl of Cool Whip and was currently eating it off a spoon.

"Wesley," Bryn said. "Put that up right now."

Wesley stuck out her lower lip. "I'm just trying to help."

Bryn laughed. "If you want to help, then let's me and you wash the vegetables, okay? But eating Cool Whip does not help."

Her pout deepened. "Yes, ma'am." But she set the lid down and came around to the sink. A step stool had been set up next to the refrigerator, no doubt so that Wesley could climb up and help.

There were potatoes to be washed and peeled, casseroles to be mixed, dressing to be made, Jell-O salads, regular salads, even pasta salad to be concocted.

Grandma Esther turned on the radio that sat on top of the refrigerator, and country music filled the kitchen. Every now and then, Bryn caught Evelyn singing along. But even more often she caught Grandma Esther dancing with Wesley.

This wasn't her first Thanksgiving without Emery. It was the second. But never had they had Thanksgiving like this.

It'd been the two of them for years. Sometimes Rick would come by in the afternoon and hang out for a little bit, but mostly it was just the two of them giving thanks for everything that they had. And though they didn't have a huge welcoming family that needed twenty side dishes for one supper, they had each other and that was a lot.

"Bryn?" Evelyn said. "Are you okay?"

Bryn jerked her attention back to the present. "Yes. I'm fine."

"Why are you crying?"

"Don't cry, Miss Bryn." Wesley launched herself at Bryn, wrapping her arms around Bryn's legs and holding on for dear life.

"It's okay, chickadee." Bryn managed to disentangle herself from Wesley's artful embrace. Then she sat down on the bench so she would be closer to eye level with the five-year-old. "I'm not sad. These are tears of joy."

Wesley eyed her skeptically. "You're crying because you're happy?"

"Yes."

Wesley seemed to think about that for a moment, then slowly shook her head. "I've never known anybody that cried when they were happy."

"It doesn't happen all the time, but it can happen."

"If you say so."

Bryn kissed her smack-dab in the middle of the forehead. "I say so. Now let's finish these salads and get them into the refrigerator."

As usual, his mother and grandmother cooked way too much for dinner. Their dining room table could seat twelve and they barely had room for plates, glasses, and napkins. But that was the way of the Langston family Thanksgiving.

"Before we eat, everybody has to go around the table and say what they're thankful for," Wesley demanded.

Jake had managed to say grace without choking up. He was thankful for so many things and yet hopeful that next year things would be different. They would love to see Chase home, Ty home, Maverick home. Next year would bring changes. He would be married, with two new children sitting at the table. And he could only hope that his mother would make it through this next year. That she could fight the cancer and win. And that Grandma Esther would remain as healthy as she was.

"I'll start," Wesley said. "I'm thankful that I'm going to get a new mom and a new brother and sister."

Jessie's gaze jerked to Bryn. "So you know what the babies are?"

Bryn shook her head. "She's just wishful thinking."

"I sure wish they had been able to tell the gender," Jessie groused. "It'd be so much easier to buy things."

"Speaking of which, we've got to get a shower together. Maybe after the wedding."

Jake looked at Bryn. He could almost see her head spinning from it all.

"Y'all are ruining it," Wesley said. "You're a'pposed to say what you're thankful for."

"Sorry, baby," Evelyn said. "I'm thankful for you."

Wesley grinned, then the smile froze on her face. "Weren't you thankful for me last year?"

"I'm thankful for you every year."

Amen, Jake thought.

Jake looked around him at his wonderful family. Some might be missing and who knew when they would return, if ever. But it was his family and he loved them.

"I'm thankful for second chances," Bryn said. She looked up and caught his gaze. Was she talking about the two of them? Or was it something else?

Chapter Seventeen

After they ate, the remainder of the day was consumed with football, football, and football.

Bryn curled up on the couch and listened to Grandma Esther and Jake argue about defensive lines and offensive plays, and she wondered if there would really be future Thanksgivings just like this one. Everything about the Langston household was exactly what she wanted from her own life. She tried to give Emery the best childhood possible, but she couldn't give her this. She couldn't give her her mother back, her father back, and even if she could have, they surely wouldn't have argued over something as trivial as a football game when they could have discussed airborne pathogens versus blood-borne pathogens. Such was the problem from having science nerds for parents.

She must've dozed off somewhere around the third quarter of the second game. One minute she was watching the Cowboys run for a touchdown and the next Jake was gently shaking her shoulder.

"Bryn?"

She pushed herself into a sitting position. "Did I fall asleep?"

"Yes."

She nodded, not feeling quite all the way awake. "I'm sorry." She pushed herself the rest of the way up. The TV was off and no one else was around. Outside the windows, the sky was dark and as usual covered with a million twinkling stars.

He must've put Wesley to bed by now.

"It's okay. You've been doing a lot lately. I'm sure you're exhausted."

She nodded and allowed him to pull her to her feet.

There was something, something she wanted to talk to him about. But what was it?

He took her by her elbow and steered her out of the room.

"Oh, yeah. Names."

They walked through the darkened house together, Jake's arm supporting her though she really didn't need it. Still, she wouldn't pull away from his touch for anything. How long had it been since he'd even clasped her hand in his? She couldn't even remember. She hadn't realized how much she missed it until now.

"What about names?"

"We need them. For the babies."

He stopped. As if the thought hadn't occurred to him either.

"Why don't you come up with a list and then we can talk about them."

"I don't like that idea. It sounds like I come up with names and you just get to be angry about them."

"I'm sure I won't get mad."

"I'm not willing to risk it."

"Or you don't want to come up with names by yourself."

"They're your babies too."

"And so you finally admit that."

"This is exactly what I was trying to avoid!"

They stopped in the kitchen. The light was on over the sink and the refrigerator hummed, but the rest of the house was dark and quiet.

"Sorry." He heaved in a huge breath. "Do you want to write down some names now?"

"I feel like we should do something. I mean, they can come any time. Twins are notoriously early, and we don't have anything for them. Not a crib. Not one stitch of clothing." To her dismay, tears rose into her eyes. "They don't even have names."

"Shhhh . . ." He pulled her into his arms.

She hated to admit it, but she needed this. She needed to be held by him. She needed to know that he cared. If only just a little. "If you want to name them, we can name them right now. And tomorrow, first thing, we'll go shopping, buy them everything they need."

She sniffed and snuggled a little closer to his warmth. She should have been pushing him away. But she couldn't. He might not love her the way she loved him. And he might not ever. But she had agreed to marry him. They needed to make the best of every moment.

"Your mother wants to have a baby shower. You know we have to let her."

He chuckled. It started like a rumble under her ear before escaping him and actually becoming a sound. "I don't think we can stop her. But we can name the babies. Or at least come up with a few ideas."

She wiped at her tears, then reluctantly pulled away from him. "Okay."

"Here," he said. "Come sit at the table."

They settled down across from each other in the dimly lit kitchen.

"Do you have any favorite names?" he asked.

She shook her head. All those names she loved in high school were dated and trite now that she was older. "My dad's name was Jasper."

He seemed to think about it a second. "I'm not sure it fits for a girl."

"Will you be serious?"

He flashed her that sexy grin that had gotten them into this mess to begin with. "Admit it. It's a terrible name for a girl."

Must have been the smile. "It's a terrible name for a girl. But do you like it for a boy?"

"It can definitely be a maybe."

She nodded. "What name do you like?"

"Annabelle."

She made a face.

"What's wrong with Annabelle?"

"I think they're boys. Annabelle is an awful name for a boy."

He laughed, the sound rich. But was it sincere? She didn't know. She only knew that there was a Jake she had never seen and she hadn't caught a glimpse of him yet. "Okay, I've got an idea. If the twins are girls, then I get to name them."

"Both of them?"

He nodded. "And if they're boys, you can name them."

"What if there is one of each?"

"Do you think there will be?"

She shrugged. "Anything's possible, I guess."

"We could let Wesley name them."

"Oh, no," Bryn said. "She wants to name the black cat out there Susan."

"What's wrong with that?"

"Have you ever heard of a cat named Susan?"

"Right. So if there's one of each, we each name one."

"Perfect."

He picked up her hand and turned it over, staring at the lines on her palm. "Do you feel better now?"

She nodded.

"Then come on." He stood and reached out a hand to her. "I'll walk you to your room."

* * *

The following week was taken up with picking up everything they needed for the wedding. And of course an appointment with Dr. Gary. He said everything looked fine and made Bryn an appointment for the following week. His goal was to get them through Christmas. Her goal was to get through the wedding. One day at a time.

But she passed most of her time working on Christmas presents for the Langstons. She had managed to get Rick's sister to go to her house and pack up her studio, at least her smaller equipment, her raw materials, and die-casting molds.

It felt good to begin to create once more. And not for a living, but for love. She was making every one of the Langstons something special for Christmas.

"Too bad Chase can't make it back," Grandma Esther said as she tied ribbons around the small sacks of birdseed.

The rodeo circuit had ended for the year with the national championship in Las Vegas, but no one had heard from Jake's brother Chase. If some of the Professional Bull Riders fan sites were correct, then Chase had holed up with a rodeo groupie or two and might not be heard from until the schedule started back in the spring. Bryn wasn't sure if he'd even been told about his mother's relapse.

"Are you sure all those are necessary?" Bryn nodded pointedly at the growing pile of birdseed pouches.

Evelyn had gone to lie down and Wesley wasn't out of school yet. So it was just the two of them putting the final touches on the details Evelyn had insisted on.

"Oh, yes." She finished another one and tossed it on the top of the pile with the others. "Everyone is coming."

Everyone?

Panic surged through her. Who was everyone?

She tamped down that panic. It felt a little too much like

a jinx to be planning such a wedding for two mismatched people. She and Jake didn't really belong together and yet they were having babies and getting married. Bryn wished that she had insisted that they just have a civil service. All these wedding plans were making her crazy.

"Are you sure you're up for making the cake?" Bryn asked. Jake's grandmother might be tough as nails, but there was still a fragility about her that Bryn couldn't deny. The cake was just one more thing on the growing list of more than needed to be.

Grandma Esther pinned her with that wise blue gaze. "I think you need to quit worrying, girl. We've got this."

They might have it, but Bryn wasn't sure she did.

Just then, Jake let himself into the house. He cradled his left hand in his right, blood seeping between his fingers.

Bryn was on her feet in a second. "What happened?"

"I cut myself." He waved her away with his good hand. "I'm fine."

She nodded as he turned to the sink and started running water over the wound.

"You need to put pressure on that."

"I need to clean it first."

She frowned at him, then wrapped his hand in a dish towel and pulled him toward their rooms.

"Really, Bryn, I'm fine," he protested.

"I think you've mentioned that." But she needed an opportunity to talk to him alone and this one would do just fine. She lowered the lid in the toilet. "Sit." And surprisingly, he did.

"Keep putting pressure on that until I find the supplies."

He indicated the cabinet on the left with a quick dip of his chin. "Check there."

She pilfered through the cabinet finding gauze pads, butterfly bandages, hydrogen peroxide, and triple antibiotic ointment.

"Let me see." She unwrapped his hand, careful to keep it from bleeding again. "It's not so bad."

He snorted. "I think I said that earlier."

"So, about the wedding," she said as she dabbed the wound clean. She added two butterfly strips and a Band-Aid to keep dirt out.

"What about the wedding?" He squinted at her.

She gave a one-shoulder shrug and leaned up against the bathroom counter. "I don't know. It just seems like such a big deal."

He studied her for a moment. "It is a big deal."

"I mean, it's too much."

"You want me to tell my mother to back off a little?"

Telling Evelyn Langston to back off would be the equivalent of telling a bull not to grow horns, and that just wasn't happening. Plus Bryn wouldn't do anything to hurt Evelyn. She'd grown quite fond of Jake's mother and was a bit protective of her seeing as how she was going through cancer treatments. But still . . . "It just makes me uncomfortable."

He shifted his weight on the toilet seat and studied her once more. "What does?"

"That everybody's making such a big deal out of it."

"Exactly why does that bother you?"

"I'm afraid it'll jinx us, okay? Make this big ordeal out of this wedding and the next thing you know . . ."

He took her hand in his good one. Running his fingers across the back of her knuckles. "Are you having second thoughts?"

"I don't know what I'm having."

He stood and gave her a brotherly kiss on the forehead. "It's our wedding, Bryn. It's our marriage. We can make of it what we want to and everybody else be damned." He tilted her chin up, forcing her to meet his gaze. "Is that what you want to hear?"

She shook her head. "It's not about what I want to hear, Jake. It's about—"

"About what?"

It was about pretending. They were pushing it already pretending to be a couple, holding this big wedding, getting married because they were having babies. He pretended that he loved her when she knew, everybody knew, that he still grieved for his wife. She just wasn't certain how long she could stand it. Bringing all that out in the open, how would that fix anything?

"Never mind," she mumbled.

"Bryn, why don't you take a nap and let Grandma Esther worry about everything."

That would be the easy way out, let somebody else worry about it. And heaven help her, she wanted to take it. Otherwise she might have to face two more truths about her and Jake's relationship than she wanted to admit.

December first arrived and with it an extreme case of nerves.

"What am I doing?" She studied herself in the mirror, critically going over her burgeoning form.

"You're getting married to the second-handsomest man in Page County," Jessie said, spraying one last layer of hair-spray onto Bryn's updo.

"Who's the first?"

"My husband." Jessie laughed.

Bryn joined in, but it quickly turned to tears. "No, really. What am I doing?"

Jessie wrapped her in a warm hug. "You're worrying over nothing."

"It sure doesn't feel like nothing."

Jessie pulled away and handed Bryn a tissue. "If you don't stop this, you're going to mess up your makeup."

Bryn dabbed at her eyes, doing her best not to ruin her eyeliner.

"You want to know a secret?" Jessie asked. Her eyes sparkled like gray jewels. "I'm pregnant."

"Oh, Jess, that's wonderful."

She nodded. "Our babies will only be a few months apart."

Family. There it was again. The sole reason why she had come here. The sole reason why she had agreed to marry Jake. And yet now she wanted more.

"You're the first person I've told," Jessie continued. "Except for Seth, of course."

"I'm honored."

"Do you know why I'm telling you?"

Someone knocked on the door. "Ten minutes, girls."

It was almost time. Bryn ran her hands down her sides. She could do this. She could. For the twins. "Why?" she asked.

"Because you need to know. Everything happens for a reason."

Did it truly?

"I don't know why I lost the first baby. But I know without it, Seth and I would have never gotten married. And that's not how it's supposed to happen. You and Jake might have gone about this a little backward. Lord knows, Seth and I did. But that doesn't mean it didn't happen the way it was supposed to.

"Maybe you're here so you can heal after losing your sister. Or maybe you're here to help Jake, but you getting pregnant and moving to Texas . . . it was part of a greater plan. Jake needs this. He needs you."

"He doesn't need me."

Jessie shook her head. "I've known Jake most of my life and I tell you, that man needs you more than he needs air. He just doesn't know it yet."

Bryn let her words sink in.

"Seth was the same when we got married. It's easy to look back and see that now, so I know what I'm talking about. Just make sure when the time comes you're there for him."

"I don't understand."

Jessie clasped Bryn's cold hands in her own. "Don't shut yourself off thinking he'll come around. You have to leave yourself open and he'll find his way there."

A short rap sounded at the door. "It's time."

Jessie squeezed Bryn's fingers and gave her a dazzling smile. "Are you ready?"

Bryn nodded and headed for the door.

Jake stood at the altar marveling at what the women in his life had accomplished in such a short period of time. Somehow they had managed to get the church, decorate it, and invite half the town.

Next to him stood Seth and Joe Dan, while out in the crowd, friends and family waited for the big moment.

Rick stood across from him and in a few minutes he would be joined by Jessie, who was walking down the aisle just before Bryn.

So much work had gone into today. So much time, energy, effort. And for a marriage in name only.

Suddenly he realized what Bryn had been talking about a few days ago. They were deceiving themselves and everyone around them.

But it doesn't have to be that way.

The organist started to play, and Wesley skipped down the aisle, tossing white flower petals from side to side. She went as far as the front pew, then plopped down between her nana and Grandma Esther.

Jessie was next, smiling prettily as she walked the steps that Bryn would soon take. The woman who was like a sister to him only had eyes for Seth. The pair looked as if they had some secret that the world needed to know, but they weren't telling.

He wanted that too, that connection with another. And why couldn't they have it? Jessie and Seth's marriage hadn't exactly started off on the right foot. And yet they had found a love without measure. Why couldn't he and Bryn have the same?

But Jessie and Seth had known each other most of their lives. He and Bryn were having babies together but were barely acquainted. She had been telling him that all along, but he had been too stubborn to listen.

Jessie took her place next to Rick and the music changed. Pachelbel's Canon gave way to the wedding march and everyone stood.

Bryn walked slowly toward him, a spray of white carnations mixed with white roses in her trembling hands. Her steps were graceful despite her extended girth. And she wore the cowboy boots he had bought her in San Angelo. She shot him a trembling smile, which he returned with as much confidence as he could muster. He was confident about what he was doing. He was confident that they could make a life together. And he was confident that he wanted that life to be with her, but standing up in front of everybody and declaring as much was still a little unnerving. He'd rather get on the back of a wild bronco any day.

She took a place across from him as the preacher looked out over friends and family.

"Dearly beloved, we have gathered here today . . ."

Jake had known Ethan Davis practically his whole life, and yet here the man was about to marry him and Bryn. Jake couldn't say it was less than strange. But he leaned in as Ethan prattled on with the traditional set of vows. This wasn't a traditional marriage and it needed a little more than that.

"I think you're beautiful. I hate camping. And I'm glad you're standing up here with me," Jake whispered to her.

Somehow her smile stayed on her lips as her forehead wrinkled into a frown. "What?" she whispered in return.

He repeated his two truths and a lie.

"I know what you said. Why did you say it?"

But he didn't have time to respond as Ethan turned back to the two of them. He instructed them to take each other's hands. Bryn's hands were ice cold and her fingers shaky as he clasped them in his own.

"Bryndalyn Carol Talbot, do you take this man . . ."

Jake hardly listened as he stared into those chocolate brown eyes. They could do this. Somehow, someway, they would get through this. Together. Just like Seth and Jessie.

"I do." Her voice was just one decibel above a whisper. But it was enough for Jake. He squeezed her fingers reassuringly, lifting each hand to his lips in turn.

A collective sigh sounded from the audience. But he hadn't done it for them. Everything was for the woman in front of him.

"Do you, Jacob Dwight Langston, take this woman . . ."

"I do."

"Then repeat after me," Ethan instructed. "With this ring I thee wed. . . ."

Jake repeated the vows to Bryn as Seth stepped forward and handed him the ring. Jake slipped it on her finger and smiled as she gasped in surprise. Yes, they had agreed to plain wedding bands, but he had taken the opportunity to buy something more, a beautiful, clear-cut, one-carat diamond, round with two baguette stones on either side. It was big enough to show that his intentions were good. But not so big that she could complain.

But she would, because that was just his Bryn.

"Jake," she whispered in protest, but her eyes sparkled. The ring was beautiful, elegant, and lovely.

He leaned in a little closer, until their foreheads almost touched. "This is for real, Bryn. And you need a ring to symbolize that."

Ethan looked at each one of them in turn, a confused

frown puckering at his brow. "Are you ready to continue?" he asked where only the two of them could hear.

Tears filled Bryn's eyes, but she nodded.

"Yes," Jake said.

"Bryn, repeat after me."

Rick stepped forward and supplied Bryn with the ring she would slip on Jake's finger. The gold felt heavy there. It'd been five years since he'd worn a ring. And only then when he wasn't working. Which was hardly ever. Sometimes he'd forget it, and Cecelia would get angry. He hadn't meant anything by it. But tonight he would wear the ring. In the morning he would take it off and replace it with a silicone band that he had gotten at the jewelry store when they got their other rings. He wanted Bryn to have the traditional ceremony.

"I now pronounce you husband and wife."

Jake looked back to Bryn. She started to tremble anew.

"You may kiss your bride," Ethan prompted.

Jake stepped forward and cupped Bryn's face in his hands. How long had it been since he'd kissed her? Since before the lawyer's office. Before their argument over custody, before she caved in and agreed to marry him. But now, she was his. Her hands flew to his, circling his wrists as he leaned in for his kiss.

Her lips trembled beneath his, but they tasted sweet. Oh-so sweet. And he wanted that kiss to go on for ever and ever. He raised his head, tilted it the other direction, and swooped in to finish the kiss.

Someone in the crowd whistled while someone else yelled, "Get a room."

"Looks like they already have."

Jake chuckled and lifted his head. "Are you sure you're ready for this town?"

Bryn smiled. "As ready as I'll ever be."

Chapter Eighteen

The reception was held in the bonus room at the VFW. It was by no means fancy, but it was warm and welcoming. Esther and Evelyn had set up all of the traditions, including cutting the cake together and the first dance.

Jake was entirely too sweet, feeding her a tiny bite of cake on his fork without any intention of smashing it into her face. Which left her no choice but to do the same. Pity, she would love to have smeared cake right up his nose.

Once everybody had cake, punch, and those little ham and cheese pinwheels from the freezer section of the grocery store, Grandma Esther pulled out the music.

Anne Murray crooned "Could I Have This Dance" as Jake waltzed Bryn around the small space set aside for dancing.

He leaned close. "You're a wonderful dancer."

She moved near as well. "I am not. I'm so ungainly right now it's not even funny."

He gently twirled her around and took her back into his arms, never missing a beat. "I've seen you dance and you're graceful."

"When have you seen me dance?" She pulled back so she could see his face.

"In the kitchen. With Wesley."

She smiled with the memory. But where had he been as he watched? "I hardly think that qualifies as dancing."

"You said dancing was your favorite."

"Dancing is like freedom."

"It's your turn, by the way." He twirled her once again.

"To dance?"

"Two truths and a lie."

She grinned. "I thought you had forgotten about that."

"Not a chance. Aren't we supposed to be getting to know each other better?"

"Right. Okay let me see." She thought about it a moment. "I'm worried about our marriage. I love brussels sprouts. And I hate this ring."

He stumbled, then caught himself. "I really hope you like brussels sprouts."

She grinned up at him. "As a matter of fact, I do."

He ran his thumb across the ring he'd placed on her finger not half an hour ago. "I wanted you to have something special."

She nodded. "It is special. And so very beautiful. Thank you."

He leaned his forehead against hers as they continued to dance. The rest of the town watched. "So why are you worried about our marriage?"

"You're not?"

"I see no reason to worry. We can only do what we can do. One day at a time, you know."

"That hurt me. The day in the lawyer's office," she admitted.

"I know. And I'm sorry. I never meant to hurt you. All I ever wanted was what was best for these two babies coming into the world."

"I know that now. But at the time . . ."

"So all is forgiven?"

"I think it has to be. We can't start a marriage at each other's throats for custody."

"So true."

She tilted her head back, staring into those green eyes. "I want us to have a chance, Jake. Everybody went to so much trouble to make this wedding beautiful and somehow managed to pull it off in no time at all. You know they even got a photographer to come in from Lubbock?"

"I'm not surprised."

"Don't you think we should honor that by trying to make our marriage work?"

He jerked back a little. "Why wouldn't I want our marriage to work?"

"That's not what I meant. But don't you think we should do everything in our power to—to—"

"Fall in love?"

This time she missed a step. She crashed into him and caught several chuckles from the onlooking guests. "Not exactly. But at least try to be amicable."

"I told you I loved you. So you don't believe me."

"I—I—" She couldn't find the words. Yes, she believed he loved her but she also believed that he loved a ghost. He couldn't get over Cecilia. And that would always stand in the way of their marriage.

She was saved from answering as the music finally came to a stop and everyone clapped. They turned to face the crowd, Jake taking a deep bow as Bryn curtsied.

"Come on, everybody," he said, motioning toward the dance floor. "Dance with us."

It was after ten when Jake pulled his truck in front of the ranch house. He cut the engine and looked over to his wife. His wife.

After Cecelia died, he never dreamed he would get

married again. And he had vowed to never have any more kids. It was too dangerous. Too risky. Yet here he was with a wife and not one but two babies on the way. Funny how life liked to throw curveballs.

"Bryn," he whispered, nudging her shoulder. Her head was leaned against the window and he had a feeling she'd fallen asleep. He couldn't imagine what it was like being so pregnant and yet still managing to keep up, have a good time. She hadn't smiled as much in the last few weeks, yet there had been a time when she was never without a smile on her face.

And whose fault is that?

His. All his. He just about ruined everything asking for custody. And that had never been his intention. He only wanted what was best for the babies and yet he almost destroyed everything he had built with this beautiful woman at his side. Thankfully, she'd had a change of heart, but there was still something holding her back. She said she had forgiven him, but he doubted that. Maybe with time . . .

"Bryn," he said a little louder. He shook her arm. Even with the twins, she couldn't weigh that much. He should be able to carry her to the house. But if he stumbled and fell, he would never forgive himself. No, he needed to wake her and get her into the bed.

Whoa. That was a thought he could've lived without. But ever since she put up that wall, he had kept his distance as well, not encroaching on her nighttime hours. But he missed her. Not just the soft way she sighed when he entered her, not just the way she breathed his name when he kissed that little spot on her neck, but the way she snuggled against him in her sleep, the way she wrapped herself around him in her dreams, the way she warmed him from the inside out.

"What?" She stirred and pushed herself up in the seat a little more. "Are we home?"

"We're home." The thought made his heart pound a little heavier in his chest. They were home. The two of them.

They had left Wesley at the VFW with his grandmother and his mother. The two women were finishing up the last of the cleanup while Wesley napped on a cot in the corner. Bryn had said they would bring her home, but neither woman would hear any of it. The newlywed couple needed to go take care of newlywed things, as Grandma Esther put it. But there would be no newlywed things tonight. And yet he wanted to hold her so bad he could taste it.

"I'm sorry. I must've fallen asleep."

"It's okay. It's just been a long day."

She shot him a trembling smile. "Long day."

He took the keys from the ignition and stepped from the truck. Then he came around to her side, opening the door and helping her to the ground.

"I don't think I told you this today, but I like you in cowboy boots," he said.

"Yeah?" She tilted her head back to look at him. One turn to the side and he could capture her lips in a heartbeat. But he kept walking. "It'd be nice if I could see them," she chuckled.

"I'm sure you'll be able to see them soon enough."

"I'm hoping I make it through Christmas," Bryn said.

"Or on Christmas. Just think, we could name them Noel and Holly."

"Both terrible names for boys," she said as she waited for him to unlock the door.

He chuckled and held it open for her. She stepped inside and he closed the door behind them, so aware of her every move, of her every breath.

"I guess it's past time for bed," she said.

"Yes ma'am. Five o'clock comes mighty early." Together they turned and walked down the hallway toward their rooms.

She stopped in front of her door, stared at the handle for a minute, then turned back to him. "Is this how it's going to be?"

"What do you mean?"

"I mean, we're married now. How can we make this work in two separate rooms?" She shook her head. "That didn't come out right. I'm not inviting you in for sex."

"Okay."

"I mean, I'm about the size of a barge and not very pretty these days."

He tilted up her chin to better meet her gaze. "You're beautiful."

She shook her head. "You don't have to say things like that. I'm not fishing for compliments, but it just feels really weird to spend my wedding night alone."

"Why shouldn't I say things like that?"

"Because you don't need to lie to me. I'm already married to you." She gave him a trembling smile.

He couldn't stand it anymore. He leaned in, then lightly kissed her lips. "You're the most beautiful person I know. You've been through so much and yet you smile constantly. You dance and make cookies in the middle of the night. You see art where the rest of us see dirt and scrub. Not so long from now, you're going to give birth to two special little people and that's the most beautiful thing of all. So yes, I think you're beautiful and no, I'm not lying. And I don't want to spend our wedding night separate either."

She stared at him, brown eyes searching green. "Will you come in?" she asked. "And just hold me tonight?"

His breath hitched in his chest. "I thought you'd never ask."

Bryn sighed and melted into the man behind her. Things weren't perfect, but today had been a step in the right direction.

"Your turn," she said and snuggled into him just a bit closer.

His arms tightened around her. They were lying on their sides, her back pressed to his chest. She had a pillow between her knees, not the sexiest position, but she was comfortable and he was warm and strong behind her.

"The first time I ever kissed a girl I was eleven years old. I think rice is the worst food on the planet, and I don't let myself drink Dr Pepper because if I do, that's all I'll drink all day long."

She brushed her fingers across the fine dark hair on his arms. "Let me see. I've never seen you drink anything but water and coffee. Wait, you had that one beer. I don't think I've ever seen you eat rice, though we had it one time when Grandma Esther made chicken enchiladas. And I can so imagine you kissing a girl at eleven years old. So I think your lie is number three. The Dr Pepper."

Jake shook his head. "I kissed the first girl at twelve years old."

"And you're addicted to Dr Pepper?" she asked with a laugh.

"Hey! That's some good stuff. Your turn."

"Let's see," she mused. "I went to a private Catholic school growing up. I had a crush on Rick before I found out he was gay. My parents let me name Emery."

"Hmmm . . . ," he murmured. His face was buried in her hair, his breath tickling the back of her neck. "I don't think you're Catholic."

"You don't have to be Catholic to go to Catholic school, you know."

"And I'm pretty sure everybody knows Rick's affiliation as soon as they see him. Not that there's anything wrong with that."

She chuckled.

"And I can definitely see your parents letting you name a child that they probably had no clue what to do with."

"So what's your answer?"

"Are you sure they're not all lies?"

"Only one."

"I'm going with Catholic school."

"Final answer?"

"No. Not when you say it like that."

She laughed.

"Okay, I don't think your parents let you name your sister."

"Are you sure?"

"No."

"One answer, Jake."

He thought about it a second more. And she didn't mind. She felt warm and cozy cocooned in his embrace. Not exactly the traditional wedding night, but then they hadn't exactly had the traditional wedding, or the traditional courtship, or did anything the traditional way. But he was with her and that was what mattered.

"Catholic school."

"My parents didn't let me name Emery. Though I'm pretty sure they named her after the nail file boards."

"It's a cute name."

She rolled her eyes even though he couldn't see it. "Says the man who wants to name his child Annabelle."

"Annabelle is a great name."

"You just keep telling yourself that."

"Are you still stuck on Jasper?" he asked.

"It was my father's name," she reminded him.

"Don't worry. It's growing on me. Jasper and Annabelle."

"Jasper and Jarvis," she corrected.

He stilled behind her. "Jarvis was Grandma Esther's maiden name."

"I know."

"She would love that so much."

"She's one special lady."

He gathered her closer. "Seems like my life is full of them."

* * *

Two weeks passed in tentative marital bliss. Upon discovering that they still occupied separate rooms, but slept in one bed each night, Evelyn promptly declared that since Jake was truly man of the house, he should have the master room back.

Bryn didn't ask why he had moved out to begin with. But she felt it had something to do with Cecelia's death. At any rate, Evelyn took to sleeping in her office in a recliner she bought. The treatment seemed to bother her breathing at times and she stated that she slept better sitting up. As each day passed, she drew more gaunt, weak, and frail looking. No one had the heart to disagree with her.

Bryn knocked on Wesley's door. "Wes, are you ready to go?"

"No!" the young girl wailed. "I can't go."

Bryn paused, closed her eyes, and wondered what the drama was this time. She opened the door a crack, peeking in to see Wesley lying in the middle of the floor, arms and legs spread-eagle.

"Why can't you go?" It was the Cattle Creek Elementary School Christmas pageant and Wesley had the great honor of playing a snowflake. One of many.

"I don't think I want to be a snowflake," Wesley said.

"I think it's a little late for that, don't you? You have to be there in half an hour and everyone's depending on you."

She didn't even raise her head. "No one will notice if I'm gone. All the snowflakes are just alike and there's fifteen of us." This time she did raise her head, branding Bryn with that serious brown gaze. "Fifteen. No one will miss me if I'm gone."

Bryn eased further into the room. "You really think that?" She sat on the edge of Wesley's bed. A few months ago she might've crouched down on the floor next to her, but these days she would never get back up if she did something like that.

"Who's going to miss one snowflake out of fifteen? I wanted a better part, but the kindergartners all have to play snowflakes. They wouldn't even let me try out for anything different."

"I think that's so you get experience for when you can try out for better roles. You'll know more about how it works. All kindergartners are new, right?"

She laid her head back on the rug. "I guess."

"And you know about snowflakes, don't you?" Bryn asked.

"I know they're cold and wet and there's fifteen of them in the Christmas pageant this year."

"No, snowflakes are all different. No two snowflakes are alike. Can you imagine with even an inch of snow all over the ground how many snowflakes are out there? And every one of them is different. There's more than fifteen, wouldn't you say?"

"Yeah," Wesley said, though her tone was more skeptical than anything.

"A whole field of snow and no two snowflakes that are just alike. That's pretty incredible, isn't it?"

"Is that really true?"

Bryn crossed her heart with one finger, then made a heart shape out of her hands. "Honest."

"What can I tell you? There will be fifteen just alike tonight." She raised her head up again. "Make that fourteen."

So it was all about individuality. Wesley had on her white tights and white leotard for underneath the white and light blue snowflake costume that had been cut out of cardboard and spray-painted for the occasion. They used one pattern, Bryn had found out from Wesley's teacher, and it would be waiting on them when they got to the school.

"I've got an idea," Bryn said. "I have spray glitter."

Wesley pushed herself up onto her elbows. "You do?"

"I do. And we can take it to school and spray-paint it on your costume."

"We can do that?"

Bryn shrugged. "I don't see why not. We can paint yours on the ends and maybe paint everybody else's in a different spot, so everyone gets glitter, but everybody's different."

Wesley nodded, her blond ponytail bobbing with the motion. "I like that idea."

"You do? Well, you can't spray-paint glitter laying on the floor here."

Wesley was on her feet in a second. She found her coat and slipped her arms inside, turning to Bryn as she finally managed to don the garment. "What are you waiting for? Let's go."

Bryn had never been more proud or more uncomfortable as she sat in the auditorium chair and watched snowflake number fourteen dance to the Nutcracker Suite. The glitter was a huge success with all the snowflakes wanting different parts of their costume sprayed so they all could be a little different than each other. And the glitter caught the lights of the auditorium and sparkled like real snow in sunlight.

Bryn shifted in her seat.

"Are you okay?" Jake asked from beside her.

"Yes, just miserable." She shot him a rueful smile.

"I don't think we have much longer now."

"I hope not." Then she realized she was talking about until she gave birth and he was talking about the end of the program. "I mean I'll be okay."

He shot her a concerned look, then turned back to the front.

First-grade sugarplums danced across the stage followed

by candy canes and Christmas stockings that she was pretty sure were second graders.

Jake leaned in close again. "Are you sure?"

"I'm not going into labor, if that's what you want to know," she said.

The look on his face was filled with such relief that she almost laughed out loud. "This chair has a broken spring that keeps poking me in the back."

"Do you want to trade seats?"

"No, I'm fine." But his concern touched her.

Finally the program ended and everyone milled around, drinking punch and eating Christmas cookies.

Bryn felt a little like a show-and-tell project as Wesley dragged her from person to person telling them all how Bryn was her new mommy and they were having not one baby but two. The tone of her voice was evident. That topped all the stories of all the students, at least all the ones in the kindergarten class.

"You must be Bryn," a mid-thirties woman asked. She was slim and trim, her Christmas green dress hugging every delicious curve. Bryn used to have delicious curves, now they were just life-threatening slopes.

"I'm sorry. I don't believe we've met."

"Kristen Stringer. I'm Wesley's teacher."

Great. The teacher that once upon a time Jake had crushed on. He was married to her, Bryn reminded herself. But she was as green with envy as Kristen Stringer's party dress. Why couldn't she have been frumpy and wear cat sweaters like any self-respecting kindergarten teacher should?

"How much longer?" Kristen pointed toward Bryn's very pregnant belly.

"I'm hoping to make it to Christmas."

Kristen smiled, a pretty smile with even white teeth. Perfect honey-colored hair. "What a wonderful present for the holidays."

Why couldn't she say something mean or stupid where Bryn would be fully justified in hating her? Or maybe she should be asking why she was jealous of someone Jake had a crush on when she was wearing his ring. She touched the stone with her thumb as had become her habit of late. She seemed terrified she was going to lose the ring, but her hands were so swollen she didn't think it would come off now if she tried with soap and cold water.

She felt that hand on the small of her back and inhaled his warmth and presence before he spoke. "It was a great program, Kristen."

Bryn leaned into him ever so slightly. It was childish, she knew, but she felt she needed to stake her claim, like her big belly wasn't enough to prove that Jake was hers.

"So glad you enjoyed it, Jake. I'm sorry I missed the wedding. I hear it was lots of fun."

Jake grinned. "You know Mama and Grandma Esther. If they're not having a good time, no one is."

"Very true." She looked off to a point somewhere on the other side of Jake's right shoulder. "I see the principal waving. I better go see what he needs. Thank you so much for coming."

"So that's her," Bryn said after Kristen Stringer moved away.

"What?"

"Two truths and a lie. You said you had crushed on Wesley's teacher. That's Wesley's teacher."

He frowned. "Yeah, I know."

"Didn't you think that was a little awkward?"

"Not particularly," he said. "Was I supposed to feel it was uncomfortable?"

"Jake, be serious. I'm not sure how I feel about that."

"Because I had a crush on Wesley's teacher when we were in the sixth grade?"

"Yes, I mean . . . sixth grade?"

He nodded. "Sixth grade." Then he stopped. "You feel better now?"

The heat that rose into her cheeks could toast marshmallows.

"Oh, so I've got one who's the jealous type." He grinned.

"It's not funny," she said. She wished she could've crossed her arms for emphasis, but they would just lie on top of her belly and she would look all the more ridiculous.

"I disagree. I think it's quite funny."

She frowned at him.

"You have a lot to learn about small towns, Bryn." He scanned the crowd of parents and grandparents all milling around with the elementary kids. "There's probably not a woman in this building tonight that hasn't been kissed by a Langston."

"You?"

"Me or one of my brothers." He shrugged. "See, that's the thing when your graduating class doesn't reach triple digits. There's not many to choose from."

"So you kissed all the girls."

"Something like that."

She thought about it a second, still not quite convinced. Her graduating class had nearly five hundred.

"There's nothing to worry about. I married you, did I not?"

Something charged the air between them. And the seriousness and mock anger and his laughter all merged into something . . . more. It was as if someone had sucked the air from the room and she was standing there alone with him in a vacuum of awareness. No one else around. Just the two of them.

"Yes," she whispered in return.

"Always remember that."

She wanted to protest, challenge him to stop putting up walls, tell him to break down the barrier that kept her from knowing the real Jake.

She didn't know how she knew it was there; she could just feel it between them. It was the only thing keeping them apart. She was afraid it had to do more with his grieving for Cecelia than it did any reason why he couldn't love her.

Chapter Nineteen

I can't believe it! You put an open invitation to come to the baby shower in the paper?" Bryn asked two days later.

Grandma Esther shrugged. "I figured it was the easiest way to reach everybody. This way anybody who wants to come can come, and anybody who doesn't just missed out."

Jake's words from the night of the Christmas pageant came back to her. She didn't know a lot about how small towns worked, but Grandma Esther and Evelyn seemed to think this was the perfect way to notify guests. Bryn secretly wondered if this was just another way for them to work through their party gene. They seemed to want to have a get-together for everything that happened. Then again maybe that was one of those small-town things that she just didn't know about.

Bryn shuffled into the VFW just behind Wesley and in front of Jake's grandmother and mother.

"Surprise!"

The reception area was full of people. The majority of which Bryn had never met. But Cattle Creek was her town now and she supposed it was time to start meeting everybody.

A blond-haired woman with a short ponytail and bangs shellacked firmly into place grabbed her hand. "Come sit down. Come sit down. I'm Darly Jo. It's so good to meet you." Her gaze dropped to Bryn's belly. "Oh, my. I heard it was twins but . . . oh, my."

She shuffled away on wedge-heeled boots, and Bryn was left at the mercy of the next person in line. She met Wanda from Wag the Dog, Debbie Ann from the Chuck Wagon, Cora Mae from Cora's Country Kitchen, and a host of other people whose names she would probably never remember.

A table had been set up in the back and was piled high with presents wrapped in every color of pastel paper known to man. Balloons had been scattered about, along with the required crepe paper streamers. Plastic tablecloths covered all the tables in the reception area. It was the same place where they had held their wedding reception, and it seemed as if the same crowd had come back once again.

"Isn't this fun?" Grandma Esther clapped her hands. Wesley snuggled up beside Bryn and gave her a kiss on the cheek. Someone had made pink raspberry punch, and someone else had broken out the cookies and mini quiches from the wholesale club. It wasn't fancy but it was friendly.

Bryn looked around at all these people who had probably known Jake all his life. And she knew she had made the right decision to come to Cattle Creek. Her children would grow up in this celebration-loving small town filled with people who dropped envelopes off marked "college fund" and played a variation game of Yahtzee with dice the size of shoeboxes.

Bryn sat back in her chair and watched. She laughed and drank punch as everyone partied around her. She had a wonderful time just sitting and getting to know the good citizens of Cattle Creek. Jessie, Ethan Davis, and Millie Sawyer, who used to live in Cattle Creek and had recently moved back. Everyone was welcoming and warm and somehow it felt like home.

"Are you having a good time?" Evelyn sidled up beside Bryn, who had pulled a second chair over to prop up her feet and keep her ankles from swelling. "It's wonderful."

"Are you getting tired?"

"I think I could ask you the same thing."

Evelyn swallowed hard and looked out over the crowd of people. "I'm okay."

But Bryn could tell a lie when she heard one.

"The treatments are going well, then?"

Evelyn shook her head. "No. Not really. But we're hopeful. The doctors want to try something new after the first of the year."

Bryn nodded. "It's hard, you know. When it gets the upper hand."

Evelyn laid her hand on Bryn's shoulder. She clasped it in her own, squeezing her fingers reassuringly. "You loved your sister very much."

"She was kind of like my own. Our parents died when she was only seven."

"And you raised her then."

"Of course."

"I'm sorry for your loss."

"I believe you've already said that. It's not necessary."

"It just hits home, you know." Evelyn smiled, but her lips trembled. She no longer seemed like the strong woman that Bryn had come to know in those first weeks in Cattle Creek.

"Just do me a favor," Bryn said.

"What's that?"

Bryn squeezed her fingers once again. "Never stop fighting."

"Don't you know? A Langston never quits."

Christmas Day dawned poignant and cold. Wesley hadn't been able to sleep the night before; she was too excited to see what Santa would bring. She'd crawled into bed smack-dab in between Bryn and Jake somewhere around one a.m. He'd laughed and said he didn't mind, and Bryn didn't either. There would be a day when Wesley wouldn't want much to do with either one of them, having grown up so much she didn't need parents. So until then Bryn would relish all the little times like this.

Bryn stirred awake as Jake rose from the bed. Wesley, who finally passed out from exhaustion, was snoring softly beside her.

"Where are you going?" she whispered. He pulled on a flannel robe and pointed to the front room. "I'm going to build a fire. You have to have a fire on Christmas Day."

Bryn leaned back in bed. A fire on Christmas Day sounded wonderful and beautiful. Though Georgia wasn't quite cold enough for a fire, even on Christmas.

She lay back and settled down into the warm covers, but it just wasn't the same without Jake. She rose from the bed, found her robe, and pulled it on before padding behind him into the front room.

He just had the fire started when she came up behind him.

The Christmas tree stood off to one side of the fireplace. The beautiful artificial tree had rope for garland and was decorated with tiny cowboy hats mixed in with random Christmas balls and homemade ornaments that looked as though Evelyn had been collecting them for years. Bryn supposed that she had.

"Do you want me to make some coffee?" Bryn asked.

He shook his head. "You sit down. I'll do it."

Bryn laughed. "I'm not an invalid, you know. I'm just pregnant."

Jake's gaze dropped to her belly. "Oh, I know."

"All right, cowboy, you'll pay for that. One day, anyway."

Jake held up a hand to show that he was shaking. "I'm scared." Then he headed into the kitchen to brew some coffee.

Bryn sat down to enjoy the quiet moment. Christmas Day. Not her first without Emery and most likely not her last. But she said a little prayer in case Emery was watching from heaven.

Jake returned a few moments later, a steaming cup of coffee in each hand. He handed one to her.

"Only one, right?"

"Only one," she agreed. "Are we ready to have these babies?" she asked. She wasn't sure where the question came from; it simply popped onto her lips before she had a chance to think about it.

"Well, we have cribs in the room, and clothes hanging in the closet. Maybe not a lot of clothes. But once we figure out what the babies are, we'll buy more. I think we've got two thousand diapers from the baby shower."

Bryn laughed. "You think so. In about two months you're going to wish we actually had that many."

Jake reached out and grabbed her hand and interlaced their fingers. "So my answer is yes. We're ready."

She certainly hoped so.

"Do you want to open a Christmas present?" he asked.

"Everyone would be so upset if we started opening the Christmas presents without them."

Bryn looked to the tree once again. There was one unwrapped present, a pink bicycle with white daisies, silver streamers hanging from the handlebars, training wheels, and a white basket attached to the front. It was the only thing Wesley had asked for. Though Jake had confessed that he didn't know why she would want to ride a bike when she could ride a horse instead. But that was her cowboy husband. And Bryn knew why. It was just one more stab that Wesley could make at individuality.

"Maybe this is something I want to give you when we're alone."

Her heart gave a weird thump in her chest. "This doesn't have anything to do with sex, does it?"

He laughed. "Methinks someone is a little undersexed these days."

"And it's all your fault." She ran a hand over her impossibly large stomach. She could barely walk down the hallway these days. Intimacy was completely out of the question. Oh, the days.

He shook his head. "Nope, I just was responsible for the one baby. You're responsible for the two. Simple genetics."

She sighed. He was right. Damn it, she hated when he was right. He squatted down in front of the Christmas tree, reaching to the back and pulling out a small rectangular box.

He offered it to her, then pulled back slightly. "I know you make jewelry." He shook his head. "I just wanted you to have something special from me." He pushed the box into her hands.

The wrapping paper was red foil with a beautiful gold ribbon. A bell had been tied up in the bow. She stared at it a full minute.

"Open it," he said. He sat down on the couch next to her.

She slipped the bow from the package and carefully began to pull back the tape and wrapping paper.

"Oh, come on. Open it."

Finally, she allowed herself to tear the paper. She opened the box to reveal a velvet case nestled inside. With trembling fingers, she pried open the case to reveal the most beautiful necklace she had ever seen. It was a heart pendant reminiscent of two people with their heads together. Three small jewels, one red and two pale blue, dangled off the point.

"It's our family," Jake explained.

She nodded, her throat clogged. It was all she ever wanted, to be part of a family, and it was the one thing she'd never been able to truly call her own.

"We might have to change the blue stones. If you don't decide to have those babies before the end of the month." He chuckled. "But it's no matter."

"It's—it's beautiful." She threw her arms around his neck

and hugged him close. He might have walls around his heart, but he was trying. And maybe one day they would come down. Maybe one day . . . maybe one day . . .

She pulled back, and he took the box from her hands. "Let me put it on you."

"Because it matches my pajamas so well."

"That's the most fun part of Christmas."

She lifted her hair off her neck so he could clasp the necklace behind her. Once it was in place, she couldn't see the pendant. But she could feel it. She knew what it stood for. And that had tears rising in her eyes once again.

"If I'd known it was going to make you cry this much, I would have never given it to you."

She shook her head. "Oh, no, you don't. I'll cry all I want. Thank you very much."

"The prerogative of a pregnant woman?"

"You got it." She fingered the necklace and smiled. "Your turn."

"Okay."

"Down there on the bottom. It's wrapped in blue snowman paper."

He got down under the tree searching for the box. It wasn't large and it took him a second to find it amid all the toys wrapped and ready for Wesley.

"Here it is."

She didn't think she'd ever been this nervous in her life as he started to tear that paper open. She wanted him to like her gift so much.

He wadded up the paper and tossed it over one shoulder. She laughed at his childish antics. Then he slid the lid from the box and removed the cushioning tissue from the top.

Then he stopped and stared into the box.

She couldn't read his expression. "They're conchos."

"I know what they are."

"I looked at the ones on your saddle. You should be able to replace them. If you like these."

She had patterned the decorative silver discs after the ones already on his saddle. But these she had embossed with the Diamond Duvall Ranch brand. A diamond shape with a *D* in the center.

"And there's a smaller one for your hat." Still he was quiet. "Jake?"

He shook his head. "These are the most beautiful things I've ever seen." He pulled her close, capturing her lips with his own. The kiss was sweet and chaste and all too quick.

"I didn't know what to get you." She smiled. "You kind of have everything. But I thought this might be nice."

"They're more than nice."

"I can make you some for your chaps too if you want."

He shook his head. "I can't believe you made these."

"Are you sure you like them?"

"I'm sure." He pulled her close once again. He said he loved them, and he seemed almost stunned. She knew the craftsmanship was good, excellent even. Because that was what she'd been trained to do. And he had seen her work before. So she could only speculate that maybe his surprise had come from something else. Maybe she crossed a line she hadn't known was there.

They had exactly fifteen minutes to sit and watch the fire and enjoy a cup of coffee. Bryn heard the bedroom door shut first, then the running of feet, then Wesley burst into the family room. "It's Christmas! It's Christmas!" She jumped up and down, bouncing on the balls of her feet. "A bike! Look, Daddy! Santa brought me a bike!"

She hopped on and pedaled the bike around the family room. "Why didn't you wake me up?" She shouted with joy in the way only a five-year-old at Christmastime can do.

Jake laughed at his daughter's antics. "Be careful," he said. "Don't run into any walls."

"Yes, sir! Where's Grandma Esther? Where's Nana?"

"Right here." Evelyn entered the room, her eyes tired but her smile bright. Esther was right behind her.

Wesley hopped off the bike and grabbed Evelyn's hand. "Come on, Nana! Let's open presents!"

Jake frowned, but sent a little wink in Bryn's direction. "I think we should have breakfast first."

Wesley stared at him wide-eyed, the bounce completely gone from her step. "Are you kidding me? Who eats breakfast on Christmas Day? I want to open presents!"

"I don't know," Bryn added. "A nutritious breakfast is very important."

Wesley stopped, unsure if they were joking or not. She just stood there a second staring at them. "Please don't do this to me."

Her words were so heartfelt that Bryn couldn't keep a straight face any longer. She started to laugh. "Find a present and start handing them out."

"You want me to play Santa?"

"If that means you hand out the presents, then yes," Bryn said. "I can't get down in the floor these days."

"Daddy usually hands them out."

Bryn looked to Jake, who shrugged. "I think you can handle the responsibility this year."

He leaned a little closer to Bryn. "This might keep her a little bit busier."

Bryn smiled as Wesley, in all her Christmas excitement, got down on all fours and started looking at gift tags. Before long she had every present out from under the tree and piled next to the person it belonged to. Of course the largest pile was hers and she sat down and promptly started to open them.

There were a lot of typical Christmas gifts: sweaters, socks and underwear, and toys galore for Wesley. There were even a few under the tree for the twins. But since they didn't know the gender, they were mostly educational toys for when they were a little older.

"That's from me," Bryn told Wesley.

She held the small box in her hands, then ripped into it with true Wesley gusto.

"Be careful when you open it. You don't want it to fall on the floor."

Wesley finally managed to get the box open and stared down at the object inside. She pulled the crescent-shaped item from the box, holding it up with two fingers as if it might bite. "What is it?"

"It's for your hair."

Wesley's eyes grew wide. She jumped to her feet and ran over to Bryn. "Can you show me how to use it?"

Bryn laughed. "Turn around."

Wesley did as she asked. Bryn gathered her hair and began to wrap it around and through the intricate silver hair piece. To Bryn it resembled fingers with stars on the ends with a cubic zirconia in the center of each one to add some sparkle. When she was done, Wesley's ponytail hung down her back but the curve of her head was accented by the silver.

"How does it look?" Wesley asked, turning around in a circle as she tried to see the back of her head.

Everyone laughed.

Bryn stood and reached out a hand to Wesley. "Come on. I'll show you in the bathroom mirror." She took Wesley into the bathroom and showed her how to look in a hand mirror and use it to see the big mirror behind her.

"Oh, it's so beautiful," Wesley said. "I look like a princess." She flung her arms around Bryn and hugged her tight.

"You are a princess," Bryn told her. "Never forget that."

Wesley dropped a kiss on her cheek and hurried from the room. "Daddy! Daddy! Daddy! Miss Bryn said I'm a princess."

She might grow to regret that. Bryn chuckled and went back into the living room. Grandma Esther had just opened her present from Bryn, a brand-new cane with a molded silver horse head. The horse was depicted as running, its mane flowing wildly behind it.

"It's beautiful," Jake's grandmother said. "Thank you."

"You'll be the envy of everybody at senior center card day."

Esther smiled. "I already am."

Bryn held her breath as Evelyn opened her present. Jake's mother gasped, then looked back to Bryn. "This is beautiful." She shook her head. "That's not even an adequate word. It's exquisite."

"It was the scene that got me drawing again. One of your horses." It was a lapel pin, the horse bucking, but the shape was more like the horseshoe. It was an interesting study, Bryn thought. And the one person who would appreciate it the most was Evelyn Langston.

"I don't know what to say."

Bryn smiled. "There's nothing to say."

"Thank you."

"Merry Christmas," Bryn replied. Then she turned to Jake. "I never asked; are Jessie and Seth coming over? I have something for them too."

"They'll be by later. I think they wanted to have their first Christmas by themselves at home."

Bryn remembered the secret Jessie had told her the day of Bryn's wedding. It seemed like this would be their last Christmas alone.

"Plus, it's nearly impossible to keep Wesley out of the presents until anyone can get out here," Evelyn added, her tone affectionate.

Since all the presents were open except those for Seth and Jessie, Jake went out to do his morning chores. Ranch work didn't stop just because it was Christmas Day. Bryn commissioned Wesley's help, and together they picked up the mess of the Christmas gifts and took everyone's Christmas presents to their room. Grandma Esther went to the kitchen to start breakfast, and Evelyn called Seth and Jessie to let them know they could come eat as well.

Bryn stood at the door to the patio and looked out over the beautiful landscape. The sun was bright and the wind cold. It was a beautiful Christmas Day. She felt a twinge in her side and gave it a little rub. She must've tweaked a muscle when she was helping Wesley pick up all the wrapping paper.

Jake came back in the house just in time for breakfast, and it seemed as if Seth had perfect timing as well. He and Jessie arrived as the last fried egg was slid on a plate.

"Merry Christmas!" they cried as they came into the house. And once again Bryn was hit with that overwhelming sense of family. Would she ever get used to it?

Hugs and kisses on the cheek went all around, then everyone sat down to the table to eat breakfast. The meal was half over when Seth stood and clinked his spoon against his juice glass.

"I need your attention," he said. "Jessie and I have an announcement."

Bryn ducked her head and smiled to herself. Jake bumped her shoulder and whispered in her ear. "How come I think you already know?"

She gave a little shrug.

"Jessie and I are having a baby."

Cheers went up all around the table. Bryn was so happy for them. Their family was growing.

Another twinge tweaked her other side, and she rubbed it absently.

"Are you okay?" Jake asked.

"Yes. Just tired."

He shot her a worried frown, but didn't say more. It had been a long couple of weeks for them all.

They all got up and went back into the living room to watch Jessie and Seth open their presents. They had a little something for everyone as well, including two pair of tiny cowboy boots for the twins and an ultrasound picture for Evelyn.

Bryn shifted uncomfortably as Jessie opened her present from Bryn. It was a hair piece similar to the one that she had given Wesley, though in the place of stars she had put leaves, the stones natural jade.

"It's for your hair," Wesley explained. "Here. Let me show you." She went behind Jessie and started to fix the woman's hair. Though with all of Jessie's curls Bryn was certain they would have to cut the thing out instead of actually making her hairdo.

By some miracle, Wesley's attempt to fix Jessie's hair actually turned out. She was so proud of herself, the whole family was smiling.

"Thank you for the keychain," Seth said to Bryn a bit later. She had gone to the kitchen to get a drink of water. "You're very talented." She had made Seth a leather key fob with a concho embossed with the county seal.

"Thank you. And you're welcome."

"You could sell those and make a fortune at the gift shop."

"I've never done that before. This was kind of a new venture for me." Her past designs were a little more Aztec-inspired. Cuff bracelets, chunky necklaces, and large earrings. At one time she'd even done slave girl anklets. This Western flair was still new to her.

"I would love to say that it's going to be my next venture. But I have something else on the agenda for the next eighteen years."

Seth laughed as another twinge started in Bryn's side. She inhaled sharply and placed a hand over that spot.

"Are you okay?" Seth asked.

Bryn continued to rub her belly. The doctor said the babies could come at any time, but she wasn't sure she was ready. Not today.

"Yes. Of course. I'm fine." But she could tell by the look in Seth's eyes that he didn't believe her.

"I'm getting Jake."

She grabbed his arm as he turned away. "No. Don't. It's nothing."

He stopped and eyed her carefully. "That didn't look like nothing."

"Okay, so it wasn't nothing. But it wasn't a contraction either."

"You're sure?" Seth asked.

Bryn nodded. "I promise. I would tell you."

For a moment she thought she hadn't convinced him, then Seth nodded. "All right. But if they get worse, you'll tell us, right?"

"Oh, if I go into labor, y'all are going to know."

"Fair enough." Seth disappeared back into the family room where the men were watching football, yet again. Grandma Esther had put the ham on to cook, and Jessie and Evelyn were looking at recipes trying to decide exactly what sort of potatoes to make. Wesley was sitting at the kitchen table coloring in her favorite coloring book. Hundreds of dollars spent on toys and she reverted to her old standby. Kids would never cease to amaze her.

Bryn sidled up to Grandma Esther. "You need some help?"

Esther shook her head. "I got this. Why don't you go rest? You look a little peaked."

She was a little tired. But it was Christmas Day, and she didn't want to miss a minute of it by taking a nap. She would rather be in the family room curled up next to Jake as he watched football and drank a beer with his brother. But since Jessie was in the kitchen, Bryn thought it best to stay close to the womenfolk. She slid onto the bench across from Wesley.

"What are you coloring?"

"It's a butterfly. See?" Wesley turned the coloring book around so Bryn could have the right-side view of the picture. So far the butterfly had at least six colors and none of them were symmetrical. It seemed Wesley had an artist's heart.

"It's beautiful," Bryn said.

"Thank you." Wesley bobbed her chin and turned her coloring book back around.

Bryn sighed. She felt restless, expectant, and maybe a

little anxious. She rubbed a burning spot on her chest. Or maybe it was just indigestion from breakfast. It seemed like she couldn't eat much of anything these days without getting heartburn. She knew it was because the twins had taken up more room than average and had pushed her stomach a little out of whack. Such was the problem with being pregnant.

"Are you okay?" Evelyn asked.

Bryn nodded as the pain streaked across her abdomen. She caught her breath and held it, unable to move.

The rest of the women had no such problems, and she found herself quickly surrounded by the other Langstons.

"Is that the babies?" She thought Evelyn asked that, but she wasn't sure.

All Bryn could do was nod.

The pain subsided as quickly as it came, and Bryn straightened. "I'm okay."

"You're white as a sheet," Jessie said.

"I don't think you're okay at all," Grandma Esther added.

Wesley sat at the table watching all the interactions. "Are the babies going to be born today?"

Bryn shook her head. "Probably not, chickadee."

Wesley seemed to think about it a minute, then gave a quick nod and went back to her coloring.

"Do you think we should take her to the doctor?" Evelyn pinned Esther with a look.

The older woman shrugged. "I guess that's up to her. Bryn, do you feel like you need to go to the hospital?"

"Who needs to go to the hospital?" Seth had come back into the room, apparently to grab a couple more beers for him and Jake.

"Did somebody say hospital?" Jake burst into the room. "Bryn, are you okay?"

"I'm fine." She laughed to show just how fine she was. The pain had come and gone, most probably Braxton Hicks again, but she couldn't shake that expectant feeling she had. Her stomach pitched like she was on a roller coaster.

"Honey, why don't you sit down?" Jake asked. He plowed into the room and took her elbow, his intention clear: to walk her into the living room and sit her down on the couch. But she was tired of sitting and she was tired of waiting.

"I don't want to sit down." She dug in her heels and as she did the pain hit again. It was like lightning and fire blazing inside her. Her breath caught. Jake stilled as he watched her. They had gone through all the classes of breathing techniques and other helpful information, but it was hard to remember all of that when she was being torn in half.

"Breathe," Jessie said.

The one word seemed to spur Jake into motion. He took her face in his hands and tilted her chin so he could look deep into her eyes. "Are you ready to have these babies today?"

She wanted to tell him no. She wanted to tell him it was just Braxton Hicks, but somehow she knew. "I think so. I'm sorry to ruin everybody's Christmas."

"Ruin Christmas?" Jessie said. "Why, this is the best Christmas ever. Wesley, get your coat. We're going to the hospital."

Chapter Twenty

It seemed to take forever to get Bryn's suitcase and get her into his truck. The pains were coming quicker now, and it was hard for him to breathe with his heart lodged in his throat. There were too many things that could go wrong.

"Somebody call Gary and have him meet us at the medical center," he called as he ran around the front of his truck and slid behind the wheel.

His hands were shaking so badly he could barely get the key in the ignition. Next time he was leaving the damn thing running for nine months. Next time.

He put the truck into gear and glanced over to Bryn. Her eyes were closed as she practiced the breathing techniques he never quite understood. But did he try? Not really. Fully understanding the importance of the breathing was the equivalent of admitting that she was having a baby, two babies, and that so many things could go wrong.

"Are you okay?"

"Drive fast," was all she said.

Jake spun out on the dirt driveway and headed toward

the road. They were coming too fast, the pains one on top of the other. He was supposed to be timing them, but he couldn't check his watch and drive.

"When did these pains start?"

They were coming so fast they had to have started sometime in the night. And yet she'd said nothing until now? Was she trying to drive him insane?

He shook his head. This wasn't about him. He could go crazy later. Right now he had to get her into Cattle Creek. And for the first time since she started going to see Dr. Gary Stephens, he was grateful that they had chosen a doctor who was close.

"Jake!" She practically screeched his name. He braked at the end of the driveway, fear controlling that instinctive reaction.

"They're coming. Now."

"How can that be?" Weren't babies supposed to wait hours and hours before they actually arrived?

She clutched his arm, her fingers digging in even through his thick winter coat. "We have to do something now!"

He shoved the truck into park and left it running as he ran around to her side. His mother, Grandma Esther, and everyone else were in the car behind them. He wrenched open the door. "Why are they coming so fast?" he asked.

Bryn shook her head. She turned in her seat, her back braced against the center console.

"I've got to get you to the hospital. To the doctor," he said. They needed a doctor more than anything in the world. They needed one right now.

"There's no time."

How did she know? It was her first baby! He didn't want her to have them here. They needed medical equipment, sterilized blankets, and everything else that modern technology could give them. He needed them to be safe. He needed heart monitors and incubators and—

"Jake!"

He snapped to attention.

She leaned up and clasped his face in her hands. "I need you. You can do this."

Suddenly Grandma Esther was behind him. "What's going on?"

Jake leaned in and gave Bryn one last kiss, his mind made up.

"We're going to have these babies, Grandma. Like, right now. Keep Wesley back."

"I'll go back to the house to get some towels." She turned away. "And blankets. And hot water. I don't really know what it's for, but they always have it in the movies."

"Have Mama call 9-1-1. And go get Abraham."

His grandmother stopped. "The vet?"

"Just do it!"

The driver's-side door opened, and Jessie slid in behind the steering wheel.

"Hey, Bryn. It's me. Jessie." She reached over and grabbed Bryn's hand. "Squeeze my hand. Let me know that you're listening. Ow," she said, then gave a small laugh.

"Jake's going to deliver the babies," Bryn whispered, but her eyes were closed. That in itself worried him. He wanted her looking at him, eyes sharp as she bossed him around, telling him what to do, but he was on his own.

He grabbed his pocketknife and exposed the blade.

"Bryn, I've got to cut these jeans off."

She took a deep, shuddering breath. "I don't care. I hate them anyway."

Jessie laughed. "They are quite ugly."

"Your turn is coming," Bryn grit out as another pain gripped her.

Somehow Jake managed to get Bryn free of her jeans.

"Here he comes!" Bryn's strangled cry sliced through him. This was no different than delivering a horse or a cow, he told himself, but he didn't believe a word of it. First there was a head, then the tiny body. The baby boy slid from his mother and let out a lusty wail.

Jake held the squalling bundle in his arms and looked to his wife. Her eyes were closed. "Bryn," he called softly.

She opened her eyes just enough to peek at him.

"It's a boy."

She closed her eyes again. "I told you so."

He wished she would look at him.

Please God let her be okay.

Why wouldn't she look at him? But surely her smart mouth was an indication that she was okay.

Please God let it be so.

Suddenly Grandma Esther was behind him.

"Here." She handed him a thick fleece blanket. "Make sure his mouth is clear and wrap him up in this. You need to clean him a little, but it's more important to keep him warm."

Jake held the baby away from him as his grandmother wrapped the baby in the blanket. With the baby warm and snug and still screaming his little head off, Jake laid him on Bryn's belly.

"The doc said to use these to tie off the cords." She handed him a couple of shoelaces.

Bryn's eyes were still closed, but she cradled the baby boy. He had stopped crying and was snuggling close as if he knew his mother was near. That had to be a good sign too, right?

Jessie was behind her, caressing her face and talking nonsensically. Must be a girl thing, he thought.

Then Bryn sat up a little straighter. "Here he comes."

Jake felt just a little more confidence this time around. Unlike his brother, the baby came in record time.

"It's a boy."

Twin boys! He could hardly believe it.

Bryn reached out and lightly touched the baby's face. "Jasper and Jarvis," she said, then slumped back into her seat.

* * *

When asked later, Jake couldn't remember exactly how he got Bryn to the medical center. He had, and that was all that mattered.

The babies were whisked away to be measured and weighed. They had taken Bryn as well, leaving Jake waiting for word.

Shortly after suppertime, they put Bryn in a room and allowed Jake to join her. She was sleeping peacefully when he entered and he found himself watching her chest move to reassure himself. He hated it, hated his weakness, but he had to know that she was okay.

Two incubators stood nearby, each one holding a tiny Langston twin. Well, not so tiny. Jasper Thomas Langston weighed in at six pounds two ounces, while Jarvis Talbot Langston weighed five pounds ten ounces. The biggest twins the Cattle Creek Medical Center had ever seen. Not that it was saying much. But Jake was still proud of his boys.

And so very proud of his wife.

He sat down next to her bed. The heart monitors beeped out of sequence, but it was the most musical sound he had ever heard.

How could one man be so blessed? Love for the three of them filled his heart. He could hardly wait for Wesley to see her baby brothers. She was going to be such a good big sister. And two rowdy boys ensured there would be lots of roughhousing and noise in the years to come.

He reached out and took Bryn's hand in his own. She didn't move, just peacefully slept. And he was grateful, so very grateful. They made it through. All three of them were fine and healthy. What more could one man ask?

It rose up in him, a strange mixture of happiness, gratitude, and sorrow. It clogged his throat and pounded through his veins.

Jake laid his head on the side of the bed and wept.

He wept for Cecelia, whose life was cut way too short. He wept for Wesley, who had been denied a mother for far too long. But he also wept in happiness that somehow, someway, he and Bryn had been brought together. They had two healthy sons and would now share a beautiful daughter and be the family that she deserved. But mostly he wept for time lost. He'd been such a fool for the last five years. But no more.

"Shhh," Bryn murmured.

He felt her hands smooth down his hair as she tried to comfort him. But still he wept. "It's okay," she murmured. It was. And he was glad. "It's all okay. We're all okay."

She was having the most wonderful dream. She was floating on a pink sea of cotton candy. Okay, so that wasn't actually possible but it felt that way, soft, cushiony, and sweet. In fact, it felt so good she wasn't sure she ever wanted to wake up.

But there was a constant beeping noise. It interrupted her beautiful pink dream. And there wasn't just one. There were two or three layered together, though some were much faster than the others. Too many beeps was all she could think about. Why were there so many beeps?

The only way to know for certain was to open her eyes and find out where the noise was coming from. But she was tired, so very tired, and uncertain if she wanted to open her eyes just yet. Still, that beeping noise was starting to get on her nerves. She pried open her eyes one at a time and took in her unfamiliar surroundings.

She was in a bed, but not her bed. A window across from her had the curtains drawn and it didn't look like any room she had ever been in. She didn't remember coming here. How did she get here? And what was that infernal beeping?

She started to push herself up a little in the bed when somebody grabbed her hand. "Bryn?"

She looked over. Jake. "Hi." She gave him a smile, at least she tried. Her mouth was so dry that her lips stuck to her teeth. "Water," she croaked.

His chair scraped against the tile floor as he pushed back from the bed. He returned a few moments later with a cup and a straw. "Easy does it, now."

She drank her fill and laid her head back on the pillow, as he hovered by the bed. "You look haggard," she said.

His eyes held a worried light, his mouth turned down at the corners. He looked like someone who had been delivered the worst news of his life. Then she remembered. She sat up straight. "The babies?"

He pointed to the incubators on the other side of the bed. They were side by side, two little boys and, as far as she could tell, perfect in every way.

"You did that," he said. He took her hand in his and kissed her palm.

She shook her head. "You did it. I don't know what I would've done without you."

He smiled and kissed her hand again. Then his eyes turned serious. "I need to talk to you about something."

Her heart gave a painful thump. "The twins?"

He shook his head. "They're perfect in every way. Ten fingers and ten toes. I counted."

She nodded, but swallowed hard. "It's about us."

She couldn't allow herself to think anything negative. She couldn't allow herself to think that perhaps she would lose him. Because if she had loved him before, she loved him doubly now. He had stepped up, faced his fears, delivered his sons in the driveway of the ranch house. He was a hero. Her hero.

"What about us?"

He shook his head. "It's really about me."

"Spit it out, Jake. You're scaring me."

"Yeah? It was scaring me too. But you . . . you're the bravest person I know."

She waited for him to continue.

"When I married Cecelia, she was a city girl through and through. She was also a Texas girl, you know? She thought she had ranch life all figured out before she set one foot on the Diamond. But it was a little different than she had anticipated. Or maybe marriage was a little different. Maybe it just wasn't living in a big town anymore that did her in. Whatever it was, we started to fight. Constant arguing. Of course with arguing comes the makeup, and one day she came to me and told me that she was pregnant. That she was going to have an abortion."

Bryn gasped. It was perhaps the last thing she had expected him to say. But despite her outburst, he continued as if she hadn't made a sound.

"She said she was going to divorce me and go back to Austin. I couldn't let that happen. We were having a baby. It was a miracle and perhaps the one thing that could save our marriage. So I convinced her to stay. She didn't want to. But I couldn't let her destroy our child." Tears rose in his eyes and slid down his cheeks.

Bryn squeezed his hand encouragingly.

"She wasn't really happy about it, but she did what I asked. She stayed on the ranch, and she agreed to have the baby."

She didn't need to hear the next words to know what happened.

"I killed her. I convinced her to stay. I convinced her to have the baby. Then she had an aneurysm and died."

"Oh, Jake." Tears spilled down her own cheeks. What a burden to carry. "You didn't kill her."

"That's what Seth says too, but in my heart, it feels that way. Like I brought about her death. And I can't change those feelings. So when you came and told me that you were pregnant, I couldn't stand the thought of someone else dying at my hand."

She didn't know what to say. Maybe one day he could see how Cecelia's death was a terrible, terrible accident and he was not responsible. But the first step in healing came with new life.

"If you hadn't talked her into having the baby, you wouldn't have Wesley."

He nodded. "It's something I remember daily. Sometimes it makes it easier, sometimes not so much. I have my daughter, but I took someone else's from them."

"Jake, you have to forgive yourself."

"I know. I'm trying. But I also put everything on hold. I thought I was living. I got up in the morning, took care of the chores, took care of my daughter, spent time with my mother and my grandmother. In the summer we go swimming and in the winter we go hiking, but once you came into our lives, I realized I was just going through the motions. Thank you. Thank you for giving me two beautiful sons. Thank you for teaching me how to live again. Thank you for bringing sunshine into my life."

"You know I could say the same thing to you." She sent him a tired smile.

He shook his head. "I need to finish. I have something else I need to say before everyone arrives. I made Mama and Grandma Esther promise not to bring Wesley up until you got some sleep. I don't think I can put them off much longer."

"I can't wait to see them."

He gave a small nod. "That night . . . the night I told you that I loved you. I guess I did, in my own way. But you're right. I manipulated you. I did everything in my power to convince you to stay in Texas so that I could have the twins near me. That was wrong of me. I should've never done that. And since that night I've learned what true love really is. I love you, Bryn Talbot Langston, but I won't manipulate you that way again. If you want to go back to Georgia, I won't stop you. Your house is still there. You can move back in and pick up your life where you left off. I won't try to stop you."

Tears filled her eyes. “I don’t want to go back to Georgia. There’s nothing for me there. I was just afraid,” she confessed. “I lost everything. My parents and then Emery. All I ever wanted was a family, then I come here and meet yours.” She shook her head. “I was afraid that I would never be a part of such a wonderful group of people. Do you know how precious your family is?”

He grinned. “Yeah, they’re pretty special.”

“And I was afraid that I would get attached and then have to leave. But all I’ve ever wanted in my life was love, real love.”

He glanced over to where the twins slept peacefully in their warm incubators. Then he looked back at her. Bryn could see the love shining in those green eyes. Jasper and Jarvis already showed signs of having that same dark hair like their father. She hoped their eyes would be such a beautiful, crystal green. And she hoped that they would be full of love as well.

“You have my love. Always and forever.” Jake kissed the back of her hand. “This is as real as it gets.”

Epilogue

They're awfully wrinkly." Wesley looked at the boys and frowned. They weren't exactly what she had been expecting. And the fact that they both were boys . . . well, she didn't know who was responsible for *that.* There were enough boys running around the ranch. Now they had two more. "Are they always going to be that wrinkly?"

Her dad laughed. He seemed so happy these days. Ever since they brought Bryn home from the hospital with Jarvis and Jasper. She still wasn't sure if she liked those names. Bob and Sam sounded so much better to her. But once again no one had asked her opinion before deciding what to call her baby brothers.

"It's just because they're so little and new," her dad said. "Give them a couple of weeks and they'll fill out."

Wesley eyed the babies skeptically. "If you say so."

Daddy reached out a hand for her to take it. "Come on now, Mama's got to feed them and get them ready for bed."

Wesley slid her hand into her father's big warm one. Mama, she liked the sound of that. Once Bryn came home from the hospital she said that Wesley could call her Mama if she wanted to. And she wanted to. So bad.

"They sure sleep a lot," Wesley said as her dad led her from the room. She glanced back one last time. The twins had their own room with two little beds and cowboy decorations hanging on the walls. It was all right, she supposed, but she preferred pink so much more than baby blue and red. But once again, they hadn't asked her when they decorated.

She craned her head back to look at her father. "Can we watch *Little Mermaid*?"

"We can watch anything you want. This is your time."

"I think I want to watch *Little Mermaid*. Uncle Seth and Aunt Jessie, are they going to have a boy too?"

Her dad shook his head as he led her into the family room. "We don't know what kind of baby they're having. It'll be around your birthday before we can find out."

"Their baby will be born on my birthday? Is that even possible?"

Daddy laughed. "Absolutely. Just like the twins were born on Christmas Day."

"I don't think I like that idea."

"We don't have to talk about it now. Let's watch *Little Mermaid*, okay?"

She nodded and scooched over a little more so he could sit next to her on the couch. "I would have much rather had girls," Wesley groused.

Her father started the movie and gave her a kiss on the cheek as *The Little Mermaid* flickered to life on the TV screen. "So you've said. But keep in mind, the most important part is that they're healthy."

"Yeah, I guess."

"Wesley." She was always in trouble when he used that tone of voice.

"Yes, sir."

She supposed he was right, but adults were always going

on about health and being well. She guessed it was a big deal to them. So maybe it was more important that they were healthy than whether or not they were boys or girls.

"What about the family?" Wesley asked. "Isn't that important?"

"Family is always important."

And that was what they were now—a family of five. Even more if she counted Grandma Esther and Nana, which she did. That made four girls and three boys. Four girls. That was good, huh?

Okay, so maybe it was all right that they were boys. It wasn't her first choice, but again no one had asked her.